To Lyn :

CW00665555

The Priest's Pool

Marion McGowan

Love from Marion x

First Edition published 2024 by

Westering Home
United Kingdom

This book contains both real and imagined events and characters
based on some real people who lived in 19thC.

Cover: Hare illustration "Dawn Treader". Copyright © Lisa Hooper
Printed in UK by TJ Books
"John Anderson, my Jo" by Robert Burns on P128-129. Song
lyrics from Scottish Poetry Library
www.scottishpoetrylibrary.org.uk/poem/john-anderson-myjo/

A CIP catalogue record for this book is available
from the British Library

ISBN 978-1-0687161-0-2

A Corner of Southern Scotland.

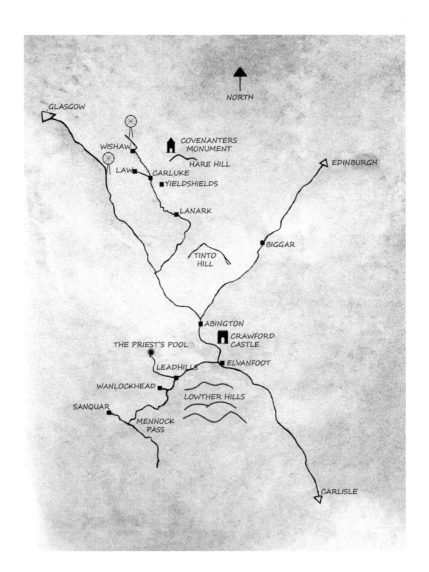

Dedication

To my family,
past, present, future

PART ONE

Wanlockhead
1870

THE PRIEST'S POOL

MARTHA WAS SINGING to the hare. The song started deep in her chest, with a hum; it was one of the old songs, the one her mother loved best, about the coming of spring.

As the last echoes settled, Martha and the hare looked at each other for a long time. Then the creature turned its head sharply, looking up the valley, nose bristling. The next instant it was gone, zigzagging along the old road.

The distance stone was marked S7: this old corpse road went to Sanquhar, seven miles of hard track. The stone, with the strange, twisted old tree beside it, was her preferred seat, a rest on her morning walk back from her job at the farm. Sometimes she would hide objects at the base of the tree: a button, or a tiny scribbled note. Martha stood now and stretched, turning to watch the sun rising over the Lowther Hills. She would head back to Wanlockhead now, face her cares. She picked up her pail and trowel. She would take some silt from the burn, add it to the fresh cow dung; the compost pile needed it. The spring light made her feel a little giddy; she closed her eyes, enjoying the moment.

It had been a harsh winter. Wanlockhead had been cut

off several times, deep snow making the roads impassible. The proud boast of 'highest village in Scotland' often meant long periods of isolation and hardship, even with the provisions carefully laid aside all through the warmer months. Still, neighbour had looked out for neighbour, and they had got through it. Just.

Each step felt heavier, as she drew nearer to the village. She had the rent to pay and three mouths to feed – although the youngest was so weak she ate less than a kitten. Agnes was growing fast; she needed new boots. Even with two jobs, it was difficult. She stooped to collect some fresh new thyme, cutting it with the sharp little knife that she kept in her pouch, then sniffed her fingers, savouring the lemony tang. She would stop by the clump of tansy by the graveyard and check for growth; she was sure that the pinch-faced woman from the back row would be knocking on the cottage door soon, looking for her mother, looking for a way out of her latest trouble. Women's trouble. The only part of her mother's business that Martha struggled with. Tansy tea was frequently requested, and the jar of dried leaves and flowerheads was running low.

Her mother knew everyone's business in the village; most folk stopped to chat when they saw her sitting on the bench by the cottage door, so she didn't have to stir far to hear all that was happening. There were frequent brief consultations, gifts of potatoes or sugar in exchange for potions and advice. The little garden opposite the cottage provided many of the plants needed for the work of a healing woman – herbs carefully sought and nurtured, even raspberry canes – and Martha had been taught where to look in the bracken and the heather of the bleak valley: where to find the moss, the leaves, the bark that would bring comfort and relief. Her mother had learned her craft from Nana Sadie; Martha now understood that the 'tinker' name she had been given in the playground derived from her. Nothing to be ashamed of – that's what her mother always said. Hold your head up.

She looked towards the village. On the path by the church, there stood the Reverend James Laidlaw. He too was looking to the hills, his head tilted back, better to feel the early warmth of the sun. She felt the frown come across her brow and the tightening around her mouth; she took a breath to calm herself. She knew at heart that James Laidlaw was a decent man, but the power invested in the collar round his neck made her uncomfortable, contrary. Hearing her footstep, he turned to greet her.

'It's a fine morning, Mrs Marshall.'

'Aye, Minister. Spring is here, at last. There are dozens of primroses on the bank.'

'Always later up here in the hills, but worth the wait, don't you think? And how is little Lucy faring today?'

Martha's face clouded.

'She's very frail, Minister. Her breathing is such an effort.'

'We are all praying for you, Mrs Marshall. Such trials

we endure on this earth, surely our reward shall be great in heaven.'

'Aye, well.' Martha turned away. 'Ah thank ye for your kind words, Minister. I'll bid ye a guid day.'

'And to you. Regards to your mother.'

Trowelling the contents of the pail into the compost, she jabbed at the pile. Prayers to Jesus. Heaven and the pearly gates. This holy certainty, that all would be well in the end. All that hope, built on a book of old stories. She sighed. If it gave comfort to wee Lucy, and solace to young Agnes, that was perhaps a blessing. For herself, the dawn sky was enough, and knowing that the spirits were in the hills. She dug the trowel deep, and smelled the earth. Today she would complete the preparations for May Day, and the long walk into the hills, to the Priest's Pool.

May Day. It was usually a day of joy and celebration, but today was carrying a heavy burden of sadness. Martha and Agnes were struggling with the handcart on the stony, rough track up into the wilds and moors above Leadhills. Wrapped snugly inside was little Lucy; wan, weak and breathing rapidly, she peeped out of her blanket cocoon, her wide eyes drinking in the clouds scudding over the skies.

'C'mon, Agnes, pull; you're a brave, strong lassie.'

Martha tried to sound encouraging, but she knew there was a further two miles of rough path still to go. They tugged on, Martha gritting her teeth in determination. Today was crucial; perhaps it was Lucy's last chance. Hopefully nobody had seen them leave. They had risen at dawn, taking some porridge and tea before starting their trek. Martha's mother had called from the box bed, encouraging words.

'You'll have a fine day of it, Martha. It'll do ye all good to go to the Priest's Pool, not just wee Lucy. Don't forget to put those bottles in the cart, we need the May Day water. You'll have sunshine today, right enough.'

The first part of the journey was the easiest, so best done in the half-light. They had trundled quickly up the road from Wanlockhead to Leadhills. It was as they veered on to the hill track that it became harder to pull. Martha fretted that the rough path was jolting wee Lucy, but the padding of the blankets seemed to be supporting her well enough. The only sound she made was an occasional cough and, always, that struggle to breathe.

The Priest's Pool: a remote and lonely spot, at the joining of Snar Water and Glendorch Burn, high in the moors, past the track to the Beltane beacon hill. Martha had been to the pool before, as a child, and had long heard her mother and other women tell stories about the healing that had taken place with the careful application of the waters. Tucked in beside Lucy were cloths and bandages, to be soaked and applied to her thin, bony frame.

'Mind your cousin, Mary Hewson, Agnes? Mind they brought her up to the pool last spring – and how much better she fared?'

Agnes knew Mary well; they were neighbours and school friends as well as relations – as were most folks in the village.

'Aye, she's doin' fine, now,' she responded, breathlessly. This was not a road for chat.

The small family trundled on, stopping for some oatcakes by a marker stone. They had passed many paths veering off up to the mine workings, but barely noticed the bings and spoil heaps that covered the moor. This was their familiar landscape, sinister and wild. The rest did give them time to lift their heads and notice early bluebells and primroses, the familiar whins flowering in a gully – all signs that May was here, and summer surely coming. The broom smelled sweet and strong, like the moor itself. This was the right time to be making a pilgrimage.

'Maw, why does the minister not like us going to the pool?'

Martha sighed. 'The Reverend Laidlaw is a guid, kind man, Agnes. But the Church has many strict rules. It's best not to speak to him – or to others – about this trip to the pool.'

'At school they teach us that we have to obey the minister, though,' said Agnes, anxious.

'Aye, and we do our best. We try to be guid. But the world is much bigger than the Church, and much … older. There are … traditions … that go way back, even before Jesus.'

At this, Agnes whistled.

'Before Jesus? But that's … ages!'

'Aye, Agnes. And the Priest's Pool has been there for centuries, with folk like us visiting it in our times o' need. The minister …' She hesitated. 'The minister just wants us to keep with the ways of the Church, and to do away with the old ways. But with a worry like this' – she inclined her head to the frail bundle in the cart – 'then we have to try all that we can.'

Martha didn't want to think too deeply; her head and her heart were telling her that her wee Lucy was going to die soon, Priest's Pool or not. Clenching her teeth again, she grasped the handle of the cart and adjusted the pulling rope round her waist. Her mind was always easier when there was a task to do. Just a mile to go.

She saw the steely glint of the pool in the distance, and it helped to draw her along, lifting her spirits. The sun was climbing higher now, and was warming her neck and back as she strained on the handles. The Snar burn ran peaty-brown, fresh and fast beside the cart, a lovely rushing sound.

'Maw …' Agnes stopped, and looked up at her mother, panting. 'Maw, is the priest still there? Will we see him? At the Priest's Pool?'

Martha saw her daughter's pupils dilate.

'There's nae priest there now, Agnes dear. That was a story from long ago.'

'Before Jesus?'

'Aye, mibbe before Jesus, there was a priest at the pool. But he's no' there now. Don't be feart, it'll just be us. It's a bonny day, and you'll get a nice cold drink and a wee paddle in the water.'

Reassured, Agnes lifted her handle and pulled on the cart again.

They startled a heron out of the bog as they approached the pool, and Agnes let out a scream.

'It's a big bird, is it not? As big as yersel'!' said Martha. A heron, she wondered. Was that lucky, or not? She would have to ask her mother. The bird lifted high in the sky, flashing silver, flapping its huge wings; soon it was distant. Seeking to distract Agnes, she pointed at the bog around them.

'Look, bulrushes – so many! And yellow irises – what a pretty spot.'

They spread out the blanket on the bank and carefully lifted Lucy down. She stretched out her thin body, looking up at her mother and sister, gaunt and grey – almost old-looking.

'Now, pet,' said Martha, smiling warmly, even as her heart ached sore. 'We'll just have a rest, and then we'll start the treatment.'

This journey had been discussed and planned during the dark months of winter. Martha's mother had learned of the old ways from her mother, and her mother before that. There were stories about a family coming from Ireland in a bright caravan, bringing folklore and cures to the drab southwest. A forebear from long ago had stayed behind with a miner, and her dark eyes had been passed down through the family, along with her knowledge and wisdom.

Her mother had told them where to look and what to do, so Martha knew to seek out the source of the stream running in from the east. She found it easily enough, gurgling and chuckling over the stones, before a short cascade into the pool. She soaked the rags in the fresh water, then – 'gently, gently' – she removed Lucy's vest and wrapped the damp cloths round her frail chest.

'It's cold, mama!' cried the wee one.

'Wheesht, Lucy! It's tae help ye!' Agnes was holding her hand, and stroking her hair.

Martha encouraged Agnes to drink from the stream, while holding a cup under the water to fill it for Lucy to sip.

'It's special water, pet. To make ye better.'

Martha watched as Agnes bent forward to the cascade, squealing as the cold water hit her face. She closed her eyes, gasping, invigorated – then opened them again, shining, bright, alive. Martha drank too, closing her eyes in a kind of prayer. The water tasted peaty yet fresh, and was deliciously cold after the arduous walk. She looked round at her two children resting on the blanket, in this peaceful place. She would remember this moment, in the May sunshine. She would especially remember the light and dazzle of Agnes's face after she had taken the waters, and her own feeling of a sacred moment.

There were duties to complete before leaving. A singlet belonging to Lucy was tied upon a hawthorn bush, by the spring. Other cloths fluttered in the breeze, other offerings, other prayers. Solemnly, Agnes dropped a penny and some pins into the pool. Afterwards, the three of them lay resting on the blanket a while; Martha was enjoying the silence. Agnes, never still for long, was soon up and exploring. Boots off, she was guddling the stones by the water's edge when she picked up a pebble – dove-grey, small and smooth. Martha watched as her daughter clutched and stroked it in her palm before putting it in her pocket and sitting back down.

'Tell us a story, Maw! Tell us aboot Hogmanay in Biggar.'

'Hogmanay?' laughed Martha. Laughing felt good, lifting her heavy heart just for a moment. 'Why, here we are in lovely bright sunshine, an' my day off, and you want to hear about one of the coldest, darkest nights o' the year?'

'Aye, Maw! Whit aboot the bonfire?'

'The bonfire was bright and warm, right enough, just what you need on a cold winter's night. What a sight! The folks o' the town had been building it for weeks, piling up all their old rubbish. It felt like the whole place was out in the streets. We started frae the Cadger's brig, the men carrying torches. What happened was, when they reached the square, they threw the torches onto the big pile, to start the bonfire. There was such a noise of cheering and shouting – a great way to see in a new year. Yer paw was there, Lucy, and I had you wrapped up warm in my shawl, a tiny babe, keeking out at the noise!'

Agnes scowled. 'I would have loved it there, Maw.'

'Aye, ah ken, Agnes dear. You were here, in Wanlockhead, such a guid girl, cosy in the cottage with your grannie. It was hard for us all, being apart. Now, c'mon, let's not get ourselves feeling sad on a fine day like this, and after taking the waters, too.'

Agnes set off again to explore round the pool, and Martha lay back on the blanket, stroking Lucy's hair. She was remembering her wedding day and that surge of excitement, setting off for Biggar as Mrs Marshall. Sitting up there on the waggon clutching the arm of her new husband, knowing she was going somewhere new – that was special. Admittedly, there was the swell of her belly under her wedding gown, no denying it. 'That was you, Lucy,' she murmured, stroking her child. 'You were our wee baby.' Billy Marshall had started coughing not long after their arrival in Biggar, and with growing alarm she had watched him tire, then sicken and then die of consumption. She had returned to Wanlockhead with her child, knowing it was likely that she too had phthisis. Such a beautiful name for a terrible illness, Martha thought. It sounds like a flower. A flower that flourishes red in the lungs, and wastes the body to whiteness.

She heard the faint toll of the curfew bell in the distance, announcing a change of shifts at the mines, and called to Agnes.

'Mind, Agnes; mind if we meet anyone, we've just been out in the May sunshine wi' Lucy. No need to mention the Priest's Pool. Now, time to head back. Into the cart wi' ye, wee pet.' Tenderly she lifted her younger daughter into the nest of blankets, and Agnes tucked her in.

Having pulled and dragged the cart up to the Priest's Pool, it was much easier to push it down the hill. On the way back, Martha acknowledged others making the journey up towards the remote spring. There was a neighbour, with an ill relative blanketed in a cart; and here was a parent, carrying a small child; then a family walking together. Little eye contact was made, just a quiet 'Guid day tae ye'. Martha was glad they had been the first there, to have the place to themselves.

They reached the road at last, and Martha stopped and stretched her tired limbs. 'Agnes, you've done well, lass, but I can manage frae here. I want ye tae run home to yer Grannie. Tell her we're all fine. See that she's comfy, help her make the tea.'

Agnes sped off, one hand rubbing her thin shoulders. She was a good girl, uncomplaining, Martha thought.

She picked up the handles again, and walked on with the cart, down towards the village. She was cooing and chatting to Lucy, so jumped a little when she saw the minister in front of her.

'Reverend Laidlaw – guid day to you! I was miles awa,' there!'

'Good day, Mrs Marshall. And how is Lucy today? Out for a wee hurl, in the spring weather? The sunshine will be good for her.'

Martha saw his sharp eyes take in the bumps in the blanket, and then back to her face. She flushed. He knew well enough what was hidden under there – bottles of water from that pagan place, in the hills. She wondered if he had heard the chink of the glass.

'Aye, a lovely day for a walk, Minister, a'hm sure you'll agree. Now, Lucy's getting a bit warm in the sun, mibbe I'd best be getting her home.'

'Aye. Aye, you do that, Mrs Marshall. And mind to pass on my best to your mother.' His voice softened, as he looked down at Lucy. 'You are all in my prayers.'

He moved on up the road, and Martha gulped for air. Her heart was racing. She knew full well that if the bottles of water from the Priest's Pool had been revealed, she could have been in front of the Church accused of an act of heathenism. It was not the shame of the denouncement she feared – after all, she had faced worse, at the front of the Church – it was the fine that accompanied it. She could not afford any unexpected call on her meagre finances.

Martha turned, and saw the minister standing in the road. He had met one of the elders, and they were talking. She saw James Laidlaw shake his head, and she knew what the subject of their discussion was. Pagan rituals, that's what they would be calling it, encouraged by tinkers. Martha picked up the cart handles again and headed for home, her mind still racing.

Perhaps they were talking about her, and about Agnes. A familiar chill settled in her heart. Most of the villagers accepted that she had a daughter born out of wedlock, but there were still some who would look askance, whisper cruel words as she walked down the street. Her mother had often told her to keep her head high, but she had heard them talk, heard them tell outsiders that she had a 'reputation'. When that itinerant blacksmith had up and left her with child, the minister had been kind. He had baptised Agnes in the Church, despite the tutting. He had said that the Church was for everyone.

She looked ahead to the church building and saw the new place of worship that had just been built nearby. There was an almost feverish excitement around the new Free Kirk in Wanlockhead; many of the younger miners attended, and there was a feeling of militancy, much fervent talk about answering only to God. Martha wasn't sure what the fuss was about. She understood that people needed a church, a place for weddings and funerals, but she would always prefer the old one. More than that; despite her struggle with belief, the old church was part of who she was. After all, her family members were buried under its name, down at the old Meadowfoot graveyard. She even liked the smell of the old church building, and sometimes found comfort in the rhythm and familiarity of the services. However, the unthinking authority often jarred, and it was sometimes difficult to listen to the sermons. She had heard that the Free Kirk sermons were especially long – and who wanted to spend their precious free time on a hard seat? And Ferguson, the minister, was a cold fish.

The following Sunday, Martha and Agnes were in their pew at the rear of the church as the Reverend James Laidlaw took to the pulpit. Doubtless he was going to explain once again to his wayward parishioners how the Priest's Pool had come by its name, and why the Church forbade heathen rituals. Martha shifted uncomfortably as he looked down at his notes and began.

'There are a few versions of this tale about the Priest's Pool; some are unsuitable for telling in a sacred building.'

Martha noticed Agnes was fidgeting with something in her pocket; likely it was the pebble from the pool. She put her hand over her daughter's and sighed, as the minister leaned forward in the pulpit and surveyed his congregation.

'I know that you are all familiar with the story. It was a feud between neighbours. Long ago, when Jock O'Snar was away from his castle, his enemies broke in and were sampling the contents of the cellar. On his return, Jock was understandably furious. However, due to their inebriation, Jock O'Snar had the advantage. There was a priest present and involved with the break-in party. I will make no comment about the morals of this individual, as that is not the purpose of today's sermon. Suffice to say, he begged for mercy, and was thrown into the pool at Snar. Hence the name – the Priest's Pool. The other version of the story …'

Around Martha the congregation shifted, and looked down. Everyone knew full well the version he was referring to: a priest caught in the act of fornication with Jock O'Snar's wife, and cast into the pool by the jealous husband.

'Well, again, it features a transgressing priest. Doubtless of the Church of Rome.'

The congregation shuffled.

'The details are irrelevant. What is important is this.' He stood tall, took in a breath, and raised his voice to a thunder. Martha felt her stomach contract, and Agnes clutched her hand.

'Such places of superstition and fairy tales *drag you down into the dark ages*. These are irrational beliefs – *foolishness and ignorance*. This place you frequent is no sacred pool. It has no healing powers. *It is the scene of a rout*.' His fist struck the lectern. 'In these enlightened times, you should be turning your backs on this nonsense. Attend to your prayers, and there will be no need for heathen practices.' His voice rose further. '*Trust in the Lord*!'

He announced the hymn, then sat down, shaking his head. Martha watched from her pew as the congregation in front of her rose in a bedraggled fashion, most looking to their feet. There was much clearing of throats as they prepared for the hymn. She pulled Agnes up gently, and they started to sing.

MEADOWFOOT

MARTHA STOOD AT the door and breathed in deep. Another fine, spring day. At least she could let some fresh air into the stuffy wee room. She turned as Lucy stirred and coughed in the cot.

'Wheesht, there now, pet. Look, she's settled again, Martha. Why don't ye take yersel' out a walk? I'll watch her. Agnes'll be home frae the school any minute now, wi' all her stories and blethers. She'll keep me company.' Martha's mother motioned to her daughter to step outside.

Martha crossed the track to the little garden. She treasured her time there, tending her simple crops of kale and turnip and herbs. She usually eagerly anticipated this time of year; such a joy, as the new shoots burst through. But today she had no appetite for it. She picked up her trowel and pulled some weeds – then shuddered, as she looked up to see sparrows flitting over the house. Her mother always said it was a sure sign of the imminent death of a child.

'How can there be new life and growth here, when inside there is illness, suffering and death?' she thought. She remembered her mother's words, on hearing of the heron disturbed at the Priest's Pool.

'Aye, it's a guid sign, a heron. It carries the spirit o' the sacred place. We can only hope it was bringing peace.' Her mother's old eyes had filled, and she had turned away.

Martha sat back against the fence, wrung out, wearied, heartsick. What was it the minister said? *Count your blessings in testing times.*

Well, she had the help and kindness of her workmates at the miners' canteen – covering shifts for her, leaving small gifts at the door. A jar of jam. A simple bunch of primroses, hastily tied. She knew that they would be starting a collection for the funeral already – God knows, she had contributed to so many herself over the years. Now it was her turn. Count the blessings.

She felt, almost tangibly, the shy love and concern of many of those around her – neighbours, relations, friends. It was often unbearable; just the kind touch of a hand on her shoulder, and she fought to control the tears. Her cousin, David Hewson, who helped her with the garden – he could barely look at her. His face was etched with sorrow and pity. She did not want pity.

Agnes called over from the cottage.

'Maw, that's me home frae school now. Grannie says, away a wee walk. We're all fine here. I'll sit wi' Lucy, and then I'll make the tea.'

'Mibbe I will, dear. I won't be too long.'

Martha stood and stretched, then turned down the hill towards Meadowfoot.

Such a pretty name, Meadowfoot, she mused. *This is where she will lie with her kin, the hills around her and the village not far.*

She walked on down the hill, to the gate. The simple cemetery was one hundred years older than the church in the village – yet even before that, there were people here who had to bury their dead. They would carry the coffins of their loved ones past the twisted tree, miles onward down the road through the hills, to Sanquhar.

The corpse road, thought Martha. *At least we won't have to walk that.*

She looked on down the track, stretching ahead to the hills. Her eyes were scanning the valley, looking for hares; today, though, they were elusive, perhaps hiding from her sadness. Standing for a moment, she let her imagination take her back to her kin of old, bent over their burdens as they readied themselves for the painful parting ahead. And returning to her present, she could hear the lead-mining works now in the valley – the background clatter and hum of industry ever constant. What might it be like in the future? Might quietness return? A flashing image – too fast – of someone walking up the road, with a load on their back; and then she collected herself, steeled herself to push open the gate.

The drystone wall, the trees around and the stream running nearby made for a tranquil spot. The Hewson graves were near the gate, and she moved towards them.

I need to prepare myself, she thought. *This is where she will lie. And soon.*

Her foot touched a dead bird and she startled, nausea rising in her throat. The rancid smell of a rotting sheep's carcase caught her, and she forced herself to steady against the onrush to her exhausted senses.

'I must be strong. Help me to be strong.' She was speaking aloud now, as she stood at the Hewson stone. Some names were still clear. Her long-dead baby brother and sister – she had never known them. And the others, now crumbling into the years of rain and wind; her father, his siblings, his parents. She moved her fingers over the stone, at the place where Lucy's name would be written.

'Help me to be strong.'

Was it wrong to ask in the old way? She had many requests; there was one for strength, and another for protection for the family, at this vulnerable time. Most important was the wish for a peaceful passing for Lucy. She walked on to the rowan tree outside the cemetery and found the small circle of stones beside it. Taking a small bundle of scribbled notes from her pocket, she scrunched them together and placed them inside the tiny round fireplace. She built up a fire with rowan and heather twigs – rowan, such a strong force against evil. Then she added some herbs from a small draw-bag that she kept tied at her waist, and brought out the flint. Martha stood back and watched the papers burn.

She was walking back up the hill when she saw the minister coming towards her.

'Mrs Marshall. Martha.' James Laidlaw's voice was gentle. 'I just called at the house. Your mother told me where I might find you. You have been making the journey. Preparing yourself.'

'As best I can, Minister. It's awfy hard.' Her throat caught. She kept her head erect, her eye steady, but her voice betrayed her. 'At least it's a peaceful, bonny spot to lie in.'

'Would it help to say a prayer, Martha?'

'Ah cannae pray. I'm too … twisted up inside. Like a knot. I ken whit's coming. I'm dreading it, Minister. I need to be strong.' She stopped. 'Could *you* pray for us all? Pray for Lucy, that she'll just slip away gently?'

'You are all in my prayers just now, Martha. I have left a reading at the house for you. Matthew chapter nineteen, verse fourteen.'

She looked down, wrapping her shawl around her. 'Aye. Thank you, Minister.' She nodded to herself, and met his eye again. 'Ah mean it. Thank you.'

Martha walked on towards the village. James Laidlaw continued his perambulation, down the hill, past the end of the graveyard. Martha looked back and saw him looking down at the smoke rising from the little circle by the rowan tree.

At the cottage, Agnes was bustling and busy.

'Maw, there ye are! Did ye see the minister? He brought us this.' She put the embroidered card into her mother's hand. 'Suffer the little children …'

'Aye. Very guid of him.' Martha placed the card on the family Bible, which sat open by the cot.

'An' he brought some eggs. I thought we could try wee Lucy with some egg? She likes a boiled egg mashed wi' butter.'

'Mibbe just warm milk and water just now, Agnes, dear. She's so weak, and she's coughing that much. We can have the minister's eggs for tea. Yer Grannie likes a buttery egg in a cup, too.'

Agnes moved to the fire, and Martha sat by the cot with her mother. She picked up the Bible and began to read aloud.

Agnes clattered busily by the stove. 'Maw? Maw, ah ken we have to be holy just now, wi' Lucy being so ill. But might we have a story later on? Out of this? Mary's maw gave it tae me.' She held up a battered *People's Friend* magazine.

'Give it here.' Her grannie squinted at the cover. 'Have we no' had this one before?'

'Aye, Grannie, but there's some excitin' stories. Ah like the one aboot the lassie and her dug. They have some grand adventures. Can we have a dug, Maw? I'd like a dug.'

Martha closed her eyes, and Agnes fell silent, turning back to the fire.

The hours stretched and contracted through the night. Lucy's breath became slower and shallower as dawn neared. Martha watched, helpless, as the child she loved slipped away. How could she bear this? She found her mind moving ahead, to afterwards. How she would open the doors and windows wide, to let Lucy's soul go free. How she would burn the bed linen from the cot. How she would clean this whole cottage from top to bottom.

Scrub and clean, scrub and clean. Her hands clenched, ready to start work.

The Hewson women gathered round, as she knew they would. They were mercifully gentle with the still little body, dressing her in her dead-clothes, ready for the last journey.

The minister looked by; Martha noticed his gaze take in the little saucer of salt placed on the child's breastbone, to guard against evil. Doubtless he'd be judging their superstitious ways; or perhaps he understood the deep, aching need for these ancient practices.

'How are you doing, Agnes?' James Laidlaw spoke kindly.

'Ah'm fair sad, Minister,' said Agnes. Her face was pinched and white, her dark eyes giving her a gaunt look. 'I'll no' see Lucy again, till I get tae heaven.'

'Aye, but she'll be keeping a place for you there, Agnes. You can be sure of that.'

Martha looked over and saw Agnes's misery. She watched as her daughter clutched in her pocket – doubtless that stone from the pool was a comfort to her – then she caught her mother's eye over the room. The old woman moved forward and put her arm around Agnes.

'You'll not be needing that place for a long while yet, lassie. Dinnae fear.'

A SOUND IN THE HILLS

THE IRONY OF grief is that life goes on. The sun still rises and sets, the rain still comes in hard over the hills. But slowly the heavy sickness in the heart starts to ease and the head starts to lift.

Things are a bit easier, thought Agnes. *Maw isn't just so snappy.*

'Right, Agnes,' said Martha, 'we have work to do. We have the space now, an' that means we can take in a lodger. When you get home frae school, we'll roll up our sleeves and clear that corner in the roof space for the trestle bed.'

Agnes sighed. 'Och, Maw. Do we have to? Have a lodger, ah mean. Ah like it fine when it's just the three of us. Their boots smell and they eat an awfy lot.'

'Ye ken fine we need the money, Agnes dear.'

'Yer maw is right, Agnes. We'll be cosy in the box bed, they'll no' bother us.' Her grannie was smiling about the smelly boots. 'We'll make them leave their boots outside.'

'We cannae let the boots get wet, Grannie. I'll just put a peg on ma nose.'

'Now, miss.' Martha was laughing, as Agnes pinched her nose and made a face. 'Right, come on. It's off tae school with you. I'll see you after ma work, and we'll make a start.'

The new school year had begun, and the teacher was strict about timekeeping. Agnes gathered up her slate and put her oatcakes in her piece-bag. She heard Mary at the door.

'Are ye ready? We dinnae want to get into trouble.'

'Aye, I'm here, just tying ma boots.' Agnes hated her boots. They were cast-offs from a boy cousin, black and ugly. Already her feet were too big for her mother's footwear. At least these boots didn't pinch and hurt her feet.

The two girls set off, Agnes eager to share the latest news with her friend.

'Ah think we're going to tak' a lodger again. We need the money.'

'Ugh, a big smelly miner in the house? Coming in stoatin' full o' drink on a Saturday night?' Mary was not impressed.

'Maw will be careful. She won't take one of the young, daft lads in.'

'Aye, well she'd better be careful, right enough.' Mary didn't look at her friend, and Agnes felt a change in the mood, a frisson of judgement. She changed the subject quickly.

'Have ye brought yer skipping rope?'

It was a relief to be outside again, after hours in the warm classroom. Agnes was rubbing down her left arm, in an effort to stop the pins and needles – once again, she had suffered the indignity of having it tied behind her, in an effort to force her to write with her right hand. Corrie-fisted, they called it – and worse, sometimes – but she couldn't help it.

The school gang was gathering by the crossroads, letting off steam, reluctant to part, reluctant to head home to cramped rooms, sleeping fathers and harassed mothers. The usual teasing and showing off was going on, fighting and flirting. Agnes was distracted, watching wee Effie cowering, pinned against the railings by Bobby, the innkeeper's son, wondering whether she should intervene. She was unprepared for the voice in her ear. Malicious, gleeful; the hot, breathy whisper of the beautiful Catriona Ferguson – the Cat.

'Well, well, whit are we hearin'? Is it right that yer maw is takin' up hoorin' again?'

'My maw is not a whore. Dinnae you ever say that again!'

'If she's no' a whore – that means ye're no' a tinker's bastard. And ye are!'

'You shut yer trap, Cat, or I'll ...' Agnes looked round desperately, but her heart sank as her classmates started to gather, interested in some bastard-baiting.

'Dae I smell a bastard?'

'Dirty wee cack-handed bastard!'

'Yer hoorie maw hates you! Ye're just scum!'

'Naebody wants to be pals wi' ye, leftie bastard!'

Agnes knew what to do. She picked up her bag and walked off alone on the high path, up towards the hills, the bings and the mines. She didn't look back as the taunts grew fainter. At least they weren't throwing stones this time. She knew that Mary would be nowhere to be seen, avoiding trouble. She felt sick, the familiar dragging in her gut, precipitated by Cat's whisper. The bullying hadn't happened for a while, but she knew it would never go away. The 'bastard' thing was part of her – she was, and always would be, the bastard. From her reluctant place on the sidelines of the playground, she had watched the casual cruelty of her peers, waiting for it to be her turn. She fingered the pebble in her pocket and felt the smoothness. It helped her steady her breathing. It would all calm down. Till the next time.

Agnes walked on past the pit paths, distracted. She had forgotten about getting home, about helping to clear the roof space for a paying guest. The sun was high – this September was warm and glorious, and she smelled the grass and dry earth. She turned a bend in the road and found a boulder to sit on, to catch her breath.

She closed her eyes and felt the clamour of her heart slow and settle. Gradually she became aware of an unfamiliar, far-off sound. What was that? Was it barking? Or could it be something from the mine? It was closer to hand, surely. She stood up, listening. 'A dug!'

Agnes left her school bag on the path, and set off exploring. The sound was unmistakeably a bark, but muffled; it was coming from under the ground.

'Doggie! Where are ye?' She whistled, mimicking the way miners called their dogs to heel. The noise was coming from here. She put her head down on the moor grass and listened. Here was a scratching and a snuffling and a whining; and a barking too.

'Can ye no' get out, doggie?' She tried to dig with her fingers, but the ground was hard and dry. 'I'll get help!'

After moving her school bag to the exact spot, Agnes ran off down the path. Branching left, she headed up towards the mine. She knew there should be a man in the gatehouse; although 'gatehouse' was a grand name for a building that was just a tumbledown hut. Two men sat outside, enjoying a pipe in the sun before the next shift.

'S'cuse me, mister. There's a dug! Barking! Underground!' Agnes pointed up the hill.

'Whit are ye on aboot, lassie? Can ye no' see we're on our break? Away hame, it's dangerous here.'

'Really, mister! Ah heard it clear! It's no' far. Mibbe it's trapped!'

'Have ye no' been reading too many stories?' The older man shook his head, but stood and stretched. 'We'll come and tak' a look. Wullie, bring that shovel.'

Approaching the spot, the men saw what Agnes had not: a rough old dig, in off the path, by the burn. On the far side, fresh scree and earth had been cleared out.

'Mibbe an incomer, looking tae make his fortune.' The older man knelt down, peering and shouting into the darkness. 'Anybody in there?'

Agnes heard the muffled bark and lay down by her school bag.

'The dug – it's under the ground here!'

'The lassie's right! Mind yersel', Wullie. There's been a collapse. Lassie, you run back to the gatehouse and tell the gaffer that Malkie says there's mibbe a trapped man here.'

After that, time seemed to pass very quickly. Agnes was most excited to hear the curfew bell toll. She knew that outside of shift changes, this was a call for help, a signal that there had been an accident. Soon the hillside was crowded with men and equipment. Even Dr Menzies had made his way up the path, and was standing alongside the stretcher-bearers from the mine.

Malkie called out to the gathered men from the top of the shaft. 'That ladder was ancient, rotten. No wonder it broke. And it brought doon a load o' stone. Poor fella. His heid's all mashed in. Best get that lassie awa' before we bring him up.'

'Whit aboot the dug?' Agnes heard her voice high and thin. She felt horribly frightened about the miner, but she was desperate to know whether the dog was trapped, or injured.

'Aye, we've got the dug. We need to bring this poor fella up first, though. Away and sit over there, till we let the doctor tak' a look.'

Wullie firmly guided Agnes over to the boulder, and sat her down. 'Just wait there.'

It was difficult work, pulling the body out of the shaft, but the men were skilled and used to working together. Eventually it was heaved up into the daylight. A sack had been placed over the head, but even so some of the men were visibly shaken.

Dr Menzies stepped forward. 'We'll need to take that off, till I get a look. Though there is no sign of breath in the man.' He made a quick examination, and confirmed the worst. 'He's been there some days, too. Cold as ice. If it hadn't been for his dog, then he might never have been found.'

'Stupid man. Mibbe doon frae Glasgow, trying tae find gold. Folk don't know how dangerous these old workings are. Dry weather, wet weather, there's hazards wi' both. He's paid dear for it.' Wullie was upset, but trying not to show it. 'Where's that dug? Gie it to the wee lassie.'

Covered in dirt and shivering in its whole body, the terrier was handed over to Agnes. It whimpered and trembled in her arms.

'It'll need a drink, lassie. Help it tae the burn.'

She carried the dog over to the stream and laid it down. At first the dog just lay collapsed, panting and shaking. Gradually it struggled to stand, but its legs buckled under. Agnes cupped some water into her hand and offered it under its nose. It licked and lapped, then laid its head back on the ground, looking up at her. Agnes felt her heart melt. 'Barker. I'm going to call you Barker. Your barking led me to you.'

It was Dr Menzies who took Agnes home in his trap, the dog cradled in her arms. His presence certainly saved the day; Martha was worried and angry, not knowing where Agnes had been for these hours.

'Agnes did the right thing, Mrs Marshall, going for assistance. Unfortunately, there was nothing we could do to save the chap. He had been dead for some time. But your girl was very helpful, guiding the men to the spot.' He patted Agnes on the shoulder.

'Thank ye, Dr Menzies. We have been worried aboot her, especially with the curfew bell tolling and nae sign of her. She was supposed to be straight home, to make her Grannie her tea.'

'Well, she's here now, safe and sound. No, I'll not stop, Mrs Marshall. Regards to your mother, there. I'll leave you with the heroine of the day.'

A heroine! Here was a word that Agnes never thought she would hear spoken about herself. She would have to think about it. Meanwhile, she had a dog to look after.

Martha looked dubious. 'Whit's this sorry creature?'

'This is Barker, Maw. He was under the ground, barking. That's how we found the poor man, the one that died. The stanes had collapsed on him, but missed his dug. The men gave him tae me, to look after. He's been under the ground for days.'

32

'Whit were ye doing up there on the moor, Agnes? It could have been you, fallin' down the old workings!'

'I wouldnae go off the path, Maw, I know how dangerous the workings are. I just fancied a wee walk in the sun after school.' She had forgotten about the bullying at the crossroads. Her heart was full of Barker.

'Let's have a look at this dug. It's filthy. C'mon, fill a pail. We'll take it tae the garden and give it a bath.'

A wash and a shake revealed a coarse coat, the colour of a ginger biscuit.

'And it's no' a he at all. It's a she. A bitch, mibbe three or four years old. Dae ye still want to call her Barker?'

'Aye, Maw. That's her name.'

'Any trouble, any mess, and she is out. D'ye understand?'

'Yes, Maw.'

Martha softened. 'She found ye, Agnes. Ye'll always be special to her. Ye'll have a pal for life.'

Agnes looked at her mother, bright-eyed, and they smiled.

STORIES BY THE FIRE

MARTHA WAS PREPARING the broth, while Agnes cut the oatmeal out the drawer – double the usual amount, to feed the lodger. He would take a piece wrapped in a cloth to his shift, sometimes to eat it in the dark, by flickering candlelight. Barkie was watching with interest; occasionally her bright tongue would protrude for a moment.

'Maw, how long is Arthur staying for?'

'Just till the year end, Agnes. He says he's away back tae the mines in England.' Martha leaned in to the knife, to chop the turnip.

'Aye, he said there was more money there. He says he doesnae like being in truck. Whit does that mean?'

'That's a hard question.' Martha paused. 'The men here are used tae the system, but Arthur says it's old-fashioned. Wages dinnae get paid right away, the men have tae wait – sometimes it's two years, till the lead is smelted. The men get some money, but most of their needs are seen to at the store. They all have accounts there, that comes off their wages. It's called being in truck tae the company.'

She picked up the knife again, and Agnes moved over to

the table, to wrap up the slice. Barkie slunk to her corner by the fire, in despair of getting any crumbs. Martha knew about having an account at the store. It was a difficult business. She had often experienced the grimace of the storekeeper as he turned to their page in the book, adding another line to the ledger.

'Whit happens if they want to buy something not from the store?'

'Och, they get some money for their pocket if they ask for it. Beer money. Money for the travelling carts. They don't want for much. The company's no' bad, it's just always done things this way. Arthur says it's the same in most lead-mining places, but he's fed up wi' it.'

Barkie lifted her head at the word 'fed'. The dog seemed to like the male company in the house, and certainly enjoyed the treats that Arthur brought home for her. She looked around expectantly, then settled down when it was clear no food was coming.

'Arthur's away just now, speakin' wi' the gaffer, to be sure to be settled up by the year end.'

'He'll have a right job.' Martha's mother sounded grim. 'They dinnae like breakin' wi' the system. They dinnae want tae encourage others tae ask for their wages in a different way.'

'Is that no' why those young lads left for America, Grannie?'

Martha remembered the talk and the tears as women lamented their young lads buying passage on a ship to

New York out of Glasgow. She had felt a stir of jealousy, then. The thought of going to Glasgow was exciting enough in itself, without the notion of boarding a boat to cross the world. New York. It sounded full of glamour, possibilities. 'Aye, four of them gone. Guid luck to them. They'll likely make their fortune. At least they'll get paid on time.'

Her mother looked at her, and raised her eyebrows. 'It's no' all bad here, Martha. The Duke looks after the men well. And he puts money into the school, pays for the master. It helped you get an education, and now Agnes.'

'Aye, right enough. But the old ways are changing.'

'Mibbe change finds it hard to climb the long hill track to Wanlockhead,' said the old woman, smiling. 'And talkin' of school, is it no' time ye were off, Agnes? Away ye go, I'll see to the oatmeal.'

'Yes, Grannie.' Agnes stopped at the door. 'It's a shame aboot Arthur going. He's nice tae Barkie. An' his boots are only a wee bit smelly.' She whistled her dog. 'Barkie, look after Grannie – I'm away tae the school.' She ran off up the road.

'It won't be long and she'll be starting at the sewing,' said the old woman.

'Aye, she'll stop the school in January. It's a shame, she's guid at her books. But it'll bring in more money, mither.'

'We've all done it, Martha. But it's hard work, an' it hurts yer eyes.'

'I've spoken tae the woman in charge, the lace agent. She'll call in next time she's here, to talk aboot getting the machine set up.'

'It'll be company for me,' said Martha's mother. 'The days'll pass more quickly.'

'Mibbe for yersel', but mibbe not for Agnes. It'll be quiet after her being used tae the school. Mind you, mibbe that will suit her. And she has a steady hand. Aye, she'll be fine.'

It was getting dark so early now, and the winter nights were long. It would be a while before Arthur would be home from the inn. Martha felt the familiar sag to her spirits, the restlessness, always worsened by the miseries of cold and wet weather.

'Let's have a wee story. Would ye like a story, Agnes?' Her mother's warm voice gathered them all together. 'Light another candle, there's a lass. We've got to show those witches roaming outside that there is nothing for them in here.'

'There's not really witches, are there, Grannie?' said Agnes, discomfited. She loved hearing the old stories, despite the unsettling effect that they often had on her imagination.

'Don't be giving her nightmares, Mither,' said Martha. 'Agnes, you know fine well that nae witch would ever dare come near this hearth.' She nodded towards the fire as she took up her knitting. Barkie stretched sleepily on the rug.

'Have ye ever seen a witch, Grannie?' Agnes knew all

the stories well.

'Did I ever tell ye aboot the time I was small, and a witch tried to steal my baby brother?' Old Mrs Hewson gathered her shawl around her, and leaned forward conspiratorially.

'Go on, Grannie!'

'Well, I was just a wee lassie, still at my mother's skirts. I remember that Bobbie was in the old crib. It was a dark, rainy night, just like this one, when there was a knock at the door. My mother knew better than tae answer it; she called out, "Go away!" But the voice that came back sounded just like her poor dead sister. "Sadie," said the voice, "open the door tae me. You wouldnae leave me outside in this terrible weather? Open the door." Well, my mother was very distressed. I remember her walking up and down, not sure what tae do. The voice was pleading with her, asking her tae open the door.'

'Where was great-grandad?' asked Agnes.

Martha smiled. She knew that, like herself, Agnes had the familiar tale off by heart.

'He was fast asleep up in the attic. He had been workin' hard all the long day, and my mother didnae want tae disturb him.'

'Whit happened, Grannie?' Agnes's eyes were gleaming in the candlelight, and Barkie roused herself, sitting up, alert, as if she too were caught up in the story.

'When she heard the voice of her sister, my mother relented. She opened the door, and – whoosh! – the witch blew in on the wind.'

Agnes had heard the story too often to be afraid; she wanted the details.

'Whit did she look like?'

'Well, this is the strange thing, Agnes. You perhaps think that a witch would be ugly, with a big warty nose and a pointy hat. But this witch was …'

'Really beautiful.'

Her grandmother nodded. 'Yes, Agnes. She was really beautiful. She was young, and had long dark hair, and such a bright, bonny face. Her eyes, though. They were …'

'Clearest blue and staring, cold as ice.'

The old lady laughed. 'It should be you telling this story, Agnes! Why don't ye tell us the rest of the tale?'

Agnes clasped Barkie's neck, and continued the story.

'Your maw was too frightened tae speak. Or mibbe the witch had put a spell on her.' She lowered her voice, dramatically. 'You watched in horror as the witch moved towards baby Bobbie. But then the witch spied the Bible, open on the table beside the crib, and she cried out in anger and frustration. At the same time, you shouted out, "Faither! Help us, Faither!" and your paw came out of the roof space, jumping down the ladder. The witch looked up, and saw him coming towards her, and stepped back. At the same time …You tell the ending, Grannie!'

'At the same time, my mother grabbed the poker frae the fire, and ran at the witch. She fled out the door, into

39

the night, empty-handed.'

'But your maw singed her hair, Grannie.'

'Aye. My faither slammed the door shut behind her, but some of her hair got caught. And when the red-hot poker touched it, it burst into flames, crackling and spitting.'

'And the flames burned green.'

'Aye. The flames burned green. There was a terrible scream – she must have torn her hair, tae get free. The next day, there was a scorched bundle of coarse thistles and horse hair outside our door.'

The three of them sat in silence for a moment, contemplating this horror.

It was Martha's turn to contribute to the storytelling.

'So of course, your mother made sure that this awfy tangle was properly burned. But it had to be right outside, away frae the house, did it not? You wouldnae bring such a thing into the home fire.'

'Aye. She prepared a special place by the rowan tree down behind Meadowfoot, with a small circle of stones. She lifted the strange thing, using some rowan twigs, and carried it down the path. She placed it into the circle, where she burned it properly, with due care and attention – all the time saying, "keep the witches away." And that place has been lucky for wishes ever since.'

'Whit sort of wishes?' asked Agnes. 'Could ye wish someone ill?'

'Ye have to be very careful with wishes, Agnes,' said Martha.

'So, Grannie, the moral of the story is – dinnae open the door to witches!' Agnes then asked what she always asked. 'But how do you know if someone is a witch or not?'

'Evil witches like that just belong in the stories now, Agnes,' said Martha. 'But these old stories were tae teach us some important lessons, like tae be careful who we trust. And not tae be feart of standing up for ourselves.'

'And also, that someone can be beautiful, but also evil,' said Agnes.

'And tae keep the poker handy in the fire,' her grandmother added.

They all nodded, solemnly.

There was a knock at the door, and they all jumped; Barkie ran excitedly towards it, tail wagging.

'Hello?' Arthur's big voice called in from the step. He put his head round the door, pulling his boots off. 'It's only me. Jings, look at your faces. You'd think you'd all seen a witch!'

PART TWO

Carluke
1872

TAKING A CORD

JOHN HAD TO admit it: he felt relieved that his mother had died. She had been ill for a long time, eventually confined to her bed, with that sickly odour choking the air of her room. He grimaced, remembering how she had wasted away into a living corpse. All the neighbours had said it. At last, there was an end to her suffering.

He was leaning in the doorway, waiting for the others, fiddling with a too-tight collar. It felt strange to be wearing his Sunday clothes on a weekday. A day off the school, though. He shoved his hands in his pockets. He'd rather be in the school than going through this.

Faither had explained it, the responsibility of manhood.

'I'll need ye to take a cord, John. That's what the menfolk do. There are six cords to fill, and you'll take the third, behind me. I'll be at the front, with William. He'll be representing Lizzie.'

John had seen funerals in the town often enough, the sombre procession of dark clothes following the coffin. He hadn't really noticed them properly before. He wondered if everyone felt as sick at heart and shaky as he did. Faither had emphasised the need for decorum and dignity. He kicked his shoe. All he wanted to do was howl.

The family started to come out into the street, his sisters all in black, even young Jemima. They looked like strangers.

'Right, John. Are ye ready?' Thank goodness for his brother-in-law William, putting a steady hand on his shoulder. 'We need to get the coffin on the cart, to take it up to the Kirk.'

Even with six men, he found it a surprisingly heavy load. There had been much discussion about the coffin. The girls wanted the best, while Faither was more cautious about the cost. *It's just a box*, thought John. *And it's just a skeleton inside. What does it matter? It's going in the ground for ever.*

He and his sister Jemima had watched his mother thin to bone as the tumour grew in her belly. At first they had wondered if another sibling was on the way, until they saw Dr Rankin's solemn face. The doctor came often after that, sometimes sitting for a while by his mother's side. How could he stand it? John had found it difficult to go into the room at all, though she had called for him often. It wasn't just the look of her; it was that sweet smell, as if something was rotting. It made the bile rise in his throat. His sisters didn't seem to notice. All except Jemima – she would cover her mouth with a handkerchief by the door, and take steadying breaths before going in.

The procession moved forward, up the road to the Kirk. John fell into step behind Faither, following the cart. He was surprised and touched to see so many neighbours at their doors, heads bowed, or gathered respectfully on the corners, caps in hand. He saw the minister waiting at the gate of the Kirkyard. As they entered, he could see the fresh earth of the dug grave, down on the left, and averted his eyes. They carried the coffin to the front of the Kirk, then sat in the very first pews, where the minister's family usually sat. They were all in a row, Faither in the middle, head bowed; John became conscious of many familiar faces behind them. As well as the relatives and neighbours, there were Faither's masonic brethren, turned out in strength to show their solidarity. The service droned on, mostly about the heavenly Father showing mercy. The Reverend MacKenzie mentioned the bereaved family once, in a prayer; his mother got barely any acknowledgement at all, other than as a true servant of the Lord, called home at last.

Then suddenly there was the sound of the door opening at the back of the Kirk. Someone was stepping in. The powerful notes of a familiar hymn cut into the air, interrupting the words from the pulpit.

'Amazing Grace, how sweet the sound ...'

It was the singing man. John could hardly believe his ears. He looked along the pew at Jemima, who was grinning back at him. They stood, to join in – and the congregation rose with them.

Then came the moment he was dreading: carrying the coffin from the Kirk to the graveyard – or final resting place, as the minister called it – and lowering her into that dark hole. At least he had managed the cord, by following William's lead. His ears were ringing so loudly that he could scarcely hear the prayers. As Faither scattered the earth on the coffin, he felt William's hand on his shoulder again. He closed his eyes.

'Whit's he doin', still here?' Faither sounded cross.

Lizzie and Maggie were ahead, on either side of Faither, supporting him as they left the cemetery. The singing man was standing by the gate, head bowed, filthy cap in dirty hands.

Lizzie said, 'He's paying his respects, Faither. Mother was always good to him. He's harmless.'

As they drew closer, the singing man spoke, his voice creaking as if unused to speech. 'Ah'm sorry for yer loss, Mr Lindsay. She was a guid woman.' His eyes were bright with tears.

Faither replied, 'Aye. She was indeed. Ah thank ye.' He cleared his throat. 'And thank ye for the hymn. She would have liked it.'

They got back to the house somehow, where there was tea and whisky. Someone passed John a thimbleful and he put his nose in the glass, as he had seen Faither do, and tried not to think of his mother in that box under the ground.

HARE HILL

JOHN WOKE EARLY, and the first thing he thought was, *That's it. No more school. Ever.* It wouldn't be long now, and William would take him up to the Castlehill mine, for his first shift. These last few weeks of freedom stretched before him, golden and warm. He had been thinking carefully of the summer ahead, full of contradictions about how best to use this precious time. Secretly, he would have liked to run wild with his pals and Jemima, building dens, exploring streams, finding birds' nests. Instead, he knew he should be making himself useful about the town for these last few weeks, running messages to earn a bit extra for the table – and for his secret stash of coins, hidden in an old tobacco tin under his mattress. Maybe there would be time for both work and play – unless Faither caught him first and gave him a list of jobs for the workshop.

He moved to the window and watched the sun coming up over the Market Place, then made his way quietly to the kitchen. He was surprised to find Jemima there already; she grinned broadly as he entered the room.

'John, whit aboot a walk today? Like we used to. Where'll we go? Mibbe up tae the Covenanters Monument? You're always talking about it.'

'Why not?' He found himself grinning back, catching her enthusiasm. 'It's going tae be a grand day. Should you no' peel some tatties before we go, though? I'll do the fire.'

A quick bite to eat, then tatties peeled and put in water, the kitchen fire made up and the coal scuttle filled, and they were ready to go. They were just putting some provisions in a cloth bag when Lizzie appeared, yawning, with a toddler on her hip.

'Are you two off out? It's a bonny day for a walk.' She looked around. 'Thanks for helping, that'll get me started. Enjoy yersels.' She looked rueful. 'I wish I was coming too.'

The air outside was fresh, after the stuffiness of the kitchen. John breathed in deeply. This was his favourite time of day, and he was glad enough to be out adventuring with his wee sister. They headed for the Forth Road, the cobbles running out into dirt track as they left Carluke behind. The road meandered upwards, passing farm steadings and workers' cottages. They stopped for a moment at Yieldshields, looking back over the stirring town; the reek from the chimneys and the growing clamour were starting to recede into the distance.

They walked on. John wondered when Jemima would start with her chatter; he didn't have long to wait.

'It's hard tae think of sad things on a bonny day like this,' she said. 'I still do feel sad, but I keep remembering funny things aboot our maw. Do you mind how she chased you down the street wi' the rolling pin, for eating that plate of scones? The neighbours were all laughing. And when she made jam, the whole house would smell of it.'

'Aye, you could smell the sweet fruit right down the street,' said John.

'The kitchen's just no' the same. It doesnae smell the same as before, does it?'

They walked on, Jemima quiet for a bit as the road climbed higher. They stopped for a moment to listen to a blackbird, and then saw a large hare, galloping ahead of them on the track.

'We're heading towards Hare Hill,' said John. 'Mibbe that's one of the residents.'

'They're always bigger beasts than I expect. Not like rabbits at all. And so fast.'

'I think they are a different breed of animal,' said John. 'I'll ask Dr Rankin.'

They watched the hare weave from side to side up the road, then duck into the hedge and off across the field, disappearing into the distance.

'D'ye think Faither is doing all right? He is awfy quiet, sometimes,' Jemima said.

'As long as he has his pals at the inn, he'll be fine.'

'I dinnae like him going to the inn, John, and smelling of drink.'

John remembered the previous weekend, when Faither had blustered out the door to the inn early on Saturday evening. Lizzie had sent John to bring him home, worried that he had not had his supper. John was a bit shy of the

Market Inn and the loud male voices, so had lingered in the door. He spotted the usual suspects gathered round Faither, who was already looking the worse for wear. Andrew Scott – Scotty – adjusted his stance with the care of one unsure of his balance and, leaning on the counter, spoke loudly.

'Whit next, that's the question, Big Jim, ma frien'. Ye need somebody new in yer bed, to help tak' yer mind away frae yer sorrows.'

'Och, it's too soon, Scotty.' Jim considered his glass of ale. 'Gies a chance. I just need tae get used tae her being gone.'

Scotty delved deep into his bar chat memories as he savoured his pint.

'A lot of men wi' your trade travel. Do the fairs, an' that. Great chance tae meet the ladies. Have ye thought of takin' tae the road, Jim?'

'Aye, I've been to a few fairs in ma time. It's a lot of work, mind, and I'm no' a young man. Still, it's worth a consideration. In due course. Aye. All in due course.'

He downed his pint, and John saw his chance. He stepped into the smoky room and called over. 'Faither. Lizzie says yer supper is getting cold.'

The men at the bar laughed, slapping their companion on the back.

'These womenfolk o' yours, Jim. They'll boss ye to yer grave.'

John had to put a steadying hand on Faither as they

crossed the Market Place; then a familiar voice rang out. 'James! James Lindsay, this is no way to honour the memory of your late wife.'

John recognised the voice well. Steadying himself, Faither took a deep breath and turned to face Dr Rankin, who was striding across the square. A well-known figure in the town, he was tall and of striking appearance with a bold manner; and he was also renowned for his abhorrence of alcoholic beverage.

Faither pulled himself up and spoke. 'Aye, you are right, Dr Rankin. I am embarrassed that you should find me in this state.'

'It is easy to slip into melancholy after a bereavement, I understand that. But believe me, alcohol will not assist you in your recovery. On the contrary, it will only serve to worsen your mood. The other consideration, of course, is this is not an example to set your family, James. Think of young John here, having to retrieve you from the hostelry.'

Jim was contrite. 'I'm sorry, Doctor. It'll not happen again.'

'Away home to the young ones. Is that not Lizzie at the door, looking for you? Good night, now.'

The tall figure walked purposefully off across the dark street as John and Faither hastened home.

As he began to climb Hare Hill, John now reflected that he had not visited the inn since. 'It's Lizzie I worry about,' he said. 'She's got her own wee family, and all of us tae look after as well. Mind you, she's not got to nurse Maw now.'

Jemima kicked at a stone. 'I feel really bad about not helping more wi' Maw. I could make it up to Lizzie now, though. Mibbe if I left the school, I could help her more.'

'Ye need tae stick at the school, Jem.'

'I'd rather not. I'd rather be outside. I like the story time, but sums are boring.' She took a breath and continued. 'When our maw was ill, and Dr Rankin was calling, he always had interesting stories. Better than the teacher. He would tell me things about Carluke, about people from long ago. I think he's writing a book, is he not? I wouldnae mind reading that book.'

'He's kind enough, but he's a wee bit strange at the same time. He can be a bit fierce, too – I've seen him. But he was guid tae Maw.'

'Aye, we all know he means well. Maw always said he has a big heart. Anyway, he's not as fierce as his sister.'

'That's true. Is he not meant tae be quite famous?'

'I've heard that, aye. Not sure why, though. Maybe he invented something,' said Jemima.

'I've heard he collects rare stones,' said John.

'What's rare about a stone?' Jemima sounded puzzled.

'Ah'm not sure. I'll try and find out. Another thing to ask.'

They climbed on, reaching the top of Hare Hill, where they paused, admiring the view. A big sky stretched china blue, and there was a gentle breeze.

'It's so clear,' said Jemima. 'Mibbe we can see Glasgow

from up here.'

John could hear the thrill in his sister's voice, and watched as she stood on tiptoe, hand shading her eyes from the sun.

'I've heard folk say that you can see Edinburgh Castle from the top of Hare Hill.' They both peered into the distance, but could see only a shimmer on the horizon.

John spoke again, indicating north to a cluster of high chimneys, pouring out black smoke. 'See over there? That's the Wishaw and Shotts works. And look, there's the railway.'

He pointed to a train steaming in the distance, like a toy on the track.

'Mibbe that train is going all the way tae London! D'ye fancy going to London, John? We could jump on it!'

John laughed. 'I dinnae fancy London.'

'Do you no' want tae see where the Queen lives? All the fine carriages and houses?'

'Not really. I've enough here, Jem. I've to go to work. This could be my last day of freedom.'

Her face fell.

'I keep forgetting that you'll be starting at the pit. Are ye looking forward to it?'

'Aye. Ah think so. I'm looking forward tae earning a wage. But I know it will be hard work. At least Tom is starting at the same time, and I know some of the other lads.'

'And you'll be with William.'

'Aye. Aye, that makes a big difference.' John visibly relaxed at the mention of his brother-in-law. 'He's taken me up there already, just to the top workings, to show me what it's like. To explain the system.'

'He'll look out for ye, John. You'll be fine.' Jemima patted his arm.

John was heartsore that his mother wouldn't be there to see him off to his first day of work, but he knew his sisters would be proud. He pictured himself often, walking out the door in his work clothes alongside his brother-in-law, two men together. When alone, he would check his arm muscles to see if they had grown. He knew that Faither was disappointed that he wasn't following him into the tailoring business, but he would bring home more money with the mining wages. Being a miner was surely more manly than the tailoring work, too – although he would never say as much to his father. All that chit-chat and measuring up half-dressed womenfolk! He cringed, knowing that his blushes would betray his emotions; and besides, he just couldn't get the hang of the sewing.

They found a spot and sat for a while, munching their oatcakes, then lay back on the grass and looked at the sky.

'Are ye fit for going a bit further? We could make it to the Covenanters Monument. We've come this far, we might as well. Whit d'you think, Jem?'

'Aye. It's mibbe your last day of freedom. Let's keep going.' Jemima jumped up.

They scrambled over a stone wall, then headed north

over the rough moorland, taking special care as they passed small mining works. John's eyes were at his feet and he was concentrating, trying not to trip into a bog or down a disused shaft. He saw a glance of sharp white, and stopped, curious. In a tuft of coarse grass there was a small skull, perfect. He picked it up.

'Look, Jem. I'm sure that's a hare's skull. Careful with it. Let's put it in the bag, we'll take it home. I'll check with Dr Rankin.'

'A hare's skull, from Hare Hill.' She grinned at her brother. 'Ah can put it wi' ma collection.'

John smiled at her. One of his summer plans was to make her a box, so she could store the jumble of feathers, birds' eggs, dried flowers and pebbles that she kept wrapped in an old shawl that had belonged to their mother. He knew there was a hair clasp in there that had also belonged to Maw; he sometimes found Jemima behind the bed, looking at it.

They reached the memorial at last, and stood before it, sombre.

'Just think, Jem. Folk frae the town have taken the trouble tae carry stone up here to build this and honour these people.'

He moved closer and read out the inscription. 'In memory of Cameron, Cargill, Renwick, and their brethren, who worshipped on this spot, in the time of the last persecution. They jeopardised their lives, unto the death, in the high places of the field.'

'Whit happened to them, John? Tell me again aboot the Covenanters.'

'They were ordinary folk, Jem. They got into trouble because they wouldnae recognise the king as the head of the Church. They said the only person that could be the head of the Church was Jesus Christ himself.'

'And they had secret services, didn't they?'

'Aye. They met in remote places, like this. They were hunted down, Jem, by the Duke of Montrose and his men; they were hunted like animals. Some were dragged frae their families, and taken to Edinburgh, where they had a gruesome end.'

'All because they stood up for their beliefs. So brave. That's our ancestors, John.'

'Some of them were great preachers. They would certainly show the Reverend MacKenzie a thing or two.'

Jem made a face. 'His voice just puts me to sleep. I can't stay awake, whenever he starts wi' his sermon. Mind he used to come in tae visit Maw, when she was ill, and say all these long prayers? Maw always said, she would rather have a visit frae Dr Rankin any day. She preferred his company over the long face of the minister.'

'Aye, he has a long nose, and a long face, that's true!' They both laughed, John feeling a bit guilty to be speaking about the Reverend MacKenzie in such an irreverent way.

'John. D'ye remember the singing man, at Maw's funeral? That was special.'

'How could I forget? MacKenzie was in full flow, and

he just interrupted him, started with "Amazing Grace", really loudly, from the back o' the Kirk.'

'Aye. And then we all joined in. MacKenzie wasnae pleased.'

'He'll miss our maw, the singing man. I wonder who'll be leaving victuals out for him now.'

They stayed a bit longer at the Covenanters Monument. John was trying to imagine the crowd gathered at the remote site, singing hymns, listening to their preacher. It would have been wild in the winter – lashing rain and even snow. They would have been raw with cold, the bitter wind cutting through their jackets and shawls. They would have been listening out for the soldiers.

He looked up at the memorial again, then turned to speak to his sister. 'The Free Kirk came frae these roots, Jemima, but I just cannae imagine long-nose MacKenzie preaching on a moorside.'

He shivered and stood.

Jemima jumped up too. 'C'mon, John. Can we go back by Law? I'll race you down the hill. Ye can't beat me!'

She set off at speed and he followed, bounding along behind her. This had been the best day since the worst day, when his Maw died.

Ahead of him, Jemima shouted loud, her voice trailing back to him. 'Ye cannae beat me!'

John opened his lungs and hollered his response. 'Aye, ah can so!'

John was footsore and hot by the time they reached

the Hyndshaw Row, on the track down to Castlehill. The sunshine had brought the cott-dwellers outdoors, to sit on steps and stools, enjoying the warmth of the day. Most were busy at something. A large mangle was being turned, and laundry hung, and John saw several women working on a quilt; but some were just resting, eyes closed, faces turned to the sun. The children rattled about barefoot on the road, engrossed in noisy games. John lifted his cap in greeting as they passed through.

'Do the men here all work at Castlehill?' Jemima asked.

'Aye, these are tied cottages. They belong to the mine owners.'

John knew that there were many such miner's rows around Carluke – and that some gave better living conditions than others. He knew he would have to hold his breath, walking past the privies.

They were just leaving the row when his eye was caught by movement beside one of the outbuildings. He glimpsed a flurry of skirts and a bare bum, and heard an animal-like grunting noise. He grabbed his sister's arm and yanked her forward, forcing himself to look down. He was feeling very queer: excited, yet shocked. Part of him wanted to go back, stand and stare; yet he knew from the Kirk that this revolting, crude act should be abhorred.

He regained his composure. 'That Archie Campbell. He cannae keep his hands to himself. "Lock up yer sisters" – that's whit William says aboot him. Don't ever go near him, Jem. He's no guid. He'll have ye at the back of a wall before ye can say "Get off me".'

'Dinnae worry, I won't. I don't fancy him, anyway.'

'Oh! And who do ye fancy?'

'That would be telling!' She laughed, and as they strolled on the awkward feeling faded.

DOWN THE PIT

JOHN HAD BEEN roused at 5 a.m. and was fast wide awake, with an excitement and dread in his belly. Downstairs, his big sister Lizzie had his porridge ready, his plate set by William.

'A'hm no' that hungry,' he declared. He was sitting tall and trying not to squeeze his upper arms. He hoped Lizzie couldn't see how nervous he was.

'Ye'll be needin' it by the time ye walk up there, let alone piece-time. C'mon, get it down ye.'

Used to obeying his big sister, John lifted his spoon.

William MacDonald had explained 'the system' often to John; and he knew of many others from school that had started in the mine just the same way. His pal Tom Lee would be starting today, too, and they had shared many chats about their futures as Real Men. It was best to start beside a family member, someone who knew the trade and who would hopefully have the patience to induct a youngster into the toughest of environments. A mentor would know what was safe, and what meant danger. John really admired his brother-in-law, but both knew that this would be a real test of their trust.

'Ye'll work for me, John. I'll pay you a half of a half of whit we get together. So, if we load a dozen hutches o' coal, ye'll get the money for three. I'll be working the face and ye'll be behind me, sweepin' and shovellin' the coal intae the hutch.'

John had imagined it often, picturing himself working tirelessly alongside William, filling hutch after hutch.

'It'll be hard, John, especially at the start. Ye'll be that tired, ye won't be able to think straight. But ye'll get used to it.'

'See ma first wage, ah'm gettin' a watch!'

William laughed. 'It'll take a while tae save for a watch, John. You've to pay the union, put towards the check-weighman, pay off yer tools. And dinnae forget, Lizzie'll need some money towards yer keep.'

There was a scuffle in the passage from the stair. John was surprised to see Faither there, looking unusually rumpled in his nightshirt.

'Ah just wanted tae wish ye all the best, for yer first day, son. Yer mother would've been proud.' His lip trembling, he turned away and shuffled on to the privy in the close.

Lizzie and John looked at each other, and she put a hand on his arm. 'C'mon, time tae get off.'

William and John were just at the corner, when they heard Lizzie shout.

'Lads, yer piece-boxes!'

'It's no' lucky to go back!' shouted William.

'I'm comin, hold on!' Lizzie trotted quickly to the pair

and gave John another pat. Smiling, she said, 'See an' no' get these new clothes dirty!'

Heading north on the Glasgow Road, they approached Castlehill as the sun was climbing in a clean autumn sky. John breathed in deeply, as if it were to be his last ever chance of fresh air. Although there were green fields and hills in the distance, the ugly gash of industry tore across the near landscape. There was noise and smoke and dust everywhere; from the busy railway yard, from the nearby tile and brickworks, and of course, from the mine works ahead. A huge corrugated-iron shed crouched over the mineshaft, protection for the winch-gear and for the workers hauling the heavy hutches from the cages.

'Does it ever stop?'

'Aye, just Sundays, John. Otherwise it's round the clock. Day or night, it makes no difference, when you are working down in the dark.'

'Would ah get more money for the night shift?'

'No, John, it's all the same. Mind ah telt ye, yer pay is based on yer hutch weight.'

William approached an older man with a clutch of papers and lists and indicated towards John. The gaffer nodded, and made a note. John looked across and saw two ginger heads: his pal, Tom Lee, and his dad. The boys nodded at each other seriously. This was it, the real thing. No more chats, boasting and speculation. No more nights awake, wondering if they would cut it with the big lads. This was it.

John was glad that William had brought him here before today, to show him the works. He hadn't been allowed to take him down to the coalface, but there was plenty to see in the yard. It was hard not to feel overwhelmed with all the noise, all the filth and dirt.

William had explained about the hutches – bucket-shaped containers with wheels that ran on rails – and the importance of the weighing. This process was at the heart of the contract between miner and manager, and would determine how much the miner would be paid. The pithead officials and the check-weighman would supervise as the hutch was put on the weighing machine; then both would agree the figure to be written in the ledgers. The check-weighman was an independent witness, paid for by the miners themselves. After the check was noted, the miner's identification pin, or token, which had been fixed to the hutch underground, would be hung with the others on its own hook, ready for the next day – and the next, and the next.

John would learn the sound and rattle of the hutches empty, and the different, sonorous sound of the full hutch. He would learn how to keep them well balanced on their rails and how to shift them on again if they fell off. He would learn how to fasten them up to the ponies underground that would pull them to the working sections. He would learn how to push the empties from the sections to the workface, and then push the full ones back again. Above all, he would learn to be careful when working with them; he had heard many stories of crushed limbs, even crushed heads. These hutches would be the background clank and trundle of his working life.

John realised his knees were trembling, and there was fear and nausea and excitement in his belly. He tried to swallow, but his mouth was bone dry.

William picked up his hutch and cage tokens from their numbered hook and stashed them safely in a pocket. Then they walked together to the cage at the pithead. The pitheadman nodded to them both as they joined the queuing men. John tried not to look back at Tom as the line moved forward. They handed over their cage tokens and, all too soon, it was their turn to step into the unsteady-looking metal contraption.

Here we go, thought John, his knees almost buckling.

He took a last breath of fresh air, trying to steady himself. William pushed him to the side and back of the cage, where he could hold on to the bar. The count was made and confirmed. There was a gruff 'Hold on tight' from William and, with a creak, the cage dropped. John grabbed his brother-in-law's jacket, relieved to be at the back where no-one could see the protective arm going around him.

Oh God help me, God help me.

The descent seemed to go on forever, a silent hurtling into utter blackness.

God help me.

The velocity of the drop combined with the feeling of

dread in his stomach, and he tasted the sour mix of bile and porridge in his throat.

Then a slowing, and it stopped. The men stepped out towards the lamps, from which each miner would light his own. John hid behind William for a moment, composing himself. Then he moved forward, to learn about taking your light. He started to look around, his eyes becoming accustomed to the strange dimness as William steered him in the direction of the workings.

'Whit a size of a place! It's like an underground railway!' John was amazed to find a maze of rails and tracks, snaking through passages to the area beneath the pithead cage. He found that he could stand easily and walk about in this strange underground world.

'Walk between the lines, John. Be sure an' listen out for the ponies and the hutches, they go fast. I'll show ye the hidey-holes further in, to get ye out the road on the narrow bits.'

They walked on and on. John was tiring quickly. It was getting warmer, and there were many new hazards to notice and dodge, from metal ropes to dung from the ponies. It seemed like hours later when they arrived at the section where the miners were gathering, waiting to hear the fireman's report.

'All clear, lads. I've checked the joists. Ye're good tae go.'

At this, William led John onto a narrow track, off the main tunnel. Just one set of rails stretched ahead into the darkness. The height dropped quickly, and John started to bang his head on outcrops. He noticed that William, ahead of him, walked with a crouched gait, and he tried to copy. The air was stale and dusty. He was feeling disorientated and lost, suddenly aware of the tonnes of earth above him. It seemed to go on for ever.

'Here we are. Now, I'll just fetch ma tools.' At the end of a shift, the miners would roll up their tools carefully in cloth and hide them, ready for the next day. William retrieved his bundle, and started to set John up for the morning's work.

'Is that it? The coalface?' John could see the gleam and sheen of the seam, stretching to either side.

William nodded. 'Aye, that's it. King Coal.'

A cheery voice greeted him from further along the workings. 'How are ye doin', young yin? Ah hope ye've had yer porridge!'

'That's Sanny, ma neighbour,' said William. 'He'll look out for ye, won't ye, Sanny?'

'Aye, William, we all look out for each other down here, dae we no'? All the best, son. Ye've got a good teacher there. And mind out. Nae whistlin' – it's no' lucky.' Sanny gave a wave, and turned back to his work.

'First, we have to test the rock for safety.' William was using his pick, tapping the roof and the coalface. 'Ye have tae listen. A good solid sound is whit we want.' He tapped carefully around, then moved back, satisfied. 'Your job is tae move the coal back tae the hutch point, back there by the rail. The hutch'll be here soon. Then we'll fill it as quick as we can, ready for the next.'

John rushed to start, using a shovel and his bare hands to move the coal. Soon he found he couldn't get comfortable. His knees hurt, as he knelt on the rough, hard ground. His back hurt, bending in the awkward height. His hands hurt, sore already with cuts and bruises. The coal kept coming, and he just couldn't keep up. And at last, here was the hutch, ready for loading. A lad who looked the same age as himself was manoeuvring it into position. Despite his fatigue, John couldn't help looking at the lad's biceps, and despairing.

'See youse later,' shouted the lad – then was off, scurrying up the passageway, weaving from side to side to avoid the overhangs.

William hung his token on the hutch and joined John, shovelling the pile of coal inside.

'We want it as full as we can, but nae bits sticking up on top. They'll be hell to pay for, if we get the hutch train stuck at a low bit. Put the big, craggy bits in first. Save the flat bits for the top.'

John was relieved to be in a different position from the low passage by the face, but again found he was tiring quickly. He tried to follow William's instructions as best he could.

The drawer – for that was the name given to those that pushed the hutches – returned and put his shoulder to it. The hutch juddered, and he got into position behind it. Hands flat on, he shoved the heavy container along the track.

'See youse later,' he shouted back, up to a run now.

John managed a laugh. 'Is that all he can say?'

'Aye, that's his greeting to us all.' William laughed too. Then he spoke gently. 'Why don't ye have a wee rest over there for a bit? Shout me when the next hutch comes.'

John put his head back carefully against the relentless stone. This was going to be much, much harder than he had ever imagined.

'John! Johnny! How was it doon the pit?'

John heard Jemima's voice, as if from far off. He could hardly stay awake at supper, struggling to keep his eyes open, yet desperate for the stew and tatties that Lizzie had prepared as a special treat. He had smelled the food as they had approached the house; it had kept him going for the last few yards. He had bolted his dinner down, gulped his tea, and then his head hit the table. Lizzie had insisted on rousing him to wash, before helping him to his bed. He brightened for a moment, and started to speak; but then his eyes closed mid-sentence and he fell into unconsciousness.

Jemima got her chance to hear of the miner's life later in the week, but mainly all she heard was a hymn of praise.

'William is that good tae me. He even gives me a bit o' his piece. He's watchin' ma back all the time. He's so strong, whit a worker. Ah'll never be as strong as him.'

'Aye, John, ye will. He's a man, you're just a lad. Lizzie says you've got much growing in ye yet. You've to eat yer porridge!'

John smiled, remembering the morning before, when he had scarcely made it out of the door on time, Lizzie pressing oatcakes into his hand, to eat on the road.

'Aye, mibbe, Jemima.' He felt his upper arms. 'But ah've a bit tae go yet.'

'Jem! Where are ye? Come an' look at this!'

John was home from his work and, for once, he wasn't rushing straight to the table. His sister appeared from the close.

'It's a fossil. Somethin' trapped in the stone, frae hundreds o' years ago. Mibbe thousands!'

Jemima stepped forward to peer into his hand. They moved to the lamp, and there it was – a delicate fern in the stone.

'It's a wee plant, frae long ago. It got stuck in the stone.'

Jemima lifted it closer to her eyes, peering to see the pattern more clearly. 'Aye, ah see it. It's beautiful! Did you find it?'

John hesitated, looking over at William.

'Naw. Naw, it was Sanny, who works alongside us. He says it's one of the best he's found. Sanny says we should tak' it tae Dr Rankin. He'll know all aboot it. I'll go over later on.'

Lizzie turned from the stove. 'Dinnae go bothering the

doctor tonight. It's cold and miserable, ye dinnae want to be havin' him open his door tae a chill. Take it the morn, before yer late shift.'

John nodded and moved to his place, and asked his usual question. 'Whit's for tea, Lizzie?'

'Guid day, John. May I help you?'

John recognised young Sarah Kennedy, who had recently finished school; he had forgotten that she had started work at the Rankins'. The starched apron and cap confirmed her status in the house. He was startled to realise how pretty she looked.

'Guid day, Sarah. Ah was lookin' for ...'

He was interrupted, as a diminutive figure dressed all in black pushed past Sarah to the door.

'Yes?' A fierce voice, a flinty stare.

'Good day, Miss Rankin. Is the doctor at home?'

'Aye, but he's having a rest. He doesn't want to be bothered.'

'Now, who's this?' The familiar voice came along the passageway, and Dr Rankin appeared. Miss Rankin pursed her lips tightly, as Sarah made her escape to the kitchen.

'Oh, it's young John Lindsay! How are you, John? Come away in. Don't you mind my sister – she's not had her smile medicine today, so she's a bit out of sorts.'

John wasn't sure how he should react to this. Was it a joke? He smiled weakly. He started to slip past Miss

Rankin, who was still grasping the door as if she wanted to give it a good slam.

'Have you wiped your feet?'

'Oh … Right away, Miss Rankin.'

John obeyed vigorously, then entered the house. In truth, it was more of a cottage; none of the finery you might expect from someone with a grand title like 'Doctor'. Cosy enough, but not fussy. Dr Rankin beckoned him into the kitchen, where Sarah was busy at the sink. John couldn't help noticing that the back of her neck was a kind of rosy colour.

The doctor was quite stooped now, but still had authority, a presence. Although his famed long locks of hair were now white, his eyes were still bright, inquisitive and sharp as he reached for the stone.

'Where's this from, John?'

'I found it down the pit, at Castlehill.' He glanced at Sarah's back, corrected herself. 'No, ah mean my neighbour on the seam found it, an' he gave it tae me.'

'Of course, I heard you had started at the mine. Best come into the other room, John.'

They moved into the study, where the doctor selected an eyeglass from his desk and examined the fossil. 'It's a Mariopteris, and a fine specimen, at that. Will I write down the name for you?'

'Aye, thank you! Is it old, Doctor?'

'Yes, John. I'd say we are looking at a plant that was alive millions of years ago.'

'Whit? Millions?' John let this wash over him. No, he couldn't take the number in. 'Is that when Noah was in his ark?'

Daniel Rankin sighed. 'Long, long before then, John. Long before the Bible was written. Scotland was a hot, tropical place before our ancestors came. Large areas were under a warm sea, a sea that teemed with life. That is what our coal seams are made from. I could show you a few more specimens.'

The doctor opened a large wall cabinet. John could see that the many shelves were much shallower than usual, and that each contained labelled trays.

'It's my collection.' The old man stood taller, clearly enthused. 'Jock Fulton made me this fine cabinet. Look at all the fossils! They tell us so much about the world, and how it was formed. There are fossils here of fish that swam in that tropical sea.'

He pulled out a tray and put it on the table. John saw a variety of odd-shaped stones, each carefully labelled with a date and place name, and some difficult-looking Latin. Looking closer, he could see tiny patterns: the swirl of a shell, the skeleton of a fish.

'If you are interested, I could tell you more. I enjoyed our chat the other month, about the genus of the hare. Shall we say tomorrow, after you have been to the Kirk? Please tell your sister Jemima that she is most welcome too.'

Sarah Kennedy showed him to the door. John found he

could scarcely look at her. And something had happened to his voice; he was stuttering, could hardly get his words out.

'Aye. Thanks, Sarah. Ah'll see ye again.'

He was cursing his lack of eloquence all the way home.

Back in the tailor's house, Lizzie and Jemima gathered round to hear about the visit. The family all held Dr Rankin in great affection, remembering his frequent visits during their mother's long illness. His brisk and no-nonsense plain speech had softened as he spoke to her. He was always honest and clear in his explanations, yet compassionate, alert to her suffering and fear. He was a notoriously difficult man to pay, often exclaiming that the bill would 'come another time' or making droll remarks such as 'there are no charges on a Wednesday!'; but John knew that Faither always made sure his shirts were made of the finest cotton, and sometimes the tailoring bill just wasn't sent at all.

'Did ye see the crocodile?' said Jemima. 'I heard he had it stuffed.'

'Goodness, d'ye remember the crocodile?' said Lizzie. John loved the story. It was a Carluke legend. 'Do ye mind the time it took a walk across the street?'

'Aye, and we were all chasin' it!' He laughed.

'It was a horrid creature! The teeth on it! It would bite off yer hand in a second. Ah'm glad it's dead. It gave me nightmares.' Lizzie clutched her weans to her.

John disagreed. A crocodile as a neighbour was highly

interesting, and its demise to be mourned.

'I think ye should both go tomorrow, right enough. Dr Rankin's a most intelligent man,' Lizzie went on. 'Ye could both learn something. Mind and not say to the minister, if ye're heading there straight from the Kirk. He might not approve.'

'Why not?' Jemima was genuinely puzzled. 'It's only some boxes o' stones, is it no'?'

'Aye, but the Reverend MacKenzie thinks that Dr Rankin is using his fossils to tell a story aboot the earth that is different frae the true story in the Bible.' Lizzie shrugged. 'Whit dae I know? I hear that many learned folk go tae his door. Why not you two?'

A visit did take place, the following Sunday afternoon. John and Tom had chatted about the fossils on the way to work, and Tom was eager to accompany them to the doctor's house.

Daniel Rankin clapped his hands when he saw the little crowd. He was clearly relishing the opportunity to share his knowledge, and to enthuse the young people. Sarah Kennedy crept out of the kitchen to join in – and was encouraged to do so by Miss Rankin.

'The scones are ready, so I'll see to the tea, Sarah. Go through and listen well, you will surely learn something.'

John was just about managing not to think about Sarah in the room. It was lucky that the doctor spoke in such an interesting way. He had looked out illustrations to enhance their understanding. Soon John was imagining palm trees and strange lizard-like creatures all the way along the Glasgow Road to the Castlehill mine. Strange to think that the mine and tile works didn't even exist then. Perhaps it was all just a rolling moorland landscape, like Hare Hill, as far as the eye could see.

'It was much warmer, John,' said the doctor. 'The landscape would be swampy, like a huge soupy bog.'

'And whit aboot the people?' Tom was interested too.

'This was well before there were people in Scotland. The human race is a relative newcomer to the world stage. The planet was changing and evolving for many millions of years before people came.'

'If not humans, then what were the first creatures, Dr Rankin?' asked Tom.

'It is thought that the first creatures were just tiny collections of living matter, no bigger than a pinhead. It would look like a miniature collection of frogspawn. After that would come jellyfish-like creatures.'

He sought out a picture of a jellyfish and showed them. Jemima wasn't keen. 'Ugh! It looks quite monstrous!'

'Look at those tentacles!' Tom was wide-eyed.

Daniel Rankin continued. 'Some of them grow very large, and some have a deadly sting. That is how they capture their prey. There were also more gentle creatures long ago; there were many types of worms. I have a very great interest in worms. They can tell us much about how the earth evolved.'

John turned to the cabinet of books and papers, by the desk. He was suddenly conscious of Sarah standing nearby, in that neat wee cap. She smelled of baking. He cleared his throat and managed to speak. 'Are all these books aboot fossils and worms, Doctor?'

He smiled. 'Not all of them, John, but many of them. One of the most important books is this one.' He lifted a well-thumbed tome from the shelf. 'Charles Darwin's *On the Origin of Species*. One of the most exciting and controversial books of our age.'

'Is this the book that the minister doesnae like?' asked Tom, moving forward to take a look. 'The book that says we all come from apes? D'ye believe that, Doctor?'

'It is about a great deal more than that, Tom. It is interesting that the Church is concerned with just a few of the ideas discussed here. I would be glad to talk more about it, but I think that the tea is ready, and it does not do to upset my good sister.'

They all tucked in, Sarah included; Miss Rankin had made sure there was plenty of delicious jam. As he reached for another scone, John heard the doctor speaking to his sister, as they stood by the fire.

'It is wonderful to see the curiosity on their faces. Do you think that perhaps this might be a time for another series of lectures? It's a few years since I last shared my learning with my neighbours here in Carluke. It is all very well to correspond with Edinburgh and London about these matters; what of the next generation of young Scots?'

'Your talks had a bit of a mixed reception last time, Daniel, dear.'

'But at least it gets folks talking.' He brightened. 'What about a debate with the Free Kirk minister?'

'You know fine the Reverend MacKenzie would never agree to that.' She chuckled. 'It does me good just to think on it, though. You would run rings around him, Daniel.'

'I don't mind most ministers, you know that. There is something about MacKenzie, though, that rubs me up the wrong way. We just can't seem to get along at all.'

'Hush, Daniel.' Miss Rankin looked back at their young guests, enjoying their tea. 'It wouldn't do to …'

'Speak my mind?' He laughed. 'That's a habit I'll not break!'

He turned to his young visitors and said, 'Have you all finished the jam, already?'

After waving goodbye to Tom in the Market Place, John and Jemima returned home, full of chat from their visit. They were telling Lizzie all about the swamps, when Faither strode into the kitchen. He seemed distracted, almost agitated, fiddling with his moustache. He took up a spoon and knocked it on the table, for attention.

'Right. Just to let ye all know. I've the offer of a place on a cart heading up to Wanlockhead tomorrow. That lead-mining place, up in the hills. It'll be full of miners wi' money to burn on a nice waistcoat, so this is a good opportunity to take ma wares further afield. I should be back in a few days, and hopefully the order book will be full.' He leant his hands onto the surface of the table. 'I'm sure ye'll all be fine without me.'

There was a stunned silence. John looked round at his siblings, then back to Faither, who was almost grinning.

'Good idea!' said Lizzie. 'It'll do ye good, to get out and about; and all the better if the orders come in. We'll all be fine here. William and I will watch this place, Maggie and Jane will look after the workshop.'

John nodded along with the others, but there was an uneasiness in his heart. Faither had the look of the inn about him, that slightly cocky air of mild inebriation, yet no drink had been taken. John brushed his concerns aside. He was likely just imagining things. There was surely nothing to worry about, in a remote wee mining village in the Lowther Hills?

PART THREE

A meeting
1873

THE BLACK ARMBAND

MARTHA'S MOTHER MET him first; it was she who was responsible for the offer of lodging.

'Ah had a guid impression of that tailor packman,' she said, as Martha came in the door. 'A clean-looking wee chap, a recent widower. He'll be back later on, and will pay guid cash for the use of the trestle bed in the attic space.'

A widower. Available, then. Martha felt a shiver of interest, quickly followed by shame. That she should be curious about a man recently bereaved; surely that was wrong. Nevertheless, she wanted to hear more. 'Whit else was he saying, Mither?'

'Aye, we had a long chat. This is his first time in Wanlockhead. I'm no' sure what he was expecting, but he seemed surprised to find civil company.' She chuckled. 'I told him, it's not all miners here. He's going door to door, then he'll head to the canteen, to try selling his wares to the shift changes. I expect ye'll see him there.'

'Ah see you've got the broth on,' said Martha. 'I'd best prepare the roof space. The bed just needs making up. Arthur left it clean enough, but I'll tak' the broom up with me.'

She took especial care preparing for work, brushing her near-black hair till it shone. All the while, she was remonstrating with herself.

What's the point of getting all worked up? He'll never notice me, and if he does, he'll hear my history soon enough. Damaged goods, that's me. Anyway, he's probably not my cup of tea.

Still, she set off with a spring in her step, waving to her neighbour.

'Did ye see the packman's wares yet, Martha? He was having a fine chat wi' yer mither. He's got some bonny skirts – no' cheap, though!'

'Not yet,' replied Martha. 'I'll mibbe get the chance later. Doesnae cost to just have a look, does it? Might get some ideas, for brightening up what I've already got.'

The canteen was quiet when she went in, but in a couple of hours it would be a rumble of noise as dozens of men arrived, looking for food. Martha and her workmates set about cooking and baking, and soon there was a warm, homely smell pervading the hall. After an hour or so, the door creaked open.

'Is that the aroma of freshly baked scones, I wonder?'

A dapper wee man entered. He had a warm friendly smile and an easy manner. Martha noticed the smart cut of his jacket, and her eye caught the black armband on his sleeve. His moustaches were most pleasing, just right: not overwhelming and droopy, not mean and clipped, but just right.

'Ladies – Mr James Harvie Lindsay, tailor of Carluke, at your service.' He removed his bowler hat and bowed. It was impossible not to smile. 'Might I set up my wares in the corner, there? I'll be well out of your way. My trunk is just outside. If there was a table that I could borrow, all the better. I am keen to show off my waistcoats to best advantage, to the miners of Wanlockhead.'

The gaffer stepped forward, wiping her hands on her apron. 'Aye, ah dinnae see why not, although good luck; our miners are a pretty rough lot. Mibbe us *ladies* will get a look at your wares too, later on.'

Tables were moved, the trunk was brought in, and the tailor set to work setting up his stall. Martha couldn't help glancing over. First, he brought out a folding frame, which he assembled with three neat clicks. A few selected garments were displayed on this contraption, including a tartan waistcoat, paired tastefully with another, of rich maroon hue. A crisp linen shirt was draped across the middle of the display, then two shawls. One was plain chestnut-brown, warm-looking; the other was in the familiar paisley pattern, autumn colours of gold, russet, red. He arranged the two carefully and stepped back to admire his handiwork. Then he placed sample books and an order ledger on the table, and arranged his tape measure around his neck. He clapped his hands together, and made a little bow towards his audience at the service counter.

'Might there be time for a cup of tea, before the hordes arrive?'

Martha lifted the large brown teapot and poured the tea; then she served him up a scone. His eyes were blue and bright, direct and kind. He raised his eyebrows, and instinctively Martha raised hers in return.

The canteen was in full swing. Martha scarcely had time to look over to see how the tailor was faring, but it looked quiet in his corner. Then a rowdy group entered and greeted him by name.

'Big Jim! How are ye?'

'All set up, lads. Ah promised ye a look at some waistcoats, did I not? Nothing but the best for the Airdrie boys!'

These big lads were strangers to Martha. The tailor must have come up with them on the cart. Sometimes a call went out from Wanlockhead to the Lanarkshire pits, when there was a shaft to be dug; this looked like a team of labourers, right enough.

'Shove, why don't ye try somethin' on?' The older men pushed a tall, muscular young lad to the front.

'Aye. Why no'? Ah fancy a velvet waistcoat. Can ah try it?'

Of course, it was too small; but the lad paraded around in it, making everyone laugh with his mincing walk.

'It's nice material, Big Jim. An' pockets for ma baccy. You should get lots o' custom.'

Sure enough, the Wanlockhead men were starting to come forward to take a look; even the hardest of them were smiling, as the tailor encouraged Shove to turn this way and that, to show off the stitching.

'Shove. That's a new one on me. Why do they call you that?' he enquired.

'It's no' ma real name. Ah get called it for ma hands.' The lad held up his huge paws. 'Like shovels. They shortened it tae Shove, and it stuck.'

The laughter rang out, and Martha knew the sales would be good, as the men thronged the stand.

The Airdrie lads had enjoyed the food, it had to be said; all the soup was gone, and the fruit cake had been very popular. The hall was quieter now, and Martha had time to approach the tailor's table. She felt anticipation stirring as he smiled at her.

'That's a bonny shawl. Beautiful colours.' Her fingers brushed the paisley pattern. 'And warm, too.'

'It would suit ye well, with that dark hair,' said Jim, 'and would show off your complexion, into the bargain.'

'Och, I expect ye say that to all the women,' said Martha; but she smiled, enjoying the compliment. 'Now, I think ye are lodging wi' me, Mr Lindsay?' She couldn't fail to see how his face lit up. 'I'm Mrs Marshall. Ye spoke tae my mother earlier, and she offered ye our attic space. It's simple, but it's clean. If ye care to wait until I finish here, then we can walk home together.'

'I would be delighted. Most delighted.' He hastened to pack up his trunk while she finished cleaning down the counters; she couldn't help the smile that was still playing at the corners of her mouth. As she took up the broom for her final task, she was acutely aware of the tailor's eyes on her as she swept, and could feel the red blush start in her neck.

There was a nod from the gaffer, and she was free to go. James Harvie Lindsay was waiting for her by the door, the trunk already outside on the handcart. They set off down the street, starting off with an awkward moment, as both spoke at once.

'Do ye have a family in Carluke?'

'Have you always lived here?'

They laughed, and Big Jim bowed his head. 'Ladies first.'

'Tae ask, or tae answer?' she smiled.

'To ask, of course. You wish tae know about my family?'

'Aye. Who is at home in Carluke, Mr Lindsay?'

'Well, sad tae say my wife died recently. She suffered with a terrible growth in the womb. We were all bereft.'

'I am truly sorry for your loss,' said Martha.

'It was a difficult time, but somehow ye get through it. My eldest, Lizzie, she's a good lass, a real homemaker. She bides wi' me, along with her husband and their two wee ones. We gave them the use of the front room when they were first wed. He's a good man, William. He works hard at the pit, and Lizzie is a hard worker too, caring for her weans and all the rest o' the family besides.'

He says it as if he is just realising the extent of her toil, thought Martha.

He spoke, as if reading her thoughts.

'Aye. A bit o' distance from home, and telling a stranger the story, it helps ye see things a bit clearer. Lizzie has taken on a lot. She cared for her mother when she was on her sickbed, too. She's a remarkable girl. Never complains.'

He adjusted his posture to get a better grip of the handcart. Martha thought perhaps he was limping, but before she had the chance to enquire, she saw the cottage ahead, her mother on the bench at the front, a neighbour bent in conversation beside her.

'We're nearly home, and I have yet to hear of the others in your family. Later, perhaps? Let me tell ye quickly of my situation. I bide here wi' my widowed mother and my wee girl, Agnes. She's still at the school. My husband died some years past. So ye are coming into a house of women, Mr Lindsay.'

He laughed. 'I'm used tae that, Mrs Marshall.'

They stopped by the bench, and Martha's mother stood up to greet them as the neighbour nodded then departed. They made arrangements about storing the trunk and went in.

It was Martha's turn to see things through the eyes of a stranger. She was pleased that her efforts that morning were evident; there was a gleam to the room. Even the tongs in the fireplace looked polished and cared for. There were few possessions, but the simple pieces of crockery were arranged well on the shelf, and the little bunch of broom sat prettily enough beside them. The embroidered tablecloth looked neat, although her eye caught the worn edging.

Jim turned to Martha's mother, who had followed them in.

'I wonder whit the glass ball signifies?' he asked. 'Ah've seen them in many windows here.'

The old woman paused, then looked him in the eye. 'It's hung there tae keep away the witches, Mr Lindsay. If they keek in, they'll see their own reflection in the glass and they'll no' come in. They'll think there is already a witch installed by the fire.'

'Goodness. Is there still a strong belief in witches, here?'

Martha saw his gaze rest on the family Bible, and spoke reassuringly.

'These are old superstitions, Mr Lindsay, but such little habits from the old ways can be hard tae break. The glass ball has been in the family for many a year.' She looked beyond the window, into the street. 'This'll be my daughter coming now.'

The door was pushed open and Agnes came in, Barkie at her heels. Martha was pleased to hear her greet the stranger politely.

'Pleased tae meet you, Mr Lindsay. Ah hope ye'll be comfortable wi' us. Ma maw makes fine broth.'

'Aye, ah smelt it on coming in the door. It's a cosy wee place ye have here, Mrs Marshall.'

Jim crouched to pat the ginger dog, as Agnes told the

story of how she'd found her under the ground. Martha smiled over at her mother, as she reached for her apron.

Dishes cleared, seats agreed by the fire, a Carluke pipe filled with tobacco, and the chat began. Agnes was by the window on a little stool, playing with Barkie; Martha and her mother leaned eagerly into the conversation. They learned that, alongside Lizzie, the tailor had two other girls who worked in the business as seamstresses; and then they heard about Jemima, the youngest, still at school and hardest hit by the death of her mother. Agnes's ears pricked up.

'That must be terrible, to lose yer maw. Mibbe Jemima is the same age as me?'

Calculations were made, and it transpired that Jemima and Agnes were very close in age.

'Just months in it – fancy that!' said Martha. 'And ye have a boy too, tae keep ye company amongst all these lassies?'

The tailor smiled. 'Aye. John. Named for my faither. He's a good lad. Quiet. He's just started down the pit.' He shook his head in response to the questioning looks. 'Ah couldnae stop him. He had his heart set on it. He's that impressed by his brother-in-law William, he wanted tae follow him down the mine.'

'Ma husband worked the mines here, Mr Lindsay. Lead, of course, and the pits not as deep. We hear some o' these coal mines go an awfy long way into the earth.' Martha's mother grimaced and went on. 'It's no' natural, working all bent up, under the ground like that. It did for my man; he died o' a terrible injury.'

'Och, that's shocking to hear. Aye, they are dangerous places. Ah tell you, it touches you, seeing yer lad going off to work, becoming a man. Seeing him that first day dressed in his work clothes, all too big for him. That was hard.'

The women nodded sympathetically. Agnes fetched the tea and biscuits, and the conversation moved on. The tailor expressed a wish to hear more about Wanlockhead, and their remote lives; Martha wanted to hear about Carluke, his journey, the new railways that were being built.

Martha's mother enjoyed talking about her village. 'Ah've never been anywhere else but here. It's a fine place when you are used to it, Mr Lindsay, although it does rain much o' the time. We have guid neighbours and there are entertainments. The men play quoits, and there is curling in the wintertime. And our wee library is famous.'

'It's a big library, Mither,' corrected her daughter. 'We have thousands of books, Mr Lindsay, and all available for the men tae borrow. The newspapers make their way up here, too, even if they are sometimes a few days late. There is always much to chat about round the fire of an evening.' He seemed so interested, she couldn't help smiling at him.

'And there is the Church, of course,' her mother said. 'We have a guid minister. There have been famous folk here, too. Did ye ken Robert Burns left the blacksmith a bonny poem? Ayrshire folk say he wasnae that keen on the mines, though. Apparently he didnae like the cramped spaces. We've got his Works up there, on the shelf. It's a grand read.'

'Aye, he's very popular.' The tailor had remembered something else about Wanlockhead. 'What about the gold?' he asked. 'I've heard the rumours of nuggets as big as your thumb, fortunes made. Is there any still to be found?'

'Och, aye, but ye have tae ken where tae look, Mr Lindsay. I've seen some guid chunks in my day. Fortunes have been made, right enough. They say there were miners here from all over Europe, in days gone by. Gold enough for a crown.'

'Gold enough for a crown!' The tailor smiled at Martha, raising those eyebrows again. Her heart grew.

I like this wee man, she thought. *I like him very much.*

As he stood out of the chair, Martha noticed a grimace. She raised her eyebrows, questioningly.

The tailor sighed and told her he had such a pain in his ankle. 'I must have strained it, putting the trunk on the cart. Ye'll think me a decrepit weakling.'

'Not at all. Let me take a look, Mr Lindsay.'

Reluctantly he eased off his boot and sock. Martha's mother had already moved to the stove and was pouring hot water into a basin. Martha sat on the floor and lifted his foot into her lap, examining the joints of the ankle. The tailor winced as she moved it to the left.

'Aye, ye have mibbe strained it, right enough.' She touched the foot gently; she could feel tension under her caress, care and worry. Her hands moved from the heel to the toes, finding bunching and tightness.

'Dae ye suffer wi' headache, Mr Lindsay?'

He looked surprised. 'Aye. Especially after a long day at the sewing.'

'Yer foot can tell me a guid deal.'

She watched his eyes close and his face relax, as her fingers moved over the calloused skin.

'Why don't we soak both yer feet? We have some herbs here that will soothe them. Then we'll rub some balm into that sore ankle and bind it up.'

Jim didn't have to be asked twice.

The little house was still at last. Martha could hear the breath of sleep from Agnes, pressed in by the wall. Her mother was lying quietly on her side, in the middle of the bed. Martha stretched her arms above her head, knowing sleep was far distant.

'You'll no' sleep like that.' Her mother spoke in her ear. 'Calm yersel'. Try and rest.'

Martha ignored her, thoughts racing.

She was thinking of her daydreams, of the many wishes she had made for escape. She knew in her head that the storybooks were silly, with their tales of handsome men rescuing beautiful and worthy young women from lives of drudgery, but her heart dreamed of such an adventure.

Her mind went back to the blacksmith, Agnes's father, and the deep thrill of his touch; there had been a blissful summer, then such a shock when she learned he had disappeared back to Glasgow. Of course, her mother had shown no surprise about her news; she had remained tight-lipped and silent, only nodding briefly when she had explained that she wanted to keep the baby. Martha knew how much she owed her for facing up to the whispers and the judging eyes, helping to raise the child, caring for the girl whilst Martha worked.

She shifted slightly, eyes open in the darkness.

Then she had met Billy Marshall. He had been a regular visitor to the village, bringing the cart up from Biggar twice a week. Such a handsome lad. He would wait for her after her shift at the canteen, and they would steal some time together at the ruin beyond the corner of the village. She smiled, remembering the delicious anticipation of those precious moments. At least he did the decent thing by putting a ring on her finger before the baby was born; and he took her to Biggar, even if they did have to stay with his parents. She sighed. She had loved living in Biggar. It was a bright place – no glowering hills, fewer gloomy corners for bad spirits to hide. Even the weather was better: warmer, not so wet and miserable. Her mother had given her quite the look when she told her of the plans, but didn't try to stop her. Instead, she had wrapped Agnes close to her, and wished them well.

Then just eighteen months after the wedding, Billy

Marshall was dead. She should have seen the signs – the cough, the thinness of him, the crows following the cart. There was nowhere else to go but back to Wanlockhead, and with a sickly child. Her mother had welcomed her back with open arms. Agnes had loved Lucy, called her wee sister.

Now this. It was overwhelming, sensing those feelings coursing through her again. Might she stand a chance with the tailor from Carluke? She turned on her side, and her mother jabbed her back.

'Sleep!' she hissed.

Martha knew fine well that sleep was far from her mother too. Surely she wouldn't grudge her another chance? Her life here was so small, a drudge of a routine. The cottage felt cramped and crowded, with its tiny windows. She remembered the fine big kitchen in Biggar, and wondered about the tailor's house in Carluke.

Her thoughts turned to her mother. She sighed, and her mother jabbed her again, as if reading her mind. She felt a flicker of guilt. Yes, of course she loved her mother, but sometimes she just felt suffocated. Everyone in the village knowing everyone's business, and her mother at the centre, with all her stories of the old knowledge passed down. Mostly, she felt real pride in the respect shown to her mother and the authority she carried, her knowledge of the healing ways. She knew how privileged she was, to have learned her mother's craft and skills. Her mother had often said she had a real gift for it, a sixth sense. Aye, that part was good. But sometimes she felt as if she needed some room to breathe on her own. And the rest was just relentless hard toil, from five in the morning at the farm, then back after the milking to the canteen for the rest of the day. The monotony, drudgery and fatigue stretched ahead into the darkness. So often she dreamed of running free, far down the road, away from it all. And now this smart wee man had turned up, with his nice moustaches and black armband. Was it really so wrong to wish?

Martha rose early as usual the following day, walking into the thick envelope of cloud that blanketed the village, heading out to the farm. The weather seemed to reflect her mood – it would be easy to become confused and lost in the silent mists.

Milking over, she was returning to the house when she saw a figure appear before her, just by the twisted tree. It was the tailor. His eyes were wide.

'This is surely a supernatural place, wi' such a climate,' he said. 'Ye appeared before me like a ghost!'

She laughed. 'We are used tae the low clouds in our village, Mr Lindsay. They keep us company. How's the ankle today?'

He looked down and moved his foot. 'It's better. Ye have a real knack, Mrs Marshall.'

She regarded him carefully. 'Are ye no' biding another night?'

'Sadly not. I'll go round the doors on the far side o'

the valley this morning, then join a cart that is leaving at midday. I have a place back tae Abingdon, and it will be easy enough to pick up further transport from there.'

'Ah'm sorry for it. We've enjoyed yer company. Perhaps I'll catch ye before ye go?'

'Aye.' He smiled and nodded, and her heart filled with warmth. He went on, 'Aye, I'd like that. And mind, I'll be back soon, with the completed orders. Perhaps I might stay again?'

She tried not to appear too eager; but a queer longing came over her, and she leaned forward to touch his arm, letting her hand rest there. 'Yes. That would be grand.'

She would be late for her work, but she was determined to say goodbye. There was a knot of folk by the cart, and she could see that his trunk had already been loaded. He had his back to her, speaking to the carter; then turned, as if looking for her. His face brightened. 'Mrs Marshall. Ye came.'

'Martha. Call me Martha.'

'Martha. That's a good name for ye.'

'I wish ye a guid journey, Mr Lindsay.'

'And it's Jim, tae you.'

'Jim. Haste ye back, Jim.'

'Aye. Just a few weeks, and these orders will be ready. I will return soon, Martha.'

The cart trundled off up the road. Martha stood watching, as the tailor's smart bowler hat bobbed into the mist.

WAITING

'AH THOUGHT I'D take a look for some young nettle, Mither. Down the Mennock Pass.'

Martha watched from the door as her mother glanced back from tending the fire.

'Aye. Some new nettles would be grand. It's the right time tae be taking them.'

'And ah just need some time tae think.'

'You dae that, lass.'

Had she heard a tut? Was her mother angry? She was never angry. Martha felt the tension grasp her gut.

She started off quickly down the path then slowed her pace, better to breathe, better to still the churn of her body, her mind. She nodded to a neighbour, who gave a cheery wave. Now she was on the road to the pass, the valley that meandered down through the hills to Nithsdale, the gap that carried the busy, chortling river. There would be prospectors at the bends, gathering and sifting the crunchy silt from the river bed, looking intently for the glint of gold. It was mainly the off-shift miners who guddled in the water here, but occasionally there was a camp of hopeful lads from one of the cities, come to try their luck.

The best forage was in the west-facing gullies, where the plants were protected from the damaging rays of the early sun. Martha walked down the track by the river; sometimes the pass felt closed in, almost dark. Then the road took a turn, and the valley floor broadened out into a wide, green carpet, the noisy burn rattling through its centre.

She was trying to remember the exact spot where she had to climb, if she was to see the cross. Her father had brought her here when she was just a child. How old had she been? Five? Six, perhaps? It was just before he died. Her memories of him came in vivid, intense flashes: a rough yet gentle hand on her head, the smell of pipe tobacco, a loud, deep voice shouting a greeting in the doorway. He had explained that the cross was hidden and difficult to find, unless you knew just how to look.

'Ye have tae climb up. Then ye'll see the outline, when ye look down on it, the raised marks on the grass.' He had taken her hand in his, to help her up the hill.

Martha found herself talking to him as she scrambled up the gulley, to the top of the bank. It was further than she thought; she had to stop to catch her breath, leaning the basket against the steep hillside. She had spotted some young nettles and chickweed, which she would gather on the way back.

Am I mad, Paw? Upsetting everyone again, thinking about getting up and leaving. It's just that I'm hungry for this, a new life. I want it so badly. Surely it would be good for us all to have a man who can support us better?

Reaching the top, she paused there, catching her breath again. She looked around, smiling at the views that stretched out in all directions, a big sky above her after the claustrophobic tightness of the valley. Looking back, she could see the familiar village nestled along the track; then she turned, to see the far sweep of the uplands before her.

Is it wrong to want something more? she thought. *Something out there – different, new? We're here on God's earth such a short time.*

She started out along the edge of the high bank, remembering that she should look for the hunch of rowan trees on the opposite side of the valley, then the ring of the sheepfold. She peered down onto the flat grassy area below, and suddenly saw it: the unexpectedly large raised outline of a cross. Her breath caught in her throat. What had her father said? This had been the site of an ancient church, just the symbolic outline of the foundations now remaining after many centuries of erosion. Martha put down the basket and sat on the grass. This was a good place to calm her mind.

After a while, she stood, ready for the foraging. She gave one last glance to the Galloway hills, full of spring colour; then – oh joy! – a large brown hare came lolloping towards her, across the moor. She squatted down as it approached her, regarding her solemnly, its ears twitching black. She felt the song start in a hum.

Martha knew that folk were talking. She had already been asked to her face if there was anything ailing her. She wondered if they could see into her heart; her mother could. Perhaps it was her distraction that was causing the gossip. You could spoil the scones once in the canteen, but twice in a week had set tongues wagging.

Yesterday a neighbour had called to have her burn re-dressed. Martha's mother was on the bench outside, talking to her cousin; Martha had heard another voice, then her name mentioned, and the woman entered.

'Yer mither says can ye dress it the day?'

'Aye, Jeannie. Take a seat. I'll just wash ma hands, an' fetch the stuff.'

Martha sat down opposite, making sure the arm was in the best light. She carefully unwrapped the old sheeting, sprinkling a little water where it was sticking, and exposed the wound.

'How are ye doin' wi' it? Burns are awfy painful.'

Jeannie winced. 'Aye, they are that. Done in a moment, pain for weeks. It's much better when the dressing's on, Martha.'

'Aye, it'll need tae stay on for a while. Try and keep the arm rested and lift it up as much as ye can. Encourage the blood flow, it helps the healing. Ye can sit wi' a cushion under it, of an evening.'

She washed the arm gently in water. The burn looked angry, but Martha was pleased to see there was no sign of infection. She put her nose near, just to be sure; it smelled clean. She prepared the honey paste and spread it on carefully, then wrapped fresh worn and ripped-up bedding sheets firmly around the arm. Then she pulled the old, long-sleeved glove on over the top, and gave Jeannie a pat.

'I'm that grateful tae ye, Martha. Whit would we all do without you and yer mither?'

'It's no trouble, Jeannie.' Martha stood to wash her hands again.

'Martha. Can I ask ye something?' Her neighbour clearly had something else on her mind; she lowered her voice. 'It's a private matter.'

'It might be ma mither you'll be needing?'

Jeannie didn't look pregnant.

'Naw, it's no' that. I wish. It's the opposite. Whit I want tae ask is …' The woman was struggling to find the right words.

'C'mon, Jeannie.' Martha sat down again and leaned in.

'It's ma husband. He just doesnae seem that bothered any more. He's more interested in the drink than he is wi' me. It used tae be fine between us. We have two fine weans, mind. Mibbe he thinks we are finished with all that. Mibbe it's just us gettin' older.'

Jeannie had been just one year ahead of her in the school. Martha was shocked. Surely it couldn't all be over in your thirties? She thought quickly.

'Jeannie, ah've got something on the shelf that might help; I'll fetch some for ye. Put it in his food a few days, see how that goes. And here is another thing tae try.'

She leaned in closer, until she was speaking into Jeannie's

ear. She spoke words about lifting the nightshirt, about looking, touching, stroking.

Jeannie's eyes grew wide. 'Thanks, Martha. I'll let ye know how ah get on. I'm no' sure aboot that last one, but I'll give it a try.'

Martha was reaching up for the dried mushrooms as Jeannie spoke again.

'Are ye all right yersel', Martha? Ye seem a bit peaky lately.'

'Aye, aye, I'm fine. Just a bit tired, that's all. The summer sunshine will cheer me.'

'It's just that I've seen ye a few times asking aboot the post. Are ye expectin' a letter?'

Martha looked out of the window, reluctant to make eye contact. 'Not really, Jeannie. It's nothin'. We're waiting tae hear if Agnes is tae get a lace loom. I've been a bit concerned aboot her at the school, these past few months. If ye hear anything, will ye let me know?'

'Aye, the Free Kirk minister's girl, Catriona Ferguson, she was bothering her for a bit, was she no'? Ah think things are much better now she has Barkie. All the kids are wishin' they had a dug.'

'She loves that dog, Jeannie. Aye, mibbe you're right. I shouldnae worry. She's not got long at the school now anyway. With any luck, she'll be starting the sewing soon.'

Jeannie gave her a look as she passed over the jar, and Martha reddened. Jeannie knew fine well there was no worry about Agnes. Everyone knew she was waiting to hear back from the packman tailor from Carluke.

WHISTLING IN THE TAILOR'S HOUSE

JOHN AND HIS pal Tom liked sitting on Tom's front step. It gave them a good view of the street, and also allowed rapid access to Tom's kitchen, where sometimes there was baking to be sampled. Both lads had a clay pipe and tobacco in their pockets; later on they would find a quiet spot and practise smoking.

They had been talking about their work at the mine, comparing callouses on their hands, sharing tales of strength and stamina. Both agreed they still had a way to go before they would be working in their own right; but they also agreed it was getting slightly easier, as they became accustomed to the routine of the day.

There was a lull in the conversation.

'Ah hear Sarah Kennedy is working at Dr Rankin's house?' John was trying to sound casual.

Tom looked at his friend. 'Aye. We saw her there, did we no'? And so what?'

'Nothing.' He could feel the dreaded redness creep up his neck and into his face.

'Dae ye fancy her?'

'Naw!' The riposte exploded out of him.

Tom continued to scrutinise his friend. 'Aye. Ye do so.' There was a pause, then he said, 'She's a bonny enough lassie, but wasn't there somethin' in her history? Ah think she lives wi' her grandparents.'

'Ah dinnae ken. Ah just remember her frae the school. Tom, don't ye be saying anything tae anybody, right?'

'All right, pal. Dinnae fret.'

'Whit aboot trying these pipes? Will we wander down the brae?' John was keen to move the conversation on.

Later, reaching home, he heard Jemima's voice raised high. It sounded like a bit of a stramash was going on in the kitchen. His heart sank, as he remembered all the recent drama. With trepidation, he pushed open the door.

'He's pure shite and ah hate him!'

'Where did you learn to speak like that? Get out here now!'

Jemima was hunched crying under the stairs, always her favourite place in a crisis; Lizzie was remonstrating with her. He had come home at exactly the wrong time. Any moment now and Lizzie would ask him to intervene. He certainly didn't know what he could say that might possibly calm his sister.

The anger was fizzing in Jemima's voice. 'I knew something like this would happen. He's had this wee smug smile for weeks, whistling and singing around the place, all the time plotting and planning. Whit's going tae happen to us? *I miss my mammy!*'

This last was bellowed with such vehemence that Lizzie

recoiled. 'Wheesht! The whole street will hear ye!'

'*Ah don't care!*' Jemima was sobbing into her hunched knees.

Lizzie swivelled round to John. 'Can you no' speak to her? She might listen tae her big brother.' She took a deep breath. 'I'll make us all some tea. There might even be a bun.'

'Ah was thinking of another wee walk before ma work,' said John.

His big sister glared at him menacingly.

Resigned, he moved over to the stairs and crouched down. 'Jem. Here's a handkerchief.'

'Thanks,' came the muffled reply. A hand came out to take the proffered item.

'We all miss Maw, Jem. But we have tae face the future bravely.' He hoped his words sounded stronger than he felt.

Jemima snuffled, still unable to speak. This news from Faither was clearly upsetting her.

Faither had travelled back from Wanlockhead with a full order book, and in a most excitable state. He had been in the workshop all hours, trying to fulfil the orders as quickly as possible. Both Maggie and Jane said that he was driving them demented, that he was like a man possessed. Then yesterday there had been an explanation at last for his odd behaviour. Summoning his children, he shocked them all by asking what they would think of a new stepmother. He then announced gravely that he was considering getting married again and they should all be very happy for him. The Lindsay siblings had looked at each other with horror. Jemima had burst into tears, saying that he was betraying Maw. Later, they became curious about this woman from the hills who had so beguiled him; they would speculate on her appearance and character, and wonder how on earth Faither could even consider such a dramatic change to all their lives. The very fabric of the tailor's house seemed to rock with uncertainty.

'C'mon, Jem. Let's get out for a walk.'

Jem allowed herself to be hauled to her feet. She blew her nose again, and the siblings set off. They started out down Jock's Brae, Jemima marching fiercely ahead, muttering to herself. Then she let John catch up and they sat for a while by the burn, poking with sticks at the bracken-coloured water, before making their way back to the town. They had decided to speak to Dr Rankin, as a person of wisdom; however, now that they were at his door, John felt really foolish.

Jemima stepped forward and knocked. 'Hello, Sarah. Is the doctor there?'

John let his sister speak, as the familiar awkwardness engulfed him.

'Aye, I'm here.' The tall figure loomed at the back of the passageway, and beckoned them into the parlour. 'Come in, Jemima; and John, too. I can see by your faces that all is not well. Is someone ill?'

John was aware of Sarah disappearing into the kitchen, and closing the door firmly.

'Good day, Dr Rankin. Good day, Miss Rankin.' John nodded politely to the small figure knitting by the fire. 'We are sorry to trouble you. There is something wrong, but I don't think it is anything you can help with. Perhaps we had better just go home.'

'Sit down, both of you. Jemima, have you been crying? What is all this about?'

'Dr Rankin, my heart is sore,' said Jemima.

John winced. 'It is a family matter, Dr Rankin, not a medical one,' he said. 'Jemima, perhaps we shouldnae bother the doctor.'

'Come on, Jemima.' The doctor leaned forward. 'Out with it. Something is clearly upsetting you.'

The kind tone set Jemima off again, with a wail. 'It's Faither. He's met a woman, and he's talking about getting married.'

Miss Rankin tried hard to suppress a smile.

'Is that not a good thing, Jemima?' said the doctor. 'It will be company for your father. This woman will never replace your mother, of course, but she could be someone to help him in the home, make it more comfortable.'

'We don't *need* help. Lizzie looks after the kitchen. All of us lend a hand. We are all fine. We don't need this woman to come in and change everything.'

John looked at the floor. He hadn't really thought it through, about what would happen if someone else took over his mother's kitchen. He really didn't like the notion much. Still, he was mortified to be discussing this with Dr Rankin.

Miss Rankin spoke, more softly than usual. 'All of us find change difficult, Jemima. It is entirely natural that you should feel this way. Your father has shared some surprising news, and you will need time to get used to the idea.'

'I don't *want* to get used to it. I hate the idea.'

The Rankin siblings looked at each other, and the doctor spoke again.

'This will be a testing time for you, Jemima, right enough. But harbouring angry thoughts is not good for your health.'

John looked up, curious.

Jemima blustered on. 'But I'm serious, Dr Rankin!'

'I'm serious too, Jemima. Ill-feeling is like a terrible disease. It can eat away at you, from the inside.'

'What can I do? I can't help feeling like this.'

'You are recognising these angry feelings, so that is a start. And you will still be feeling sad, after the death of your mother. Fresh air and exercise are the best medicine. Interests at school and outside the home will also assist. Read stories and books. Play with your friends. Sing.'

'Yes.' Miss Rankin nodded. 'Singing is particularly good for driving out bad feelings.' She started to hum, then sing. 'My love is like a red red rose ...'

Her brother interrupted her. 'Singing is very good for

our health. I should prescribe singing more often.'

Jemima managed a smile. Dr Rankin relaxed, and turned to John.

'You did the right thing coming here. It always helps to talk, although I recognise it is harder for our masculine gender. If either of you needs to let off some steam, you are always welcome. We won't say a word to anyone.'

'It's all confidential in this house.' Miss Rankin leaned forward; she still looked concerned. 'Things have a way of working out in the end. Sometimes it isn't how you imagine it at all. You are such a bright lassie, Jemima. Surely it'll be just fine.'

John got out of the door without saying anything too embarrassing to Sarah. He even managed to give her a wee smile – which he instantly regretted. He stuffed his cap on his head, annoyed with himself again. He needed to work on appearing more manly. Crossing the square, he was relieved to notice that Jemima seemed easier. Perhaps visiting the doctor had been the right thing to do.

Then they heard a familiar sound and stopped, looking over the street. There was the singing man, shuffling along in his ill-fitting shoes, and crooning loudly. He was looking from doorstep to doorstep for a plate of food or a wrap of bread. John knew he was quite alone in the world; yet he was still singing. He wondered whether Dr Rankin had prescribed it for him, long ago.

Just a few days later, John woke with the sun starting in

the window. He'd be just on time, if he left now. He sat up determinedly, then turned to jump out of bed, gritting his teeth: he didn't want to lose his nerve.

He was trying to appear interested in the hedgerow as Sarah came up the brae. As she walked past, he started to follow her. She stopped and turned to face him.

'Good day, John.'

'Oh. Hello, Sarah.'

There was an awkward silence that seemed to go on for ever. He lifted his face to look into hers and was caught by her eyes. Were they always that hazel colour? She was smiling.

'Um … Can ah walk ye tae yer work?' He had managed to say it.

'Aye, John. That would be grand.'

He wanted to holler and shout with relief and joy; instead, he fell into step beside her, hands in his pockets, trying hard to appear like a real working man walking with his girl.

Faither was in the kitchen when he got back. He had received a mysterious letter the day before; perhaps that was it, folded into his inside pocket, the edge peeping out. He was whistling that catchy wee tune that was on everyone's lips and polishing his boots to a shine.

'Morning, John. You're up early. Ah thought ye were on the late shift the day?'

'Just fancied a breath of air, Faither.'

John felt suddenly emboldened by his earlier bravery in

meeting Sarah. Perhaps he could speak to Faither, man to man. He sat down opposite his parent.

'Faither. The lassies are no' happy wi' this talk of marriage.'

'All o' them?' His father raised those bushy eyebrows, blue eyes glinting. 'Ah thought it was just our Jem. She misses her mother something terrible, so it's no' surprising she's upset.' He continued to polish the boot. 'Ah'm no' young any more, John, but I'd still like' – he paused – 'companionship. This might be ma last chance for a bit o' comfort in ma older years. So.' He put the boot down on the floor and faced his son. 'Ah'm heading back to Wanlockhead, and then I'll see what's what. Ah'm still just thinking on it. I've yet tae make up ma mind. Your sisters will just have tae accept my decision, whatever it might be. I've a life to live, son, and I'll tell ye this, she's a fine woman. Ye'll mibbe understand when ye're a bit older. A man needs a woman in his bed.'

John was shocked. He had never considered Faither in this way, and had certainly never heard him speak so frankly. He didn't know where to look.

Faither chortled. 'Ye'll understand well enough one day, John.' He stood. 'Whit aboot some porridge, lad? I've a journey to make.'

John was starting out for his late shift when he saw Faither swing the trunk on to the cart, then jump on. They exchanged waves.

He's in a great frame of mind, John thought. *He's jaunty, no two ways about it.*

John remembered that great bursting feeling in his chest earlier, when he was running across the Market Place after delivering Sarah to the Rankins' door. Maybe this was what it was like, when you fancied someone. With all that whistling, Faither certainly seemed to have a fancy for this woman in Wanlockhead.

THE RETURN OF THE PACKMAN

AT LAST, A letter. The carter had waved it aloft for her, so doubtless all the village now knew of it. She stuffed it into her apron pocket, and took it home.

Dear Martha,
Might I trouble you for accommodation once more?
I plan to return to Wanlockhead this Friday, as my orders are now complete.
I am looking forward to seeing you again.
JHL.

Her fingers moved over the last sentence. She must reply right away, before the carter left. She raised her eyes, to find her mother looking at her quizzically.

'I need tae get a response back to the cart before he heads off. Mr Lindsay will be here on Friday.'

Her mother said everything by saying nothing. Martha picked up her pen.

We would be pleased to have Mr Lindsay lodge with us again, and look forward to his visit on 22nd of August.
MHM.

Martha was at the crossroads, brushing down her apron, unable to keep a broad smile from her face.

'Mr Lindsay! Guid to see ye!'

Thank God. It still felt right. He was just as she remembered, smart moustaches and all. The tailor was distracted for a moment, organising the offloading of his trunk onto a small handcart; but then he turned, and his blue eyes smiled back at her. She was sure he felt the moment too, excitement and anticipation stirring.

'Is that trunk full of all these orders ye secured in June? That was quick work! Oh, ah'm sure the pieces are all perfect, of course.' She added the last hastily; the last thing she wanted to imply was any hint of careless workmanship.

'Ma two lassies, Jane and Margaret, they help wi' the tailoring.' Jim picked up the handles of the handcart. 'Shall we go?'

They moved off from the crossroads, Jim pausing to give a cheery wave to the cart driver and his fellow travellers. They walked along towards the church, and there was Martha's tiny cottage in the row opposite. Martha pushed open the door.

'Mither! Agnes! We have company. Mr Lindsay is back tae lodge wi' us for a day or two.'

Barkie was bouncing, all noise. 'Quiet there!' Agnes grasped her dog and held her tight. 'Nice tae see you again, Mr Lindsay.'

'Good day, Agnes, hello Barkie. And good day, Mrs Hewson.'

'Guid day, Mr Lindsay. Come away into the house. Ye'll be wanting a cup of tea after yer journey.'

Agnes dashed to the hearth and moved the kettle on to the fire. Jim stepped into the gloom, and Martha watched him familiarise himself. There was the big box bed, arrayed with blankets and pillows; nearby, the ladder up to his quarters in the roof space. There was Mither's comfortable chair by the fire, and there was a little table, set for tea, with smaller chairs around, brightened up by embroidered cushions. She had done her best to make the place look welcoming. Martha watched as his tailoring eye was caught by a lace loom set up in the corner. He couldn't help taking a look.

'Is it yourself that does the lacework, Mrs Hewson?' he enquired.

'Och, naw, Mr Lindsay. Ah wouldnae manage wi' my eyes. That's our Agnes. She's just started wi' it this month.'

'Ah'm still learning, Mr Lindsay. Ah'm that slow at it.'

'Aye, but neat and careful, it seems.' Jim was examining the work with a professional eye. 'It's not just about speed, Agnes. That will come. It looks as if ye have a real knack for neat work.'

Agnes glowed, and Martha shot him a grateful smile.

Tea drunk and domestic arrangements made, Jim stepped out to make a start on his deliveries. He was pulling on his boots when Martha called after him.

'Ah've ma work at the canteen, Mr Lindsay, but the house is yours tae come and go as ye need it. Ma mither will see to ye. I'll be back by early evening, when there will be soup and oatcakes, and ah'll see ye then.'

'Please, Martha. Call me Jim.' He tipped his hat and set out along the path.

'Jim, is it?' said her mother.

'Aye. It's Jim,' she replied.

'He'll likely be hearin' some chat, when he does his deliveries.'

Her mother's face was set. Martha noticed Agnes listening awkwardly, aware of an atmosphere. She was clutching that stone in her pocket.

'Aye, like enough, Mither,' she said. 'Ah can't stop folk talking. Whit will be, will be. Now, Agnes. Do you and Barkie fancy a wee stroll? You could walk me tae ma work, get some fresh air.'

Agnes talked non-stop, wanting to show off a new trick that Barkie had learned. Martha was grateful for the distraction. At work, it wasn't so easy; her thoughts crowded into her day. What was Jim hearing, at the doors? The neighbours would be asking where he was staying. Would he hear comments about 'that tinker Hewson woman and her poor wee bastard'? She nearly cut her finger open, chopping the carrots. The stigma, the never-ending shame; it came over her in waves of nausea.

When he returned to the cottage in the evening, she welcomed him in with a direct look. Then she said, 'Expect there was a bit o' chat, when ye made yer deliveries, Jim?'

He was pulling off his boots, sneaking glances up to her as she stood by the stove. The smell of broth pervaded the room.

'Agnes, run and fill up the water jugs, will ye?' The girl obeyed, stepping out of the door, and Martha turned her attention back to Jim. She tried again. 'Ye'll doubtless have heard ma history, then?' She rounded on him frankly, a hand on her hip, the other holding a wooden spoon.

'Martha, mibbe Mr Lindsay would just like his supper …' Her mother's tone was conciliatory.

'It's fine, Mrs Hewson. Aye, people do like to talk. You'd be surprised whit I hear in my line o' work.' She smiled at this, imagining indiscretions shared with a tailor. 'But,' he continued, 'I like tae make up my own mind aboot those I meet, not have it decided for me.'

'Well. That sounds like a fair way to proceed.' She turned back to the stove. 'Perhaps we could have a stroll out after supper,' she continued. 'It's a fine evening, and ah could show ye the sights of Wanlockhead.'

'Aye. That would be grand,' said Jim. He moved to the table, where he was invited to sit himself down and make himself at home.

Chaperoned by Barkie, they both breathed deeply as they stepped into the warm evening. Martha was reluctant to parade through the village, so they soon left the houses behind, heading up Stake Hill. She asked him about his journey, and laughed when he told her how he had pointed out Crawford Castle – his ancestral home – to his fellow travellers.

'But it is the ancient seat o' the Lindsay family!' he protested.

'Aye, but it is a ruin now, Jim!'

'We all love a story, though, Martha, do we not?'

They speculated on wealthy ancestors and what life was like in times gone by. Then, when she felt it was the right moment, she asked him about his wife.

He told her that Margaret had been four years older, from a small village south of Carluke. She had enjoyed visiting the fairs and markets in the town, always a grand way to meet up with other young people. They were wed well before Lizzie was born, with Jim still just twenty years old. The years had passed in a blur of children and family, long hours building up the business. Then Margaret's dreadful illness was upon them. He wondered where the years had gone. By the time she died, he was a father of five, grandfather to two weans, with a successful tailoring business and a respectable place in the town, but nobody by his side to share it with.

'My own faither died in his early fifties,' he said. 'Ah'm no' ready for that. Ah feel as if I still have life to live, yet.'

He went on to explain proudly that he was an elder in the Free Kirk, as his own faither had been; he didn't seem to notice Martha bowing her head.

'My faither was one of those who walked out of the old church in Carluke, to set up the Free Kirk.' He shook his head. 'That's some story.'

He asked if she belonged to a church.

'Aye, Jim. Our family has always been with the old Church of Scotland. The minister here is a guid man. He has always been kind to our family, despite everything.'

He looked over at her, then asked the question she knew was coming.

'Whit aboot your own situation, Martha? It sounds complicated.' His voice was curious, yet sympathetic.

So often rehearsed, agonised and fretted over; with a rush, her story tumbled out. The disappearance of the bonny young blacksmith. Agnes's birth. The support of her mother. The short-lived happiness with the carter from Biggar. Her return to Wanlockhead, a widow. The death of little Lucy.

They had been climbing steadily as she spoke, her eyes mostly on the rough path ahead, only occasionally glancing at Jim as her story unfolded. He too was looking down, listening in silence, with just occasional nods. They came to a standstill, catching their breath as they looked down. The village looked like a tiny afterthought, nestled into the creases of the wide rolling hills; the colours of the summer were stretching into the golden sky.

This beautiful evening is indifferent to my story, thought Martha. *The hills and the sky will be here long after we are all gone.*

'I'm glad that you've been straight wi' me, Martha. I appreciate that.'

'In Wanlockhead everyone knows ma story. It would be terrible if ye heard one thing from me and another from my neighbours.'

They were quiet for a moment. Martha's heart was

beating hard in her chest, and it was more than the exertion of the climb. At last, she spoke. 'Ah think it's important we are honest wi' each other, from the start.'

'I agree,' said Jim. 'It's the only way.' He looked into her eyes, and she knew the bond was there now.

Martha allowed herself to enjoy the stroll down the hill. The conversation was easier – more laughter, a bit of flirting; she felt like picking up her skirts and running. Before they reached the road she did just that, careering down the last of the hill while Jim jogged behind her.

She swung round to meet him. 'Ah've no' done that in a while!' She patted herself down, steadied her breathing. 'We've surely earnt ourselves a seat, tae watch the sun set.'

Matching strides, they walked back through the village, Martha nodding to her neighbours as their eyes took everything in.

Once back at the cottage, Jim rummaged in his travel bag, bringing out a half-bottle of whisky. A tot was poured for Mrs Hewson, and then Martha and Jim took a measure each out to the bench, where they settled comfortably.

Jim spoke first. 'Ah've spent much time these past weeks, thinking over ma last visit.'

'Ah thought on it often too, Jim,' she said. She could barely trust herself to speak, and heard nerves crackling in his voice too.

He turned towards her. 'We said we'd be honest wi' each other. Would ye be dismayed if ah told ye this old man has taken quite a fancy for ye?'

She laughed with relief. 'Less of the old man, Jim! Ah thought ye said there's life in ye yet? And would ye be surprised if I told ye I've got quite a fancy for ye, too?'

Jim reached across; she put her hand firmly on his chest.

'Given ma circumstances, perhaps you would expect I might be freer in that regard. Mibbe too late, some might say, but I've learned ma lesson. Ah really like and respect ye – and fancy ye, too – but I dinnae want things to spoil between us.'

But, allowing him a kiss, she leaned in eagerly; and when his hand touched her face, she held it there with her own, breathing in his smell of tobacco and cloth.

She rose early for the milking as usual. When she returned to the village, her heart filled as she saw Jim by the marker stone, waiting. He pointed at the path behind her.

She turned and saw the hare watching them.

'Aye, ah see them often, Jim. Bonny creatures. Sometimes I wonder if they understand more than we think. Mibbe they carry spirits, of folks gone by.' She took his hand in hers. 'I'm glad ye came out tae meet me.'

They walked up the path towards the village, and paused at Meadowfoot. Martha pointed out Lucy's grave, and Jim saw two tiny, fresh bunches of daisies laid carefully by the headstone.

'We miss her so much, Jim.' Martha wondered why she had brought him in here; then she found herself opening up, sharing her darkest thoughts. 'Ah mean, ah go tae the church every Sunday, and wee Agnes too, of course. But who knows whit happens after we die? Ah hate tae think o' her lying in the cold earth. I'd prefer it if she was a hare, running free in the hills. Agnes really believes she's an angel now. But myself, I'm not sure.' She paused. 'Or mibbe she's a star, up in the heavens. When it's a clear night, there are so many stars, are there no'? More than we can count.'

'Many of us have lost children, Martha.' He touched the lettering on the stone. 'This is a recent bereavement. Ye must still be grieving. It is surely the hardest test for anyone. Perhaps we are drawn tae believe whatever will help us get through it.'

She looked at him questioningly.

He nodded. 'Aye, we had two babies that did not survive. Not strong enough for this life. The Kirk gives us comfort, a way tae make sense of it all. But ye're right. None of us know for certain. There's all that talk in the papers just now, that we come from apes. Can ye believe it? There's a man – a doctor – in Carluke; he says it is definitely true.'

The mood lifted, and Martha laughed. How could she not? She was having a real conversation, with a dapper man. 'Aye, ah've heard aboot that. Is it no' Charles Darwin? I'm sorry tae get so serious. Let's head back up the road.'

She found an arm offered, and she took it, enjoying the

sensation of warmth, of finding their step together.

The next day, Jim was at the twisted tree by the marker stone once more. As she walked down the path towards him, she searched his face, trying to read his thoughts. He walked towards her, hands outstretched, and asked if she would do him the honour of becoming his wife.

Martha told him she could not believe her good fortune; and she meant every word.

But amongst the joy, much grave discussion had to take place. To Martha's relief, she found that he was considerate of her views; even on the difficult topics, a certain understanding was developing between them. Sitting on the bench in front of the cottage, she spoke frankly. 'Ah'm used tae being an independent woman, Jim – running my own household, and looking after my own affairs. I'm no' looking for a protector, or for someone who would do ma thinking for me.'

'I understand ye nicely; and we will suit each other just fine. Let me explain. In ma work, Martha, I speak tae many women. I have often observed the difference between a woman in a respectful and loving marriage, where there is plenty of room for difference and tolerance, and those with a controlling husband, one who seeks tae dominate the household; the latter are invariably miserable. I prefer good cheer in my household. I want us to be happy, my dear.' He paused and took her hands in his. 'And let's keep yer past where it belongs – in the past. We'll talk of it no more.'

Other practical matters had to be discussed. What of Martha's mother? And Agnes? Martha was clear. Her mother was elderly and infirm, but otherwise in good health. She and Agnes had managed well enough together before, and there were helpful cousins in the same street, who would look out for them. Besides, her mother had lived all her days in Wanlockhead, and would not want to move now. Money was mentioned and an agreement reached. The upkeep of both her mother and Agnes would be supported by Jim after the marriage.

Jim described the situation in the Carluke Market Place house. He said perhaps it might be best if Lizzie and William found their own home, with their little family; then the kitchen could be Martha's domain. Jim thought he knew of a suitable lodging nearby, and would suggest this.

Both wondered privately at the disruption that these arrangements would make to the lives of their families. This would be a life-changing event, not just for themselves.

Jim spoke his thoughts. 'All ah know is that I want ye by my side from now onwards, Martha. We'll climb the hill together, as the bard says.'

Martha's heart swelled at the mention of the simple love song by Robert Burns that she knew so well.

John Anderson my jo, John,
When we were first acquent;
Your locks were like the raven,
Your bony brow was brent;

But now your brow is beld, John,
Your locks are like the snaw;
But blessings on your frosty pow,
John Anderson my Jo.

John Anderson my jo, John,
We clamb the hill the gither;
And mony a canty day, John,
We've had wi' ane anither;
Now we maun totter down, John,
And hand in hand we'll go;
And sleep the gither at the foot,
John Anderson, my Jo.

All her instincts were telling her that she had found her life companion at last.

'Aye,' said Martha. 'Ah'm ready to climb the hill o' life wi' ye, Jim. Though mibbe we are starting from halfway up that hill, dae ye think?'

A WEDDING

THERE HAD BEEN great excitement and speculation when the lace agent came to the village. Folk were surprised to learn that Agnes was to have a loom; it was generally thought that her preference for her left hand would preclude her from fine needlework, but it appeared this was not the case. Agnes was delighted. She had never been a great one for remembering the names of plants or making cures, but she could sew.

She had to admit, she had mixed feelings about leaving school. Her greatest excitement lay in the thought of earning enough money that she might be able to buy herself some nice boots, but she knew well enough that it was still a remote possibility, that every penny counted in the household. Although she struggled to write with her right hand, sometimes school was interesting. She enjoyed the lessons taught in the new way by the young master, with pupils encouraged to understand their learning, rather than reciting by heart. She was proud that she could read and write and do her sums. She especially liked writing her wee stories. However, it would be a relief to be away from the taunts and the name-calling, even if things had improved for a bit after the incident at the dig on the hill. Her fellow pupils liked Barkie; indeed, they were jealous. They knew well enough not to ask for a dog themselves. Their mothers were already speculating how Martha could afford to feed the animal, as well as the family. Agnes had taken on a higher status as a dog-owner and sometime heroine, and the story of finding Barkie never seemed to pall. What her fellow pupils particularly wanted to know were any gruesome details from the accident. Had she seen the head, reportedly smashed in? Was the eyeball hanging out? Was there much blood? Were there ghastly sounds emanating from the corpse?

Agnes took these interrogations in her stride, only occasionally adding some colour and drama to the oft-told tale.

'Ah telt ye, he had a sack over his head. But mibbe there was a strange noise …'

'Like … whit? A groaning? Like a ghostie?'

'Mibbe more like a gurgling sound, like a broken pump. Ah was that busy listening for Barkie, ah didnae really take notice.'

'Did ye get a lift in the doctor's trap? Lucky you!'

'Aye, he was nice. It saved me carryin' Barkie all that way. She was that weak, she couldnae even stand.'

Now the memories were fading, but her attachment to the dog only grew. Barkie had settled in like a comfy glove. She was now free to roam the village, and knew when the school was finished, so was always there to meet her mistress at home time.

Life is steady just now, thought Agnes, her fingers rubbing the stone in her pocket, feeling its strength. She smiled, pulling herself taller. The thought of Barkie always made her smile.

But then the tailor packman had arrived, spoiling everything. She hated the tension in the house between Grannie and her mother; Maw was so distracted and strange, and Grannie just looked worried all the time. She knew that Maw was doing the wishing fires again. Her blood had run cold when she had found a fragment of crumpled paper one morning, after her mother had left for the milking. It said *Martha Lindsay*.

This explained everything. She now understood Maw's attention to her hair and her face. She had liked it at first when Maw had encouraged her to comb the rosemary oil into her own hair, but now she didn't want any more to do with it all. She took to walking out further with Barkie, turning the future over and over in her mind like the stone in her pocket from the Priest's Pool. She so wished it had magic powers: to turn back time, to before that wee man came to the village, making her maw giddy.

Now he was back, and the two of them were down the lane somewhere, doubtless getting up to all sorts. A cold anxiety was building in her stomach.

'Dinnae fret, dearie.' Grannie always seemed able to read her thoughts. 'We'll be fine, whatever happens.'

Nobody wants a bastard. I'm just in the way. Mibbe I should have been the one lying in Meadowfoot. She grimaced; she was pretty sure bastards didn't get to be angels. At least Barkie was on her side. At least she had her dog. 'We'll away out a walk, Grannie. See ye later.'

Agnes stepped out the door, up towards the village. As she turned the corner, she stopped. Oh no. There was Cat Ferguson, large as life, tossing back her bright red hair as she sat swinging her legs on the wall by the crossroads, surrounded by her adoring entourage.

Agnes hesitated, but was somewhat reassured on seeing a figure approach down the road behind the group.

Cat shouted out, 'Well, how's ma favourite wee bastard this evenin'? Oot wi' her scabby dug, whilst her maw goes hoorin'?'

'Now then, Catriona. What would your father say to this? It's not a very civil way to address a neighbour, is it?'

The Reverend Laidlaw laid a hand on Cat's shoulder. 'And what does the Bible say? Do unto others?'

'Aye. Ocht. Aye, Minister.' Cat was scarlet, glaring furiously at Agnes. 'Ah'd best be heading hame, anyway.'

Cat and her little gang melted into the evening. Agnes was heading off too, when the minister stopped her.

'How are you doing, Agnes? I was just thinking, it's been quite a while since your adventure in the hills led you to acquiring Barker. She has settled in nicely.' He bent to pat the rough, ginger head.

'Aye, Minister. She's grand company. I don't know whit

I'd do without her.'

'I hear you are busy at the piece-work now. How are you liking it?'

'Ah like earning ma keep. It's a grand feeling when ah get ma pay. And the work is fine, but it gets awfy stuffy in the house all day. I get out wi' Barkie, though.'

'And your mother and grandmother. Do they keep well?'

'Aye, Minister. They are both in guid health.'

She looked down, fidgeting in her pocket.

'Is there something on your mind, Agnes?' He spoke gently.

'Naw, naw, Minister. Ah'm fine. I'd best be on ma way.' She ran off, before the unexpected tears fell.

Agnes and her Grannie were already tucked into the box bed when Maw and Mr Lindsay came back into the house. They were trying to be quiet, but the tailor made a bit of a clatter climbing up the ladder to the roof space. Maw slipped into the box bed; she and Grannie were whispering. Then it was morning, and Maw already away to her work, Grannie busy making a breakfast for their guest. The tailor was trying to be kind; he had a magic trick with coins, which he had laid out on the table. Agnes joined in politely, but her heart wasn't in it at all. She moved over to the loom and started her work.

Two weeks later, there was another conversation with the minister.

'It's wonderful news for your mother, Agnes, is it not?

An autumn wedding. A joyous occasion, indeed, surely?'

'A'hm trying to be brave, and to be happy for her, Minister.' Agnes was twisting her hand in her pocket, her face crumpled with misery; Barkie was looking up at her, anxious. 'But ah dinnae want her to go to Carluke. It's awfy far away.'

'You won't be on your own, Agnes. We are all here, and there is your grandmother. How is Mrs Hewson taking the news?'

'Aye, she says she's pleased for her. She says we'll be fine. But she's gettin' older, Minister. She cannae walk so far, now.'

'She is fortunate to have you to assist, Agnes.' He paused. 'I can well understand this to be a challenging time for you. It will be hard to put your mother's happiness and well-being above your own feelings, but of course this is what you must do.'

'Minister. Dae ye think it might be different if I'd been born in wedlock?' There. It was out – her darkest, most shameful thought. Agnes looked down, aghast at herself for saying the words.

'Agnes, Agnes. We are who we are, and we cannot change it. However, we can endeavour – try – to live with ourselves as best we can, and be the best we can, whatever the accident of our birth. For what it's worth, no, I don't think it would have made any difference. Your mother wants the best for you. She loves and cares for you, Agnes. And remember, Jesus loves you, too. He won't be checking your birth certificate at the door to heaven. He'll be looking to see that you have lived a good, Christian life.'

Agnes felt relieved – for now. But she knew that this 'bastard' thing wasn't going away.

'Thank ye, Minister. You're awfy kind tae me.'

'Not at all, Agnes. I can see this is a trying time for you. Come and see Mrs Laidlaw and myself at the manse, any time. You can bring Barkie, if you like.' He bent and patted the little dog.

He's forgotten about that big tortoiseshell cat of his, thought Agnes, as she meandered down the path towards the cottage.

'That poor wee lass. Whit a shame.'

Agnes could hear the whispers but kept her head high. She had a bonny new frock – a rich maroon – and her dark hair was styled back from her face. Grannie said it would show off her eyes. Best of all, Mr Lindsay had brought her some smart brown boots – proper ladies' boots. She kept looking down at them, as if afraid they would disappear. She had been stealing glimpses of her new self in the mirror, at first scarcely recognising her reflection, but latterly quite taken with her new grown-up persona.

She was following her mother and Jim Lindsay as they walked along the road to the church. Some of her mother's workmates had gathered at the cottage door, smiling and chatting; other neighbours were clustered along the path, and it was their mutters that Agnes was hearing. She looked at them defiantly – oh, the power of a new dress and new boots! – and their eyes slid away. The downturned sneer of disapproval was still etched on some faces, though, and the earlier euphoria left her, leaving the familiar sour feeling of otherness.

At the door of the church, here was the Reverend Laidlaw in his Sunday outfit: steady, solemn. He caught Agnes's eye and gave a tiny smile; she knew it was just for her. He had visited the family home a few times now, to speak with Maw and Grannie. These conversations were not just about the practicalities of the marriage service; he always steered the discussions to future arrangements for the household once the new Mrs Lindsay had left for Carluke with her husband. At first, Agnes had found these talks difficult, even painful; but latterly, they had helped her visualise a quieter cottage. She pictured herself writing to her mother in the chair by the window and found this image curiously calming. She knew she would have much of the domestic work to do, but felt ready. She lifted her head again and caught sight of a hare. Alert on a tussock halfway up the hill, it was sitting up, as if watching the wedding procession. Maw would be pleased. She always said they were lucky, and perhaps carried the spirit of kin.

At the door of the church, Martha turned and smiled at her daughter, her face alight.

My maw. She is so beautiful. Glowing! thought Agnes, watching as they walked down to the front of the church. She slipped into the front pew behind them, and her fingers sought her lucky grey pebble, her eyes squeezed shut in concentration. The minister was starting his opening prayer: 'A blessing on *all* here present …'

Agnes enjoyed the tot of whisky that was stirred into her milk that evening. It certainly ensured that she slept quickly and deeply.

Her head felt stuffy the next morning, though, as she watched the newly-weds pack up, ready for their trip. They were sharing smiles that made her feel cross and left out. She pulled the blanket over her head again. The time for parting would come soon enough.

Martha's box was ready at last. A hurried breakfast had been shared, and now the carter was here. Agnes was relieved to see that her mother had left some personal items behind – surely that indicated a return visit soon? – and was briefly tempted to steal a memento from the box. The hairbrush? Or the little brooch? Reluctantly she dismissed the idea as childish, and instead grabbed Barkie, burrowing her head in her bristly fur.

Excited farewells were made, and the couple waved as the cart moved down the road and out of sight. Agnes felt bereft as she retreated indoors to the warmth, with her grandmother's arm round her shoulder.

'Mind what yer maw told ye, Agnes. Ye're a guid lass, and we'll be fine together. That man of hers will send us our keep, and we'll no' go without. C'mon, lassie – let's get the soup on.'

A single tear rolled down Agnes's cheek. She brushed it away before Grannie saw it.

PART FOUR

All change

AN ARRIVAL IN THE MARKET PLACE

THERE HAD BEEN a couple of rare quiet moments during the shift, and John had been trying to remember his mother. Not the awful last year of her life, but before. Every time he tried to recall her face, the only image that came to mind was the formal, unsmiling family portrait that was framed on the wall in the front room; but if he concentrated really hard, he could conjure up a plump figure standing in the kitchen. Her hair was always in a neat bun, and there was a warm, welcoming smile on her face. He was worried that the more effort he made, the hazier the recollection became. Similarly, he could remember only fragments of her voice, at the edges of his memory; the sounds were distorted, as if coming from a well. He sighed. She had always called him John-boy. He knew he was her favourite, though she tried to hide it from the girls. He still missed her, especially on coming home of an evening. Jemima was right: the kitchen was just not the same.

John and Tom had finished their shift and were walking towards the gates. The chat was about Tom starting at the band practice; he was enthusing about how much noise you can make with a cornet when he broke off in mid-sentence.

'Is that no' your Jemima, John?'

Jem was by the gate, looking hunched and cross.

John's heart sank. He walked towards her, and she faced him, arms akimbo.

'So. Ye missed the great arrival. Faither's back, with the new wife.' Jem's voice was creaking with emotion.

Tom touched John's arm. 'I'll see ye tomorrow, John.' He moved off, leaving the siblings to talk.

'You should have seen it, John. First of all, guess whit she was wearing? Just that expensive paisley shawl, that we all thought had been sold. The cart was all done up wi' ribbons, and lucky heather. Lucky heather! So embarrassing. And she had flowers in her hair, like some sort of peasant. Ye've never seen the like.' Jem was scowling.

John sought a conciliatory tone. 'Well, they have just got married, Jem.'

His sister went on, her tone stiff with derision. 'Even worse. At the door o' the house, Faither picks her up, tae carry her inside. They were giggling like weans. And the whole street was watching. I was affronted.' She rolled her eyes dramatically.

John had to admit that he was surprised at this description of Faither. He didn't recall any such goings-on with his mother. *Faither must be really keen on this woman*, he thought.

He took her arm. 'C'mon, Jem. We'll go home together.'

When they arrived, Lizzie was at the kitchen stove, her weans playing by her feet. By the door was a large trunk, festooned with ribbons and heather. John looked questioningly at his big sister. She pointed up to the ceiling.

'Faither's showing his new bride the *accommodation*. I expect they'll be down soon.' Lizzie tried to hide a smile. Jem made a choking sound and ran for the privy, slamming the back door behind her.

John started to pull off his boots.

'Get yersel' a wash, John. Ye'd best be clean tae meet yer new stepmother.'

'Whit's she like, Lizzie? I cannae get any sense from Jem, she's raging.'

'She seems nice enough. She looks kind of different. She wears her hair in an old-fashioned pleat, but it suits her. Faither's besotted, cannae take his eyes off her.'

The family started to gather for the evening meal and, in due course, Faither and Martha reappeared from upstairs. Martha's cheeks were pink as she smoothed her dress. John was surprised to see that she didn't look that old – maybe just a few years more than Lizzie. He had to admit that she was quite attractive, with her dark hair and clear skin. Bonny-looking, even. He flushed, noticing Faither's hand on her back as they stood together.

Faither spoke. 'Now, everyone. This is the new Mrs Lindsay.'

'Please. You've all to call me Martha,' she said.

There was an awkward silence.

Lizzie spoke first. 'Martha. Ye are welcome, I'm sure. We hope that ye find the place tae yer liking.'

'It's a lovely home, Lizzie. Ye should be proud of yersel'.' Martha smiled as she looked around the kitchen.

Lizzie said, 'And whit of your family, Martha? Do we hear that your mother is still in Wanlockhead?'

'Yes, Lizzie. I'm fortunate that my mither is still of sound mind and good spirits – though not so agile now. My daughter Agnes is with her, and can manage the heavier duties in the home.'

'You have a daughter?' Jemima said.

Jim interrupted. 'Did I no' mention Agnes? Ah was sure ah did. She's about the same age as yersel', Jemima. She's a nice quiet lassie. She works in the house on a loom, as do many o' the women in Wanlockhead.' He continued. 'Martha was married before, of course.'

'Yes,' said Martha. 'His name was Marshall. He was from Biggar. He passed away, sadly. That was a few years ago. It's been just the three of us for a while, now.'

A daughter. Would that be a step-sister? John couldn't work it out.

Jemima looked at Faither. 'Will we get to meet her?'

Martha answered. 'I hope so, Jemima. She is certainly very interested to hear all about her new family. However, she will not be able to leave my mither on her own, so for the time being, we must make do with correspondence.

She is very close to her grannie; I know that they will be most comfortable together.'

Lizzie clapped her hands. 'We are forgetting our manners. Ye must be hungry. Why don't ye take this chair here, Martha?'

John noticed that Lizzie took his maw's chair for herself.

Sunday meant the Kirk. The Lindsay family set off, Faither in front with Martha. Then followed William and Lizzie carrying the weans, chatting with Maggie and Jane. John and Jemima brought up the rear, John acutely aware that his best trousers were just a bit too short in the leg.

Jemima was still in a mood. 'Did ye see all the twigs that she's been scattering aboot? Mibbe it's to keep the witches away. Well, there's just one likely candidate in our house, an' she's just moved in.'

'Jem! That's a terrible thing to say.'

'She's got a wee witchy mark on her neck, hasn't she?'

'It's just a birthmark. Give her a chance, Jem.'

'And look at Faither. Thinks he's the cock o' the walk,' she said.

'Wheesht, Jemima. Folk will hear ye. They'll be busy enough with their tittle-tattle, without you adding some spice into it. Best keep yer thoughts to yersel', for now.'

Jemima was trying to remember what Dr Rankin had said. *That's right. Singing.* She could belt out some hymns in the church; that might help.

The congregation were enjoying a good stare at the

tailor and his new wife, some turning in their pews to get a better view. John was most discomfited.

The lanky, stooped figure of the Reverend MacKenzie climbed ponderously into the pulpit and pushed his thinning hair over his bald pate.

'Hear ye the word of the Lord.'

He surveyed the congregation, his manner implying that he clearly had something important to impart.

John sighed.

'The lesson today is based on a beautiful verse from the Psalms.' His voice took on a sonorous, affected air. 'From Psalm twelve, verse six: "And the words of the Lord are flawless, like silver purified in a crucible, like gold refined seven times".'

He repeated the verse slowly, intonating with great care while looking out and across the congregation.

'Yes. Beautiful words indeed, from the Bible. And these holy words prompt a serious question. Who here thinks he is above the word of the Lord – the flawless word of the Lord?'

The minister paused, looked around the church, then started again in an explanatory, gentle tone. 'Our fathers before us respected and lived by the word of the Lord, did they not? They accepted it as the only truth.' His voice rose. 'Our good ancestors would surely be horrified and alarmed – indeed, they would be *turning in their graves* – if they could hear the heretical claims that are being made today.'

He quietened again. 'Dearly beloved, you must turn your faces away from the disgraceful talk that is contaminating our land. There can be no countenance of this notion that we are descended from apes. Such a concept is an *abomination*.'

He scowled down at the congregation, then his face lightened again.

'If we are looking for answers to the beginnings of life, we need look no further than this holy book. I will move now to the New Testament, and the words of the apostle John. "In the beginning was the word; and the word was with God and the word was God".' He raised his voice again. '*The word was God*! Surely you need no clearer guidance than this affirmation – that the answers you seek are right here, in the Bible. It is my humble task to lead you in your search for truth. As Jesus himself was a shepherd, it is perhaps fitting for me to see you as my flock. It is my honour to stand before you, and guide you on the right path.'

He lifted his voice once more.

'*Cast aside these heathen ideas*! For surely it is heathen to challenge the word of the Lord? These so-called scientists –we all know that for centuries there have been false statements and aspirations. Long ago we were told that they could turn metal into gold. A falsehood. We know that only Jesus can perform such miracles – he turned water into wine. As for this idea that we come from swamps and apes – it too will be shown to be a falsehood, invented by those who are against the teachings of the Christian Church. *Turn your back on them*!'

He pushed his shoulders back and thrust out his chest, looking down on them all with a most superior air. 'Trust in the word of the Lord!'

The Reverend MacKenzie closed his eyes and started into a long prayer.

John looked down at his hands. What to think? *Who is right*? He couldn't wait to talk to Tom.

A NEW BRIDE IN THE TAILOR'S HOUSE

HERE AT LAST was the Carluke Market Place. Martha felt the sky higher and herself smaller, somehow. The streets were noisy and filthy and there was a confusion of smells – coal smoke, horse muck, and a trace of the sweet smell of jam. There was so much to take in, and Martha was conscious that she was being closely observed, both by the family gathered at the door and by the curious neighbours on their steps. She held her head up, rearranging the soft paisley shawl on her shoulders. That girl would be Jemima – same age as Agnes. She had some scowl on her. And this would be Lizzie, with her father's smile. Martha smiled back.

Even in the excitement of the first moments in the house, Martha had felt a presence. It was not malevolent; more curious and persistent, like a little shadow just out of sight. She felt the brush on the nape of her neck, the hint of a breath in her ear. Her mother had warned her that this might happen. In her heather-strewn chest she had rowan twigs and other charms to ensure safe entry into the house; but if the spirit continued its haunting, then she would have to resort to other measures. She found the family portrait in the front room particularly disquieting, the dead eyes heavy with solemn judgement, and wondered whether she might persuade Jim to remove it.

The Sunday morning dawned cold, drizzly and grey; an important day for Martha and Jim, as they prepared for the service at the Kirk.

'Why don't ye wear your wedding dress? You look so fine in it and I want to show ye off tae the town. There is no sense in it hangin' in the closet – best tae enjoy it.'

'Aye, I will.' Martha knew that wearing the new dress would help her meet the appraising eyes that would be waiting at the Kirk. She looked thoughtful. 'It'll be strange, being in a different church. Ah've only known the minister at Wanlockhead.'

'He's no' the gentlest of souls, the Reverend MacKenzie,' said Jim. 'He is quite strict. Mibbe that's no' a bad thing. This is a Free Kirk, Martha; one of the breakaways, following in the covenanting tradition. Ah telt ye, my own faither was one of these that walked out of the old church, tae start this one. There was such a stramash that day. He was a real man of principle, my faither. Wait till you see it. It's a fine new building.'

He gave his new wife an admiring glance and moved towards her, arms outstretched. 'My word. You are looking very bonny, Mrs Lindsay.'

The family had all been waiting.

'We'll be late for the Kirk, Faither,' said Jemima.

'Wheesht, Jem,' said Lizzie. 'Martha, that dress is a

lovely colour on ye.'

Jim and Martha set off at a pace, arm in arm, with the family straggling behind, chatting. Even on the short walk to the Kirk, Martha was acutely aware that the eyes of the town were on her. Jim's wide grin was enough to attract attention, even without a new wife on his arm.

At the gate of the Kirk, relatives and acquaintances came over to shake hands with the new Mrs Lindsay before Jim ushered her into the family pew.

Martha found the sermon somewhat bewildering, and the minister had a judgemental, cold tone, different to the familiar Reverend Laidlaw in Wanlockhead. She was used to a straightforward Sunday message about avoiding transgressions such as stealing and lying, and the importance of being good to your neighbour. Then she remembered his impassioned plea on the Sunday after May Day, when he condemned the visits to the Priest's Pool. He had asked the congregation to turn their backs on the old ways, the familiar superstitions. Yet this minister was censuring the new ideas that everyone was talking about. Maybe the only way was the Lord's way, right enough. It was a lot to think about.

She straightened her hat and looked at her new family. Jim looked back, an affectionate gleam in his eyes. He had not been paying much attention to the sermon – as his hand moved along her skirts, it was clear he was reflecting on the joys of his new marital status, and anticipating his next frolic. The older girls were looking around, waving at their friends. Jemima was looking up the next hymn – she certainly seemed to enjoy singing. John, however, with furrowed brows, was looking very thoughtful indeed. He seemed a nice, quiet lad; he had the same brilliant blue eyes as his father, and he was clearly taking everything in.

They were on the way back to the house, having spent a good half-hour after the service chatting, with more introductions – Martha was anxious that she would never remember all the names and faces – when she heard a sound.

'Jim, whit's that noise? Like someone singing.'

'That's Carluke's very own singing man, Martha. Not always tuneful, mind you.'

'Oh, I see him now. He's a poor-looking soul. His feet look as if they pain him greatly.'

'Aye. He lives in a shack, down the brae. They say he came over from Ireland many years ago, tae work in the pits. Ah believe he lost a brother in some terrible accident underground, and was never the same after that. Couldnae go down the mine again. He doesnae talk much. Just sings the old songs and hymns, over and over. Margaret always used to make sure he got something to eat.'

'Then I shall do the same.'

How strange. Just a moment ago she had harboured feelings of confusion and uncertainty, with a different minister and all the new faces that she would surely never learn; now she was enjoying a warm feeling of benevolence, of generosity of spirit. She smiled at her husband.

Jim stroked the small of her back gently, before encouraging her to take his arm.

A DISCOVERY

It was a few weeks later. Martha had woken early and had slipped out of the house. These days she often felt distracted and out of sorts; then a whiff of broom on the air made her realise she was homesick. Her heart was sore for home and for all that was familiar about Wanlockhead, but especially her mother and Agnes, cosy in the cottage.

This was home now. Yet she still felt like the outsider. Was she just imagining it? She had felt something changing between Jim and herself, a slight distance. It had started when she had asked whether the family portrait might be taken down; he had been shocked and hurt. Now the dead eyes seemed almost triumphant, while her discomfort in the house only grew. When they had first arrived, he had welcomed her hands rubbing his shoulders, or massaging his temples, often remarking on her healing abilities; lately he had been more abrupt, moving away when she tried to touch him, spending more and more time in the workshop.

The garden behind the derelict house on the brae had felt like a gift: a secret place that she could call her own. She had stumbled on it by chance, curious to follow the last echoes of roses tumbling in the hedgerow down the overgrown carriageway. She had turned the corner by the stables at the rear of the building and had been amazed to discover an old garden. It was tangled and overgrown, but in amongst the weeds she recognised old friends like rosemary and sage, even raspberry canes. And there were new delights. Amongst the autumn debris there were signs of many more roses; an ancient apple tree; even a cascading willow.

She had already cleared some space and had started encouraging the more useful herbs. She was excited to imagine how the garden might look in springtime. The soil here was so different to Wanlockhead: richer, more fertile. She would write to her mother and tell her about it. At least here she was alive, more herself than in the dark kitchen in the Market Place house, where she often felt cautious and haunted.

Martha spent a few precious moments with the trowel she had found in the yard before heading back.

She returned in time to start the porridge, washing the soil carefully from her hands before reaching for the oats. Busy at the stove, she started to hum an air, then stopped abruptly when she heard it taken up by another voice. The hairs were standing up on the back of her neck as she turned; then she breathed a sigh of relief as Lizzie came into the room, a tot on her hip.

'Our mother used tae sing that. It's a bonny tune,' said Lizzie. 'Ah miss hearing her voice aboot the place.'

'Aye. Ye must miss her,' said Martha. She reached forward for the child. 'Dae ye want a hand with the wee one?'

Lizzie pulled back, protectively. 'This one scarcely knew her grannie. She looks like her, though.' She paused, then went on. 'William's found us another place, Martha. We'll be out yer hair soon enough.'

'Oh, Lizzie. Ah hope ye're not moving on my account.'

'Aye, well. It's time we had our own place. Let ye take charge in here. Faither's quite keen on the idea.'

'This will always be your home, Lizzie.'

'I've my own wee family now. It's right we make our own way.' Lizzie slopped some porridge in a bowl, blowing on it. She poured on some cold milk; the bairn started to grizzle. She blew again. 'It's too hot, pet.'

There was a slam, then thumps on the staircase; a pause, then Jemima entered the room. She was scowling as she addressed Lizzie.

'Is there any more porridge?' she snapped.

'Let me serve ye a bowl,' said Martha.

'Naw. Ah can serve myself.' Jemima took a bowl from the dresser and pushed her way to the stove. Martha stood back helplessly; she looked over at Lizzie, who remained fixed on feeding the wean.

Martha felt sick. She found herself wondering how much more she could take. She had never been one to feel a temper, but recently she'd had to repress some ugly words. The worst was, Jim didn't seem to notice. All his talk was about a big order in the workshop, and he would hasten there after the briefest of repasts. Martha was hesitant to say anything to him after the upset about the portrait.

She took a deep breath, listening to her mother's voice in her head, calming wise words. *She's just a young lassie. She still misses her mother.*

'I'll join ye if I may, Jemima.' Martha took a ladleful into her bowl and sat at the table near her step-daughter. Jemima pulled herself close, hunching over her dish.

'Mibbe ye can advise me.' Martha picked up her spoon. 'Ah was hoping tae make some rosehip syrup, and wondered whether ye might know where the best hips are to be found?'

There was a silence, then Lizzie said, 'Ah think ye might find some guid ones down towards the old Kirk.'

'Naw.' Jemima straightened up. 'Naw, this year the best hips will be up the Forth Road. The hedgerows were full o' wild roses when John and I were up there in the early summer.'

'I'll be looking for brambles too, for jam.'

'I'm the best for finding brambles,' said Jemima.

'That would be a help.' Martha smiled.

Jemima looked down at her porridge plate. 'Ah might be too busy. I'm seeking a position. If Faither would just let me leave the school, I could get a job.'

Maybe a wishing fire would help me, thought Martha. *Maybe that's what is needed.* She could make a circle at the back of Kirkton House. She knew just the spot.

The kitchen was quiet. Martha tied the twigs of sage together, enjoying the scent of the leaves. She approached the stove, then turned to face the room. She spoke.

'Ah mean ye no harm, Margaret, and seek nothing from ye. It's time for you to rest.'

She lit the bundle, then walked around the room, waving it in the air. She was chanting, 'Rest. Rest. Rest.' She didn't hear John come in until she saw him standing open-mouthed in the doorway.

KIRKTON HOUSE

THERE WAS NO doubt about it: Martha was a strange one. John screwed his eyes in embarrassment, remembering his discomfort at finding her chanting in the kitchen. She had told him it was an old trick to deter mice, but he was most dubious.

He couldn't help noticing the atmosphere in the house. Once, ages ago, there had been a feud between two lads at school. Whenever one of them entered the playground, you would look for the other. You could feel the tension, like a spring. John thought it was like that now, in the Market Place house.

He knew there was talk of Lizzie and William finding their own place, and he was glad for them. He had been wondering whether he might ask to lodge with them, when William suggested it.

They were walking up to an early shift. William said that he and Lizzie had been talking, and that a bit of extra cash would be a great help.

John had thought about it all day and had spoken to Tom about it, too.

His friend had been positive. 'It makes sense, John. A

fresh start. Let the newly-wed lovebirds have some peace.'

It seemed everyone was noticing Faither's keen attention to his bride. John blushed. 'William and Lizzie could do with the money,' he explained.

'Aye, ah suppose so. Whit aboot Jemima, though? Will she no' miss ye?'

'She's mibbe got hersel' a position. Live-in. Working for the Shields family.'

'The auctioneer, on John Street? Nice big house.'

Such changes afoot, and all since Martha's arrival. John didn't understand the hostility that Lizzie and Jemima clearly felt; he was just awkward around her, particularly since the herb-burning incident. He hadn't wanted to mention that to Tom, but wasn't quite sure why. Sometimes it felt as if the whole town was staring at the tailor's house, curious to see how the family was faring with the new Mrs Lindsay. These days, when Tom's mother asked how things were at home, there was an eagerness to her interest, as if any little titbit about Martha was to be savoured. Was it true that Martha had left her old mother in Wanlockhead, with a daughter from an earlier marriage? What was this daughter's name? Even the minister's wife had stopped him to ask how things were at home. The more that people asked, the more John found himself reluctant to say anything at all.

A glorious afternoon; his favourite time, after an early shift. John was starting to walk down Kirkton Brae when he saw Martha turn into the drive of the old, derelict house. He shivered. He knew only too well the sinister history of that place.

He looked up at the sightless windows, the tumbled, gaping mess of the collapsed roof. When he was younger, this had been the place of dares. He still had nightmares about the time he had ended up on the top landing. The big boys wanted to know if he could manage a count of five in the cupboard under the eaves – the one where they had found the strange symbols, and the deep scratch marks on the door. Once he was inside, they had shut him in. He heard the clatter of their feet going down the stairs as he had struggled for what felt like an eternity, trying to free himself. His breath still caught in his chest when he thought about the panic. Tom had come to his rescue, bounding up the stairs and putting his shoulder to the door; then, as they reached the top of the stair, it had collapsed with a terrible roar of rotten timber, leaving the two of them trapped in a cloud of dust. The big lads had screeched with laughter, imitating ghouls and ghosts, making such a terrible racket that the whole place shook. The entire roof could have come down on them all. He and Tom had managed to find a way out by the creaking, loose steps of the servants' stair, a terrifyingly dark and steep passageway festooned with cobwebs. The big boys had jumped out at them as they came into the light. He had nearly wet himself.

John shuddered. He wondered if Tom remembered

that day.

Martha must be unaware of the history of the house, surely. Everyone in Carluke knew Kirkton House was cursed. He looked around the brae. All quiet. Taking a deep breath, John set off down the carriageway and peered round the corner by the stables.

The garden was surrounded by old brick walls, so had a warmth to it. Although very overgrown, the place was bright and peaceful. There was a plethora of trees, plants and flowers, most of which he didn't recognise. Martha was kneeling with her back to him at a piece of earth that looked cared for, her long dark plait snaking down to her waist; he saw that she had woven some tiny bright ribbons and flowers into it. She was humming as she dug in some small plants. John had no idea what they were, but Martha seemed to be working with expertise and ease.

He looked around, and noticed a fire-marked circular area by one of the trees, surrounded by stones and twigs. A small, brilliant-white object had been placed on a flat stone by the bare patch. He stared at it. He could have sworn it was Jemima's hare skull.

Suddenly he saw that Martha's hands had stilled. Her shoulders hunched. John turned and fled back up the path before she turned around, trying to make as little noise as he could. As he turned onto the brae, he tried to bring a whistle to his lips but only managed a couple of dud notes. His mouth was bone dry.

It's as well I'm moving out, he thought. *This is all just too much.*

The next day, he was walking with Tom to the late shift.

'Tom, you're keen on the history. Ah ken that Kirkton House is cursed, but whit was the story? Was there no' somethin' aboot wizards?'

'Whit makes ye think aboot that place? Ah do ma best to forget it.' Tom's face was set; the memory of the attic room was clearly not one he wished to revisit.

John persisted. 'Why would naebody want that house? It's stood empty for years.'

'If you're that keen, Dr Rankin would be the man tae ask. He's writing a history o' the town.'

'Ah'll ask him.'

'Ah'll leave ye to it. Ye can fill me in later.'

John needed no excuse to knock at Dr Rankin's door. Sarah answered, rewarding him with a big smile.

The doctor called down the passageway behind her. 'John Lindsay! Are you here to see the Rankins, or is it Sarah you are after?'

'Good day, Dr Rankin. I've got a history question, if ye have a moment?'

'There is always time for history, John. It has much to teach us. Come away in.'

Sarah stepped back, to let him past. Their hands brushed in the doorway, and John felt that delicious shiver at her touch. He watched her go as she moved off to the kitchen. As he turned back to the doctor, he saw that he was smiling.

'Young love, eh! What can I help with, John?'

'Kirkton House, Doctor. Whit's the story there? Why has it stood abandoned all these years?'

Dr Rankin indicated a seat for John, and took the chair by the fire.

'It belonged to a strange fellow, John. It was a couple of hundred years ago; I'll have the dates to hand, somewhere. He went by the name of Thomas Weir. He came from a grand family, although there was superstitious talk that his mother was a clairvoyant.'

'Ye mean, she had second sight?'

'Aye. There's no such thing, of course, but that's what was said at the time. Weir was supposedly a robust enough fellow in his youth. He took up with the Covenanters, fought against the Irish Rebellion, as it was called in those days. It was whilst he was living in Edinburgh, towards the end of his life, he seemed to develop mental hygiene issues – that's illness of the mind, John. Both he and his sister were afflicted. There were even rumours that they became more than just brother and sister to each other.'

John sat back, shocked. 'Ye mean, unnatural practices? That's against the teaching of the Kirk, to be sure.'

Dr Rankin continued. 'Aye, but that was the least of it. They were both taken into custody, ranting peculiar tales of vice and sorcery, claiming all kinds of devilish wrongdoing. There are accounts of curses. Strange rituals. All sorts of goings-on. They called him a wizard. I suspect that either his mind was dementing, or they may have been poisoned, the pair of them, and that is why their behaviour changed so dramatically. Weir met a horrible end by the authorities – garrotted and burned. They were both buried under the gallows. It's as if they sought out a ghastly death for themselves.'

John grimaced. 'That is a dreadful tale. Nae wonder the house stands empty.'

'It was long ago, mind,' said the doctor. 'Perhaps it's just superstitious people that have ascribed menace to his dwelling place. Although I did read that his house in Edinburgh was supposedly so badly haunted that it had to be demolished. It's an interesting study in the promulgation of fear and hysteria in the general population in the face of those who behave in a way that is seen as outwith the norms of society.'

'Do ye not believe in the supernatural, Doctor?'

Dr Rankin was firm. 'No, John, I do not. All my studies confirm my scientific understanding that there is generally a logical explanation behind any tales of mysterious goings-on.' He narrowed his eyes. 'What's the sudden interest? Are you thinking of buying it?'

John laughed, shaking his head. 'Naw, no way – unless they take coal dust as payment, Doctor. I was just curious, that's all.'

'You'll have to read my book when it comes out, John. There are many other strange tales of Carluke, believe me. There are other seemingly quiet corners that have dramatic histories.'

John took his leave, managing a quick word with Sarah on his way out. They would be meeting later. In the meantime, he had much to think about.

POTIONS AND LOTIONS

IT HAD STARTED with the neighbour at the well pump. Martha had been scattering mint leaves into the big pitcher, when the woman asked her what she was doing. She had sounded interested to hear about the cleansing properties of the herb, and asked if that was what Martha used on her hair. A chat about rosemary oil ensued, and arrangements were made for a sample to be collected. Other women followed, more enquiries were made, and before long she was being kept busy with potions and lotions. Jim seemed resigned to the herbal activities, occasionally marvelling at what might be found in the hedgerows around Carluke. Martha just hadn't got round to telling him about the garden behind Kirkton House. It felt good to get to know people and to be busy.

Even the minister's wife had taken an interest; Mrs MacKenzie had stopped her in the street, and Martha had steeled herself for another awkward conversation about the Bible study class. Instead, there had been questions about hair oil and skin cream. Right enough, she had changed the subject to more religious matters when a group of righteous Carluke worthies walked nearby

– but she had knocked on Martha's door a few days later, ready to collect. Sadly, though, her interest in the beauty products had not extended to friendlier dealings. Her Kirk flock of do-gooders continued either to ignore Martha or to try pointedly to coerce her into joining their pious activities.

Other women were easier with her, but Martha still felt an outsider. Even her new family were still either openly hostile, like Jemima, or at least guarded. Too often she wished herself back to the comfort of a night by the fire in the cottage in Wanlockhead.

She sighed. There had been so much she had taken for granted.

There was a knock on the door. A letter – from Agnes.

Dearest Mother,

All is well here at home, especially as the snow is clearing at last. I have been to the cemetery at Meadowfoot as you asked, and put some fresh flowers on the grave for Lucy. The neighbours often ask how you like Carluke, so I hope you will write to us again soon, with all your news.

Mary said that yours was the smartest wedding dress she had ever seen, but she has not attended any wedding before. However, you did look very fine indeed. Please tell Mr Lindsay thank you again for my new outfit and especially the boots.

Grannie is well, although her legs get tired, even walking from the bed to her bench. Her appetite is good, and we are enjoying the jams that Mr Lindsay has sent. The strawberry is an especial favourite.

I have been to visit the Minister and his wife, at their invitation. He particularly said that I could bring Barkie, but failed to mention the big tabby cat that lives in their house. How might you forget that you had a cat? Perhaps when you are a Minister, your mind is filled with many important thoughts. There was an unfortunate chase, and then Barkie had to wait outside. The house is very splendid, with hundreds of books. I wonder if Mrs Laidlaw has to dust them all. The buns had currants in, and were delicious.

How are the Lindsay family? I long to hear more of them. How is Jemima? It is strange to think there is a girl almost my age, living in Carluke, and with such a fine name. John sounds like a nice lad. I am glad they make you welcome.

The cottage is quiet, but we have neighbours looking in often enough. Barkie guards us from the witches and keeps us company. My loom work goes well, and I shall get more done now that the evenings are lightening.

Please send all your news. If there are any new (or old) story papers, we would be glad of them.

I am, your obedient daughter,

Agnes Hewson Brownlee

Martha frowned as she finished the letter. *Brownlee.* Agnes had always kept her father's name, and in Wanlockhead there had been no reason not to. Martha knew that people in Carluke were aware that she had a mother and daughter still living in Wanlockhead, but everyone assumed – she had let everyone assume – that Agnes had been born in wedlock, to Martha Marshall. For a moment, she wished she had Reverend Laidlaw's kind counsel. Then she remembered Jim's words: the past is in the past. She had tried to speak to him about it since, but he was adamant that they should let things be. But it niggled her, like an itch.

Meanwhile, there was much else to occupy her here at the tailor's house in Market Place, trying to make it her own.

Only two of Jim's children now remained in the house: Jane and Maggie had stayed on to be close to the workshop, and the girls kept themselves to themselves. Lizzie, William and their weans were now established in a neat cottage in Stewart Street, just a step away, and John had joined them there; he would pay his sister a small rent, which would help with the bills. The kitchen to herself at last, Martha had rearranged the shelves by the fire to suit her preferences. She found space for some favourites from Wanlockhead: an old milk jug from her father's family that she would fill with fresh flowers in summer, and a blue willow serving plate, a gift from her first marriage. An heirloom pestle and mortar had pride of place, close to hand, beside her herb scissors. And a new pulley had been installed; many bunches of herbs and plants were drying there. A new lamp burned in the corner, brightening the room.

The Market Place house was quieter with Lizzie's family gone, and more peaceful, now that Jemima had moved to her new employment. A place had been secured for her working for the auctioneer, Samuel Shields. She was living with the Shields family at John Street, and helping Mary Shields care for their family. Martha could scarcely admit to herself the relief she had felt on Jemima's departure. She had watched her cross the marketplace with her father, her chin defiantly in the air. Jim had been carrying her small suitcase. Under his arm he carried the wooden box that John had made for his sister, a place to keep her strange knick-knacks and treasures. Jemima had made such a racket as she had packed, skirling through the house, grabbing mementoes as if she was on her way to the New World instead of across the town. There had been a bit of a fuss when she couldn't find the hare skull, but perhaps it was not surprising that it had been lost; the girls' room was such a mess. There was speculation that Margaret or Jane had broken it and thrown it away. Martha had crossed her fingers behind her back, when asked whether she had seen it; she hoped that no one noticed her discomfort.

The kitchen was quieter, right enough, but it was no easier. The presence was still there. She could feel the ghost eyes on her as she stood by the stove, sensed the eerie breath on her as she went about her work. And sometimes she saw Jim looking at her as if she was a stranger, and her heart would contract.

THE FORTUNE TELLER

MARTHA WAS WAKENED early with clamour and noise, as Carluke put the finishing touches to its preparations for the spring market fair. She had heard of little else for weeks; the Fair was a major occasion on the calendar, and there would be many attractions as well as the usual cattle and poultry sales, and the hiring of servants and farm workers. She lay there for a moment, grinning in anticipation and excitement. She had heard that a fortune teller was expected.

Walking through the crowds, Martha felt her heart beat strong, with the hustle and bustle; she breathed in the strange smell of roasting chestnuts, feeling young, alive. Then she saw the green caravan with its curious rounded roof, and the booth beside it, ribbons fluttering. Already a few women had gathered, waiting to hear their fortunes. Martha listened to the chat around her. A mother and daughter were standing nearby.

'They're calling her a spae-wife, Ma. Does that mean she's a witch?'

'No, dearie. Well, she has some special powers, but she doesnae make spells. She has a gift. She can tell fortunes, that's all.'

'But surely it's only witches that can tell the future?'

Another woman started talking loudly about whether the spae-wife could stop the children coming as easily as she could predict their arrival, and everyone was laughing loudly round about. Much advice was being offered.

'Cross yer legs, Molly, that'll dae it!'

'More chance o' stoppin' them that way than crossing yer fingers!'

'I've heard that ye wash out wi' soap, afterwards.'

'Mibbe. Usually, I just take a walk tae the Kirk, and say a wee prayer. Please God, not another wean.'

'Nettle tea, that's whit ah've heard.'

'Whit – tae drink, or tae put you know where? That would be stingy!'

The same problems everywhere, thought Martha. She had a sudden rush of memories of visits by neighbours in Wanlockhead; of whispers and tears, and her mother making strange, strong-smelling brews from those herbs in her garden.

The women were cackling and jesting. They were enjoying each other's company and the chance to be outrageous. But Molly's friend was more sombre.

'I just want to ask her aboot our wee Betty. She's no' been right for months. Blue around her lips, sometimes.'

'Would ye no' be better taking her tae see Dr Rankin? He'll soon tell ye.'

'Ah'm feart in case it's bad news, Molly. He doesnae

hold back frae telling ye, that Dr Rankin. Ah mean, he's kind enough, but he doesnae spare ye.'

There was a call. It was Martha's turn. Taking a deep breath, she pushed past the curtain, into the booth.

The fortune teller was sitting by a table, on which were laid a deck of cards and a crystal ball. Her head was covered in a scarf of an exotic deep orange, with a fringe of small red beads interspersed with gold discs. She was wearing the most extraordinary earrings Martha had ever seen – gorgeous big gold hoops that dangled almost to her shoulders. They clanked against her many bracelets as she tucked a stray hair behind her ear.

The financial transactions out of the way and the name and age of her client ascertained, she sat back in her chair and looked at Martha. And she kept looking. Martha offered her palm and the spae-wife took it, still staring; then she stroked Martha's hand, as she lowered her eyes.

'Well, Martha. I can see there is something special about you. Your hand has the touch, has it not? A healing gift, that is rare indeed. Now, let's see.' She studied Martha's palm, her fingers identifying a strong line.

'You have had a full life, Martha, that much is evident. You have loved with passion, and felt the terrible grief of loss. But the pain that you have endured has made you strong, of that you must have no doubt. You have built the strength to face what is to come.'

The woman lifted her eyes again.

A dread was creeping into Martha's heart. She wanted

to snatch her hand back, but it was held fast. 'What? What is tae come?'

'You will face trials and tribulations, Martha. Amongst these difficulties will come a heartfelt loss. But you will come through this. You are a remarkable woman, with particular resilience.'

'How do ye know that? I dinnae feel strong at all. What is going to happen? Ye are making me feart.'

'Lift a card, Martha.'

Martha leaned forward to the deck of cards and chose from low down in the pack. The spae-wife took it from her, glanced at it, then shook her head. She placed it back in the pack.

'You are heavy with secrets, Martha. Meet me later. We should talk.'

Martha stood at the top of Kirkton Brae, wrapped in her shawl. Her heart sank as she saw the Reverend MacKenzie coming up the hill towards her, just as the spae-wife appeared. Although the scarf was gone, she still had the air of an exotic creature.

The spae-wife looked carefully at the minister as he passed them by, giving him a polite nod; then she turned to Martha. 'Now then, you must call me Carrie. You said there is a quiet corner here, where we might talk?'

The woman looked younger than Martha had thought. In the dimness of the tent, she had seemed mysterious, ageless, but Martha could now see that she was of a similar age to herself, and with the same care lines and red hands of all working women. Together they walked down the carriageway to the rear of Kirkton House and into the garden. They settled on an old bench, by the wall.

'My, this is a grand spot.' Carrie looked around, nodding. 'I see you keep busy. I would love a garden like this.' She sounded wistful.

'Aye, but ye must have such a life, travelling the country. I envy ye that.'

They smiled at each other, then Martha remembered, and her face clouded.

'Carrie, whit is this that I should fear? Can I prepare myself?'

'Where should I start?' Carrie's fingers were twisting the wool strands of her shawl. 'When I first saw you, Martha, it was as if I saw my own mother, as I remembered her in my youth. I wonder if there were any travelling folk in your family?'

Martha, too, was fiddling with her shawl. 'Ye have a resemblance to my own mither, Carrie. And my daughter has your dark eyes.' She tilted her head, remembering. 'My mither did sometimes speak of a link tae travelling folk. There was a story of a tinker woman who stayed behind with one o' my kin, back in Wanlockhead.' She looked down. 'It wasnae something we spoke of much.'

'Aye. Travelling folk are not always welcome. We are viewed with fear and mistrust. Perhaps your family kept the story hidden deliberately, Martha.'

'My mither is a great one for the old ways. She's a healer. She taught me much aboot plants and potions.' Martha inclined her head to the herb bed. 'And she would talk aboot a woman called Sadie, as someone who showed her how tae prepare the cures. I must ask her more aboot Sadie.'

'Sadie. I'll ask around too. It's a common enough name, mind.'

'Whit of my future, Carrie?'

Carrie took Martha's hands in hers.

'Martha, even with my cards and my crystal ball, I cannot see the future. But I have a strong sense of difficulties ahead. It's like you have a veil, or a caul ... I cannot see it, but I can feel it about you.'

Martha nodded. 'Aye. Ah feel it too. It's like something's there, just out ma vision.'

Carrie looked at her. 'Martha, are you new to these parts? You speak like someone from the countryside. Did you come from Wanlockhead? I just wonder if you left something behind there, and you're afraid it will follow you. A secret, perhaps.'

The two women knew they didn't have much time to talk. Martha would be missed back at the Market Place house. But she felt such relief, speaking to another woman in an easy way. Carrie nodded understandingly as Martha described her fears.

'Ah wanted a fresh beginning, Carrie, but it's no' that easy. Whit will I do, if the Carluke worthies find out Agnes is illegitimate? I'll be shunned.'

'Martha, just remember you have strong blood in you. No matter what happens, be true to yourself. Take pride in your gifts.' Carrie laughed. 'We might be cousins! I could teach you easy about telling fortunes – you would have the knack, I'm sure!'

'I'd come with ye now, Carrie, if I didnae have tae make the supper!'

They walked back up the brae arm in arm, Martha scarcely noticing the eyes of the town, watching and judging.

Jim was waiting for her in the kitchen, arms folded. 'Martha. A word.'

She felt a cool breath on the back of her neck, felt the presence.

'The minister called in. Ah hear ye've made quite the wee garden at Kirkton House.'

Oh no. Not the garden.

'Aye, Jim. Ah was missing my wee patch o' green and found this unloved wee corner at the back o' the derelict house.'

'Martha, ye cannae go in there. The place is cursed. Surely ye've heard the story?'

Martha hadn't heard the story. She listened with horror as Jim described the demented ravings and the gruesome deaths of the Weir siblings.

'That's a shocking tale, Jim, right enough. But I get no sense of evil in that garden. Even the old stones of the house, I believe they are benign now.'

Jim's lips pursed into a thin line. 'Ah don't want ye

going in there, Martha. Dae ye hear? Folk are talking.'

She looked at him in silence for a moment, then left the room.

Looking back, Martha realised the illness had started after the Fair folk left. A week later, Jim came through from the workshop, looking for some lunch.

'Have ye heard much aboot this sickness, Martha?' he asked.

Martha nodded as she laid out the bannocks and cheese. 'Aye, the women are talking aboot it at the pump. They are calling it the Grip. It seems tae be the young ones who are getting ill. It sounds most distressing.'

'The Devil's Grip is what I'm hearing,' said Jim. 'They say it starts wi' a fever, then a terrible pain in the chest, like ye cannae breathe. Like the crush o' a grip.'

Martha put her hand on his shoulder, just at the tight spot, but he pulled away, distracted; as she lifted the platter to the sink, Martha felt a pang of loneliness. She wished she could speak to her maw.

The next few days brought more worrying news of the mysterious illness. The decision was made to close the school. The symptoms were discussed at length: a fever, weakness, then the frightening tightness in the chest that rendered the sufferer prostrate and bedbound. There were reports of entire households laid low. Martha advised Margaret and Jane to wash their hands in boiled water regularly. She also suggested to Jim that they avoid the

Kirk while the disease was rife, but he was adamant that they should take their usual places in their pew. Martha held a kerchief over her mouth for much of the service, her ears tuned to the tight coughs and rasping breathing of some of the congregation.

Two days later, Margaret complained of a terrible headache at breakfast. She retired to bed, with Jane hovering anxiously beside her. As the day went on, she became weaker.

'Ah just cannae seem to get ma breath.'

Her face was pale on the pillow as she clasped her sister's hand.

Jim sent for Dr Rankin and followed him up the stairs, while Martha paced in the kitchen. She heard the men speak as they left the bedroom, and strained to listen.

'It's rampaging through Carluke, Jim. It is undoubtedly some sort of contagious illness, perhaps brought in with the Fair folk. Very unusual, though. I've not seen the like before. I'm undertaking some research. In the meantime, try to encourage her with steady breathing. She needs to keep her fluids up. Perhaps a poultice might help.'

The men entered the kitchen.

'I can make poultices, Doctor,' said Martha. 'I thought onion might work best, for the lungs.'

Jim interrupted, his tone impatient. 'You'll do whatever the doctor says, Martha.'

'No, no – onion is a good idea, Mrs Lindsay,' said the doctor. He looked up at the herbs on the pulley with interest. 'You have quite the apothecary, there.'

'Aye, Doctor. My mither taught me. I'll make some bone broth for Margaret too.'

'Good. Sometimes the old ways are the best, eh? Now, Jim. I am sure Margaret will make a good recovery in time, but you might find that Jane will succumb, given her proximity to her sister. Just keep them warm and comfortable; it is all we can do. It sounds like Mrs Lindsay will be an excellent nurse.'

The following Sunday, a smaller and more wary congregation gathered at the Kirk. Many in the town were still struggling to recover, a strange fatigue lingering for many days. There were still new cases being reported. Martha had not heard of any fatalities, but there were many stories of the fear of watching loved ones striving for breath. Margaret and Jane were improving now, but still bedbound, exhausted. Jim was keen to be at the service, however. Martha saw John and Jemima in a back pew, along with Lizzie and William with their weans. Then the Reverend MacKenzie took to the pulpit, and looked right at her. It was a sneering, knowing look. Martha felt her stomach chill as the colour leapt to her face; she grasped Jim's hand.

The minister began.

'Today, during these troubled times of illness, I must address a vexing issue. I have noticed for some time that some irregular practices are being introduced here in

Carluke, and I am concerned that they may lead us away from the true path of the Kirk and its teachings. They may even account for the scourge of ill health that plagues our town. I am talking about the pagan rituals and spells that lie at the heart of folklore apothecary.' The Kirk was silent as he stared down at Martha. The door at the back of the church swung open, then shut.

He cleared his throat, then continued. 'Last week I had cause to speak with a person from Wanlockhead. A person of good reputation. A God-fearing individual. He spoke to me of a family in that village – a family descended from travelling folk – well known for their meddling in discredited superstitious practices. And, as is so often the case, this family lived flagrantly, with loose morals.'

Martha knew everyone was looking at her. Worse, with the tiniest of movements, Jim had let go of her hand and had shifted away, leaving her vulnerable and exposed. If she could only get out of the pew – but she was hemmed in, stuck fast.

The minister went on. 'First, to address the issue of paganism. Folklore medicine may seem innocent enough; the use of herbs to ease our ills, or to shine our hair. But there are some who dabble with darker forces, who bring ungodly ways and sickness into the heart of our community. We must unite against these malevolent influences.

'Then to the second sin, that of poor moral standards.'

He looked directly at Martha, a pitying gaze. She lifted her eyes to meet his with a steely stare. She was suddenly aware of her mother's courage coming into her, a fierceness born of years of otherness.

Reverend MacKenzie looked down at his notes, turned a page, and continued. 'Feminine charms can beguile and dazzle. If we are not careful, we can be ensnared by a sordid web. There can be unfortunate consequences from such encounters, and even in Carluke there is illegitimacy. It is those who seek to conceal their sin that must be condemned.'

The door of the Kirk swung open again and a clear, strong voice rang out. The voice of Dr Rankin.

'I must protest. I could scarcely believe my sister when she told me of this public berating, MacKenzie. For God's sake, man, this is not the eighteenth century. There is a perfectly logical explanation for this illness.'

Martha rose to her feet. She was ready.

'I thank ye, Doctor, but I do not need others to speak for me.' She faced MacKenzie. 'I cannae deny my history. My husband is aware of it, but we had thought it to be a private matter. However, I am not a witch, sir. I didnae bring this sickness on Carluke. Witches steal children, harm animals and fornicate with the devil. I have never met the devil, and to the best of my knowledge he doesnae live in Wanlockhead.'

She stared hard at the minister, who was looking most discomfited; he had clearly not expected a response. A ripple of excitement passed through the congregation. Martha raised her clear voice so that all could hear.

'My mither is a guid woman. Her knowledge of plants was learned from her mither, and is used only tae help others. She is well respected in Wanlockhead. You think it a backward place; yet those who live there strive tae help their neighbours, just as the Bible tells us.'

The Rankins began to applaud. A smattering of the congregation joined in, but then were silenced as the minister held up his hand. 'I speak only as your shepherd, as your guide in this life of sin. Now. Let us move forward from this day, walking in godliness, and in the ways of our Lord and Redeemer. Can we all be standing for the next hymn.'

Martha seized the opportunity, and pushed her way out of the pew. She walked out of the Kirk, her head held high. As she stormed down the street, a figure approached her.

'Are ye Mrs Lindsay?'

'Who wants tae know?'

'It's just … I've been asked tae pass ye this. Frae Wanlockhead. It's urgent.'

Martha's hands were shaking as she took the note.

Dear Mrs Lindsay,

Prepare yourself for difficult news. Your mother has suffered a seizure, and is now lying unconscious of her surroundings. I fear her condition is deteriorating. Agnes is coping well, with the help of her cousins, but this is perhaps a situation where your presence is required.

You are all in our prayers.

Your friend,

James Laidlaw (Revd)

A PEACEFUL PASSING

MARTHA HAD MANAGED to secure a lift, despite it being a Sunday. As the cart made its way up the track towards Wanlockhead, the once-familiar landscape looked strange and alien. She gazed out across the bleak moorland, the grey gravels of the old bing heaps dotting the lonely skyline, a solitary bird of prey circling high above. She shivered, pulling her shawl close. Then she caught sight of a hare on the ridge, running at a distance in parallel with the road, and her heart felt easier. She breathed in, smelling the gorse and the moor. This was home, right enough.

Agnes was at the door. 'Maw, ye got here quick! I'm that pleased to see ye!'

Martha slipped her shawl from her shoulders, patted an excited Barkie, and looked around. There was her mother, tiny in the box bed, deeply unconscious, her chest rattling with each breath. There would be no chance to speak, to say goodbye. No chance to ask about Sadie, or seek advice and counsel. She put her hand to her mother's face, her heart clenching; the skin felt clammy, and she sensed the slow, relentless approach of death.

And here was a bonny young woman – Agnes, a child no longer. The cottage was clean and tidy enough, but her sharp eye caught the tasks to be done. There would be no time to dwell on the embarrassment of the Kirk in Carluke. Martha took a deep breath and rolled up her sleeves.

'I'll make us something tae eat, Agnes, dear. Check my bag – I managed to grab some jars of jam frae Carluke. Take one up tae the minister, tell him that I'm home. Be sure and thank him for his letter.'

The little family once again found themselves enmeshed in the local support for those managing serious illness. There were regular visits from the Reverend Laidlaw, and the doctor looked in every day.

'No charge, of course, Mrs Lindsay; just making sure she is comfortable. I think your mother has suffered a bleed in the brain. Be reassured, I think she is free of pain.'

Relatives and neighbours came by, although Agnes suspected that for some it was to hear about life in Carluke rather than offer comfort. Martha met everyone calmly and with words of thanks and appreciation for the small acts of kindness but was reluctant to be drawn into much conversation. Most of all she was grateful to her cousins, who would take a turn sitting by the bed so that she and Agnes could have a breath of air – even if their steps usually took them to Meadowfoot.

'Ah just thought she'd always be here wi' us, in her chair by the fire. Ah cannae believe we are losing her, too.

Ma heart is sore. Whit'll happen tae me, Maw?'

'Let's take a day at a time, Agnes.'

She looked at her daughter, her lovely dark eyes full of sorrow, and suddenly realised she had something important to say. 'Agnes. I can see now that ah hurt ye, leaving ye here and going off tae Carluke.'

Agnes looked away, biting her lip.

'Ah'm sorry for it, Agnes. You're a guid lass, uncomplaining. I'll try and make it up to ye, as best I can. But best tae warn ye. Carluke isnae going to be easy for either of us. Perhaps this is not the moment, but just tae let ye know – we'll have to prepare ourselves well. And honesty will be our best policy.'

Agnes turned to face her and nodded. 'Tell me now, Maw.'

Three days now, and still no word from Jim. Martha was fretting, bereft. Everything was falling apart. Her mind was racing, jangled with the foreboding of grief, lack of sleep and worry. Perhaps she should speak to the minister, next time he came in; but it didn't seem right at this time, to be bothering him with her Carluke woes when they were facing such sorrow. A terrible thought came into her mind: what if it was the Reverend Laidlaw who had spoken to MacKenzie? Surely he wouldn't do such a thing. Was there anyone she could trust?

And now here he was, at the door, kind and familiar. No, it couldn't be the Minister.

James Laidlaw was remembering many bedside vigils and reminiscing; they both knew that her mother's time was near.

'Perhaps, as we age, we withdraw more into ourselves, safe in the comfort of our homes and families,' he mused. 'We begin to sleep more, dozing away the day. Perhaps we are preparing. The body anticipates the final great sleep. Your mother is fortunate, Martha; she will die peacefully in the place where she has lived all her life, surrounded by her family. Perhaps it is the best we can all hope for.'

'Aye, indeed, Minister. Ah just wish I could speak to her, again. Tae tell her thank you.' Martha's eyes filled.

The minister looked at her with sympathy. 'Speak to her now, Martha. Sit by the bed, hold her hand, speak into her ear. Who knows, she may hear your voice, and be comforted.'

Martha nodded, and pulled the chair up close. There was much to say.

'Maw? Whit is it, Maw?'

Agnes had jolted awake, fearful.

'She just slipped away, Agnes, in her sleep. She's gone.'

Martha and Agnes stood by the box bed in the early morning light, sobbing quietly, holding and comforting each other. Martha let out a tiny screaming cry, then covered her mouth, struggling to control herself.

'She'll have Lucy tae keep her company, Maw. She'll no' be on her own.'

'It's hard to say goodbye, Agnes. I'm not ready tae part from her. She was a guid mother. She looked after me well.'

'And me, Maw. She looked after me. Whit'll we do without her?'

They opened the door wide, to let the soul fly free.

Then, at last, a note from Jim. Martha tore at the seal. Even in her haste, she noticed his fine handwriting, how he had taken care with her name. *Mrs Martha Lindsay.* She scanned the contents quickly. He was sorry to hear the news of her mother's passing. Perhaps in due course she might indicate her intentions. He had scribbled his initials on the bottom of the note: *JHL*. There was no mention of the terrible scene in the Kirk. Martha looked in vain for an affectionate word.

All of Wanlockhead turned out for the funeral, lining the road to Meadowfoot to pay their respects to the wise woman. The minister spoke about her mother with respect, and Martha was sincere in her thanks for the service.

The day after, she woke at dawn. The early sun was starting in the window, as she bent over a sleeping Agnes.

'Ah'm just away a wee walk, pet.'

She hadn't expected to find herself at the Priest's Pool; her mind had been full as she had set off up the road. As she crossed the moor, she found she was looking forward to revisiting the quiet, sacred spot. Walking on, she realised that she was calmer. The wonderful, peaty smell of the moor had worked its ancient magic.

The heron eyed her as she approached, only lifting into the air at the last moment as she neared the pool. She felt suddenly close to her mother.

'Ye're a strong lassie, Martha.' The familiar voice: it was as if her mother was there beside her. 'Hold yer head up. Ye are better than all of them put together. Be proud of yer heritage. Be proud ye raised Agnes on yer own. Don't try tae be anyone else but yersel' – a fey, lovely lass frae the hills.'

She crouched down, catching a glimpse of her reflection in the water; her mother's dark eyes were looking back at her. She sought the source of the stream and cupped water into her hand and splashed her face, then bent to drink. She felt the invigorating power of the pool enter her body; she stood and stretched her arms wide. She was alive, and she had a life to live. She would write to Jim. She would return to Carluke with Agnes with her head held high.

DISCORD

THE LINDSAY FAMILY siblings had a new habit, which was to gather at Lizzie's little house on Stewart Street on a Sunday after the Kirk, when there would usually be relaxed chatter and exchange of news. It was a smaller gathering this Sunday, without Margaret and Jane; and after the revelations in the Kirk, the mood was sombre, with much shaking of heads.

John just didn't know what to think. He instinctively looked to William – but William just sat with his hands steepled together, looking at the fire. Jemima was all fury, and Lizzie was trying to calm her.

Martha had left the Kirk, the Rankins following her out of the door. The minister had gone on with the service as though nothing had happened, but the atmosphere had been crackling with tension. John had found it hard to look at Faither, sitting on his own, head down; and he had felt angry with the minister for saying these terrible, personal things about Martha. Even if they were true, to declare them publicly from the pulpit … that couldn't be right. His heart had lifted when Dr Rankin had spoken up, and he had been amazed to hear Martha defend herself in such a robust fashion. Aye, he admired her for it – that would have taken guts.

Jem was not so impressed. When the service finished, she had tugged at his sleeve. 'Ah telt ye, John. She's nae use. A bad influence. She's brought a curse tae Carluke. And it sounds like that daughter of hers was born the wrong side of the blanket. She's led Faither astray, wi' her witchy ways.' She made a witchy face.

John took her arm. 'Let's get out of here. Ah cannae stand that MacKenzie.'

'But he's speaking the truth, John.'

'There's a time and place, Jem. That was no' right.'

Jemima's lips thinned to a grimace. She marched off, and he followed behind.

Now, at Lizzie's hearth, the debate continued. John listened to the concern and puzzlement in the voices of his siblings. It seemed it was only Jem who was really angry with Martha. Lizzie in particular was expressing views that reminded him of his mother's kindness; she was using gentle words like 'forgiveness' and 'understanding'. There was, however, a discomfort that there had been secrets, and it was agreed that some frank talking was required.

'It could happen tae anyone,' said Lizzie. 'Getting in the family way.'

John thought of the scuffling behind the miners' cottages.

Jem looked affronted. 'It need not. And it should not, before marriage. That's whit we were taught.'

'Aye, but for some lassies, life just isnae that straightforward,' Lizzie replied. She turned to Jem. 'Ye're mibbe too young tae ken, Jem.'

'I know whit's right and whit's wrong,' said Jem. 'And this brings shame on our family. Faither married a woman who is nothing better than a tinker and a slut.'

Lizzie raised her voice. 'Jemima Lindsay! That is enough.'

Jemima went on. 'And whit aboot the minister's talk of pagan practices? Conjuring up sickness?'

John wondered whether he should mention the garden at Kirkton House and the burning of the sage. As he listened, he realised that the others had noticed unusual activities too. Most people they knew had some old customs – and the pit was full of superstitions – but it seemed that Martha's whole existence revolved around the phases of the moon and mysterious forces of fortune and ill luck. He had heard that travelling people were deeply immersed in the ways of folklore, so perhaps it was true that she was from such stock.

'Then there are all her evil brews,' declared Jemima. 'Smelling the place out, I hear. For curses and spells, most likely.'

Lizzie lifted her hand. 'It's no' like that, Jem. She's making herbal remedies. Some of them smell nice. Her rosemary oil is really popular – it gives a real shine tae the hair.' She shook back her tresses. Jemima was not impressed.

'Huh. There'll be something wicked in all these concoctions, I bet.' She folded her arms.

'Surely there's no harm in it?' Lizzie looked towards William, who continued to scrutinise his hands. John suddenly realised he had assumed exactly the same posture.

William spoke at last. 'Ah think we should walk over to yer Faither's house, Lizzie, and have a chat.'

'Well, ah'm no' going near that house,' declared Jem.

The rest of the family bundled out into the street, Lizzie with her arms full of children, and headed for the Market Place. Jemima stormed off in the opposite direction.

Jim opened the door a crack and peered round.

'Faither. A word. In private.' Lizzie motioned towards the kitchen. She could see heads turning at the pump.

'Come in, the lot of ye. Now shush yersels – the lassies are sleeping upstairs. Ah'm pleased tae say they are both much improved, just as the doctor said.'

They entered the kitchen, which was strangely quiet.

'She's not here,' said Jim.

'Whit? Has Martha run off? Where's she gone?' asked Lizzie.

'Dr Rankin's just called by. He told me she got word that her mother's ill, mibbe dying. He was helping her tae find transport back tae Wanlockhead.'

Lizzie slumped. 'Och. Poor Martha.' There was a silence, and then she spoke again. 'Still, we need to talk, Faither.'

The family settled themselves round the familiar table,

and tea was provided. John was looking round at the jars and the herbs. The place did smell different. He realised with a start that his usual wobbly stool seemed to have become smaller. Or he had grown, in just a few weeks.

'Aboot what the minister said, Faither. Aboot Martha and Agnes.'

'Ocht, ye know what folks are like. The minister shouldnae be listening to the town tittle-tattle.' Faither looked most uncomfortable; he was scarcely able to look at them.

William spoke, as he filled his pipe. 'Jim, the minister said he had heard it frae Wanlockhead. And now it'll be all over the town. To be honest, I'd heard rumours at my work, but I hadnae paid any mind. Folk are saying that Agnes is illegitimate. Born long before Martha got married tae that poor chap from Biggar. And that Martha's mother is a well-known healer, wi' special powers that she got from some tinker ancestor. There's talk that she is in cahoots wi' the ghost of the wizard, that used tae live at Kirkton House.'

Lizzie gave him a sharp look. 'First I've heard all this,' she said.

'I dinnae repeat half of what I hear in the mine, Lizzie,' he replied.

Lizzie glared at him, then turned to face Faither. 'It's not on, Faither. We need tae clear this up. Is she a witch? Ah thought all that notion of evil spells was in the past. And are these rumours of her child born out of wedlock true?

If that is the situation, we need tae know, not have the whole town party to our own family history before we are.'

'Ocht. Aye, I suppose ye've got a point. I just thought it would be easier for Martha if we just smoothed over her unusual history,' said Jim. He was clearly embarrassed.

'It's made it worse, Faither.' Lizzie's voice rose. 'Don't ye see? The whole town'll be laughing at us. At you. They'll think she duped you, and they've added in the hexing tae make the tittle-tattle even tastier.'

Lizzie stopped and looked at him. 'So ye knew all about this illegitimacy?'

'Aye. Of course,' said Jim. 'She never tried tae hide anything from me. The opposite. She went out her way to tell me of her situation.' He grimaced. 'Wanlockhead has its share of clishmaclaver gossips too. Ah could hardly take a step down the street there, without some supposed well-wisher stopping me, making sure I was "properly informed" of her family history.' He shook his head. 'It all sounds so stark and nasty when ye hear it frae the minister, right enough. Gypsy folk. Illegitimacy. Whit a mess. Ah might have known this would happen. You're right, Lizzie. We should have telt the lot of ye when she arrived. She wanted to. But I thought naebody would be bothered. It seems I was wrong.' He shook his head, and faced his eldest. 'Ah still think she's a guid woman, Lizzie. She's no witch. And I married her, so I have tae stick by her. Somehow we'll have tae get through this.'

'Whit would my mother have thought, being spoken of in the Kirk?' John could tell that Lizzie was upset. 'We are a decent family. And how do ye explain aboot the illness? The minister seems tae think she brought that on the town?'

William got up and folded his arms. 'Lizzie, that is most definitely just a lot of nonsense. The lads at the pit all agree that the likely explanation is that the Fair folk brought the illness to the town. I dinnae believe Martha would try tae do harm.'

Lizzie nodded. Then she said, 'Ye're right aboot one thing, Faither. It is a mess. Tell me, how are ye going tae clean it up?'

William stood back, hands out, appeasing. 'Jim, you need tae find out whit Martha's thinking of it all. What her plans are. She'd best warn poor wee Agnes, too. With her grannie gone, it's likely the lassie will need tae be with her mother. If – no, when – she comes back, we should all meet up. Discuss what we might do. If anything.'

Jim nodded. 'Aye, William. We cannae bury our heads in the sand. We need tae face it.'

He drew himself up, conscious that he was some inches shorter than his son-in-law. 'Right. Best make a start. I'll drop her a note.'

Lizzie spoke. Again, John heard the compassion in her voice that reminded him of his mother.

'Faither. If her mother's ill, she'll no' be of a clear mind. Poor woman, everything happening at once.'

'Aye. Ye're right. And mibbe I'm no' thinking clearly either.' Jim put his head in his hands.

Lizzie, William and John said their goodbyes and headed back to Stewart Street, weans in tow.

'Whit a silly man. He's brought this on all of us.'

'He was trying tae protect her, Lizzie.'

'He had his head in the sand. Ye cannae escape yer past, William. It'll always catch up with ye. Even here, in Carluke – mibbe *especially* in a town like this, where everybody knows yer business.'

'Aye. Right enough, it's mibbe best to be straight wi' folk. But we are where we are, Lizzie. You and me, we need tae think of a good way out of all this. For everyone's sake.'

John walked on glumly. There was nothing he hated more than seeing everyone upset. He made his excuses, and walked to Tom's house. Soon the two of them were walking down the brae, hands in pockets.

Tom confirmed that the row at the Free Kirk was the talk of the town.

John said, 'Ocht, Tom. Ah felt that sorry for her, having tae listen tae all that frae Mackenzie.'

'Ah heard she stuck up for hersel', though,' said Tom. 'Has she no' run off, back to Wanlockhead?'

'Naw. Her mother's taken ill. She got word as she came out of the Kirk. She left right away.'

'It's the wee lassie ah feel sorry for,' said Tom. 'Agnes, isn't it? Whit a shame, being judged all yer life.'

'Aye.' John nodded. 'It's no' her fault.'

'And Mrs Lindsay. Martha. Whit do ye think, John? All this talk aboot frequenting Kirkton House, bringing the sickness tae the place? Dae ye think she's a witch?'

Tom was slowing his pace. John stopped and looked at him.

Tom looked down. 'Sorry. Whit a daft question. It's just … that's whit folk are saying.'

'Naw. William says that thing aboot her being tae blame for the sickness is just rubbish. And I dinnae think she's a witch. Ah think … Ocht. Ah'm no' sure what tae think. She's just different.'

He thought of Martha's strange garden at Kirkton House, and the changes in the Market Place kitchen. *Aye, she's different to my maw*, he thought.

'John. A word.' He was not surprised to hear Jemima's voice, calling him over the street.

'See ya the morn, Tom!' he said, and crossed to her.

'So. Whit's the story at the Market Place house?'

He immediately recognised her fierce mood, and tried to pitch a conciliatory voice. 'If ye'd come with us, ye would know.'

'Ah cannae go back there, John. Not when there are liars in that house.'

'It's no' as simple as that, Jemima. Martha's maw is ill. She's mibbe going to die. She's away back tae Wanlockhead.'

Jemima looked away for a moment, her shoulders

slumping, then turned back, defiant. 'She's still a whore.'

'Jem, stop it. It's not like ye. We cannae change things. It doesnae do ye any guid to be so angry. So worked up.'

'Ah think it's true. Ah think she's some kind o' witch, mixing spells wi' the devil at Kirkton House. She bewitched Faither, well and proper. Has she put a hex on you too, John?'

'That's rubbish!'

But John was speaking to Jemima's back, as she stormed down the street.

MIND YOUR OWN BUSINESS

'AH FEEL SICK, Maw.'

'C'mon, Agnes. We spoke aboot this. Head up. Barkie's having a guid look around – you should, too. Look, here's the Market Place, and your new home.'

Martha was looking around for Jim … and here he was, striding across the Market Place towards them. Thank God. He was smiling, and his arms were outstretched. Martha closed her eyes in relief.

'Welcome home, Martha. And welcome, Agnes.'

Jim helped them down from the cart, then faced Martha. 'The family are waiting, in the kitchen.'

Martha nodded, and followed him inside. She was ready.

They were all there, around the table – all except Jemima. *That might make it easier*, she thought.

She looked around the room, then spoke. 'This is no-one's fault but mine.'

Jim started, 'But my dear …'

She lifted her hand and went on. 'No, Jim. Ah should have been honest of my circumstances to your children, as I was to you. It's not been fair to them, and it's not fair to Agnes.'

Agnes was white, clenching her teeth. One hand was on Barkie's soft head, the other gripping in her pocket.

Martha put her hand on her daughter's shoulder and took a deep breath.

'As ye are all now aware, Agnes is my daughter, born out of wedlock. She was christened Agnes Hewson Brownlee at the church in Wanlockhead, where her circumstances were always known. She is my dear girl.' She paused. 'Perhaps, for a moment when I first arrived, perhaps I foolishly thought that we both might have a fresh start here in Carluke. That was a serious mistake, Agnes, and I am sorry for it. We should have known that stories like ours are rich pickings for gossips in any place.'

She looked around the table at Jane, Margaret and Lizzie. William and John were standing by the fire, leaning on the overhang; as usual, William was smoking his pipe. He nodded encouragingly.

'Of course, it will be up to you all to decide how ye react to malicious comments, words that are meant to hurt. Agnes and I have had many years to learn that the only way for us to face the world is to keep our heads high.' She put her hands together, as if to pray. 'Still, I am truly sorry that I have brought strife and unpleasantness tae your door. If ye want to ask me anything – *anything* – from my past, then please feel free tae do so.

'Jim.' Martha turned to her husband. She looked bleak. 'I was so happy that we met, and I was proud tae become your wife. I didnae ever mean to bring trouble to yer family.'

'It's your family too, Martha. It's our family. I've been thinking, too. We have tae stick up for each other. All of us. We're bigger than any clishmaclavers. We'll all hold our heads high.'

Martha looked round. The Lindsay sisters at the table were exchanging glances. She looked over to the fireplace. John gave her a wee smile, a nod; and William moved his fingers, giving a tiny wave. The leaden weight in her chest eased slightly.

'You say ye've had many years to learn to deal with this, Martha,' said Lizzie. 'We are still … adjusting tae the news.'

'Yes,' said Margaret. 'It's a lot tae take in. Martha …' She hesitated. 'Martha, I heard ye had another daughter, who died.' She looked down at her hands. 'I heard she died o' neglect.'

The warm kitchen chilled, as if winter had blown in.

Martha and Agnes spoke together.

'That's not true, Margaret.'

'That's a lie! We loved Lucy!'

Agnes had stood up. Barkie stood too, and growled round at the room. Martha put a hand on her daughter's arm and felt the pain and anger coursing through her.

'It's all right, Agnes. Sit down. These folks need to hear whit happened.' Martha took another deep breath. 'A few years after Agnes was born, I met a guid man – a carter, frae Biggar. We had been married for less than two years when ma husband died of consumption. It was evident just a few months after her birth that our baby daughter had the same terrible and fatal condition. When he died, ah brought wee Lucy back to Wanlockhead. We nursed her the best we could, but she couldnae be saved. She was just three years old. She lies with my mither, in the graveyard, in Meadowfoot. I think of her every day.'

Jim spoke up. 'Martha took me tae show me the grave, and she took flowers. That's no' the act of a neglectful mother. And the Wanlockhead minister also spoke tae me on a couple of occasions – a decent chap called James Laidlaw. He spoke highly of you, Martha. He said ye were a good mother.'

'Aye, she is!' Agnes was nearly shouting. 'How can we stop these lies, especially when they are mixed in amongst the true facts?' She scowled. 'None of it is anyone's business but ours.'

Jim spoke again. 'What does it say in the Bible? "Judge not, as you will be judged." Heaven knows, there are skeletons in the cupboards of most families hereabouts, are there not?'

Agnes looked at him with alarm.

Jim shook his head. 'Not real skeletons, hen. I'm meaning, most folk have a secret or two, hidden away.'

'My old grannie had a saying.' William tapped the contents of his pipe into the fire. 'She said, "Ill words speak ill of the speaker." Agnes is right. I'll be telling folk tae mind their own business.'

Lizzie nodded at Margaret and Jane. 'Mind yer own

business. Aye, William. That sounds right. I can live wi' that. I'll take real pleasure, saying that tae a few folks about here.'

Martha held up her hand. 'Lizzie, there's something else. The minister made it sound like I was responsible for that horrible illness, too. The Devil's Grip. I can assure ye …'

Jim interrupted her. 'Don't worry, Martha. Ye have a real champion in Dr Rankin. He has made it very clear to everyone who will listen that the disease isnae caused by witchcraft.'

Martha's face lit up with a smile. 'That's guid news, Jim.' She turned to Margaret and Jane. 'And ah'm glad to see the lassies are better, too.' She shook her head. 'Whit a time we've all had.'

She turned to face Jim again. 'And just one more thing. Agnes and I won't be attending the Free Kirk again, Jim. We might give the Church o' Scotland a try.' She tried another smile. 'We could all compare sermons later.'

Jim looked down and nodded, resigned.

John spoke up. 'My pal Tom Lee goes tae that church, Martha. He likes it fine.'

Jane stood. 'Martha. I've just realised. We've no' said how sorry we were to hear aboot your mother. You have had such a difficult time. And Agnes, losing your Grannie.'

Martha inclined her head. 'Thank you, Jane.'

Margaret stood up too. 'Right. That's it all sorted. Let's

get the kettle on. And there's cake.'

The room eased. The cake was good, packed with fruit. Martha noticed that the kitchen smelled of her cleansing herbs up on the pulley. She reached for Jim's hand, felt it squeeze her own.

'Aye, ah like baking, but I'm no match for yer mother, Agnes.' Margaret nodded at Martha.

'Where's Jemima?' asked Agnes.

Martha noticed the exchange of glances between Margaret and Jane.

'Aye, ye'll meet her soon enough. Jemima lodges with her employers, the Shieldses. She's not far.'

There was some discussion about the business. Jim was keen to know when Agnes might start in the shop, and there was speculation about what role she might fulfil there.

'I remember your work. Ye're a neat needlewoman, Agnes,' he said.

She wriggled in the chair, not sure how to react to the praise. 'Ah like the sewing. Especially lacemaking. I did piece-work in Wanlockhead.' She addressed this to Margaret and Jane. 'I'll be glad to start work.' She smiled at her mother. Martha smiled back, nodding encouragement. Maybe it was going to be all right.

Later that evening, Martha was banking the fire in the stove when her eye caught something hanging down in the chimney space. She took the poker, and jabbed; a tightly wound sock bundle fell into the fire. She nodded her head in recognition as it fell open, revealing thistles and thorns. A nasty, malicious object indeed. For a brief moment she wondered who had placed it there, but as she watched it crackle and burn, she knew this was a time to look forward, and not back.

SETTLING IN

AGNES HAD SPENT much of the journey agonising over her last encounter in Wanlockhead. Most of her friends had wished her well for the future, and meant it; others felt a pang of envy at her adventure into a new life; and Catriona Ferguson had been unable to resist a last dig.

'Ma faither knows the minister at Carluke. There'll be no secrets there. Think on that when ye're rattling down the road.' She smirked, and went on. 'Ye think yer fancy new family is gettin' ready tae welcome in the bastard child frae Wanlockhead? Ye'll be sleeping in a cupboard, Agnes, and ye'll have all the housework tae dae, like Cinderella but worse.'

'Better than listening tae your forked tongue, Cat. And more chance of a handsome prince in a big town like Carluke.' Agnes had grasped the pebble in her pocket and felt the surge from the Priest's Pool fill her chest. She lowered her voice. 'Ah hope ah never see ye again. And listen tae this. A farewell gift frae the tinker bastard. A curse on you, Catriona Ferguson.'

Catriona went white. Agnes called to Barkie, then turned and walked off.

Now, here she was in this big, strange place. Agnes had only ever known one home and was aching to be back there. But the cottage was gone forever, the door slammed shut and the keys handed back.

'Look, here's Jim. At least try and give him a smile.'

Jim was kind and helped them with their trunks and boxes. He expressed his condolences for Grannie's death. But when he said the family all wanted a word, Agnes felt her stomach churn.

In the end, it had been easier than she thought it might be. She hadn't been banished; there was no talk of her being sent back to Wanlockhead alone. There had been some awkwardness, but her maw had stood strong, with that new calmness that she had. Over tea, she'd been asked about Grannie, and the funeral. They had all seemed sympathetic. And they were all interested in Barkie. Perhaps there was to be a family for her in Carluke after all.

'Where am I to sleep, Maw? Where should I put ma bag?'

Agnes pulled her dark grey shawl round her thin shoulders. She had moved from the kitchen into the narrow entrance hall. Before her were some stairs. Agnes had never lived in a house with proper stairs. Perhaps the sleeping accommodation was up there. Jane stepped forward with her hand outstretched.

'Why don't ye give me your bag, Agnes? C'mon, I'll take you up the stairs and show you where you'll sleep.

You'll be at the front of the house, in John's old room.'

Agnes turned to call her dog. Barkie perked up at the sound of her name and, with some trepidation, she followed her mistress up the stairs. Jane started to show her round.

'Faither and Martha are here, in this room at the back. It's quieter.'

Agnes glimpsed a thick scarlet quilt on the double bed, and a soft silk shift on the chair.

'Margaret and I are in here. It's not very tidy, but better than when Jemima was here as well.' Jane indicated a smaller room, with another large bed in it. There were clothes strewn on the floor, and a jumble of lotions, combs and brushes on the small dressing table.

'And here is your room. It's small, but cosy enough. You are looking over the Market Place, Agnes.'

Agnes put her bag down on the floor. Barkie had a sniff around, then she lay down on the rag rug, beside the trestle bed.

'Jane, this is very grand. It will be strange tae sleep by myself. At least I'll have Barkie for company.'

'You have some hooks on the door and a wee chest for your things. There is a table by the bed, for your candle. Oh, look. That's a pretty wee plate.'

Agnes had reached into her bag and taken out a small saucer, with roses painted round the edge. She touched it gently. 'This belonged tae my grannie. I'll just put it here. I'll sort out the rest later.'

Agnes placed the saucer by the bed, then the two of them descended the stairs, Barkie following carefully. The tour continued.

'At the front, just off the hallway, we have the parlour, where we sit of an evening. Faither likes that chair there, by the fire. He's always got a pile of newspapers on the go – what a jumble.'

They stepped back into the kitchen. Agnes was able to take in more as she looked around properly. She noticed there were three pulleys high on the ceiling: one laden with laundry and the other two festooned with tied bundles of herbs. The fire, complete with a hearth, boasted a large kettle and several pots and pans; there were shelves stacked with familiar crockery, and several mismatched chairs round a well-worn table. A lamp glowed in the corner, making the room look homely.

'It used tae be that we never had enough chairs for everyone,' said Jane. 'There was usually a fight. John always ended up on the wobbly stool.' She indicated a lopsided three-legged seat by the fire. 'Oh, and this door here leads tae the back close, where you'll find the privy.'

Agnes was suitably impressed with the size of the accommodation, but was bursting with curiosity to see the tailoring workshop. With Martha's encouragement, she and Jim went into the back close, and through the back door of the premises. She saw a bright, generous space, running from the front to the back of the house, with tall windows at either end. At the furthest wall there was a door into the front street, with a wide wooden counter before it. Parcels were piled up on top, and a huge ledger had pride of place. Arranged further into the room were worktables covered in half-finished pieces of sewing, scissors, measuring sticks and tapes, and many coloured reels of thread. There were bales of material stacked in the corners, and an unnerving object in the middle of the room. At first glance, it looked like a headless and legless person – she then realised it was a tailor's dummy. At the front of the shop there was a screened area with a full-length mirror, which Agnes assumed would be for the use of the customers. A fire crackled in the hearth on the far wall.

In pride of place, nearby on the back table, was a treadle sewing machine. Margaret was busy pedalling, guiding some material through the needle. Agnes walked over to take a look. She wanted to touch the wheel; it looked so much better than the loom she had worked on in Wanlockhead. Perhaps she could learn how to use it.

'Only Faither and Margaret can use the sewing machine.' Jane had stepped into the room behind them. 'But there is plenty more work tae do, ye can be sure of that.'

'Jane, ye are so fortunate to work here,' Agnes said.

'Goodness! What makes you say that?'

'This room. It's so light and there's so much space.'

'It can be cold in the wintertime, Agnes, believe me. But I suppose ye're right. I hear that some of the cottage workers are in quite cramped conditions, and with only small windows.'

'That was my situation, aye. I will look forward tae working here with you all very much. I hope that my work will be to a satisfactory standard. I don't want tae let ye down, Mr Lindsay.'

'I've told ye, Agnes. Call me Jim. Now, let's find you a stool to sit on, and try ye with some stitching.'

Margaret came from behind the sewing machine, and she and Jane gathered round with Jim to watch. Here was someone sewing with the left hand. It looked so awkward and clumsy – but the stitches were tiny and perfect.

'Well, I've never seen a corrie-fisted seamstress before,' said Margaret. 'That's a new one for Carluke.' She picked up the garment. 'Left-handed or no', you cannae go wrong with needlework like this, Agnes. We'll be keeping ye busy.'

'Mr Lind— Jim. Might Barkie be allowed to stay under my worktable? She will be no bother to ye, I'll make sure of it.' The dog was at her side as usual, looking up, listening intently.

'Aye, Agnes. Why not? Here's an old box. We'll make her a wee nest to sleep in.'

'Thank you.' Agnes was glowing. Having Barkie with her would make it perfect.

Barkie was trotting out into the Market Place beside her mistress. Her hackles were up, and she was emitting a low, sustained growl. Agnes hated going to the water pump; in truth, she avoided going out at all. If it wasn't for Barkie's need for exercise, she would be hiding in the workroom all day, every day.

The little groups of women would stop speaking as she drew near – or, worse still, she would hear low whispers and sniggering. She wondered how on earth her mother coped; indeed, how she had coped over the years. Nowadays, Martha seemed to grow taller with every dirty look or slight. She always made a point of smiling and giving a greeting to one and all, no matter how they responded to her. Agnes was dismayed one day on witnessing her mother being subjected to a particularly hostile and snide encounter in the queue for the baker's shop, the word 'hoor' clearly heard.

'How can ye stand it, Maw?' she said.

'Those shopkeepers need our business. And the tailoring workshop needs theirs. We have tae show them that we know how tae be civil. And these folks are our neighbours. One day we may need their assistance, or they might need ours. We just have tae put on an imaginary suit of armour, Agnes, every time we leave our door.'

Easier said than done, thought Agnes as she turned for the safety of the house.

A small stone rattled by her shoulder and landed in the gutter. Barkie turned, baring her teeth, and gave a few angry barks in response.

'That *wee bitch* – keep it under control, why don't ye?' The coarse voice of one of the sharper neighbours could be heard above the chatter.

Agnes ran inside, cheeks burning, and slammed the door. Her mother looked at her, eyebrows raised.

'Now, Agnes, whit's that aboot?'

'Sorry, Maw. It's those women. At the water pump.'

'It'll pass, Agnes. Dinnae let it upset ye. Next week, it will be someone else getting the attention. Now, come and have some lunch. Jim will be expecting ye back at your workbench soon.'

At least the big, bright workshop was a sanctuary, where the days just flew by. She could focus on her work in the comfort of a safe place, knowing that Barkie was snug in her box under her desk. Some of the customers could be quite abrupt, but her work was more and more in demand. The call to speak to the 'corrie-fisted seamstress' was starting to be heard regularly from the counter, and the pressing requirement to discuss the particular benefits of certain threads in regard to lace style and pattern clearly outweighed any social niceties. Jane and Margaret kept in their own corner, chattering away sixteen to the dozen about their pals, courting, hairstyles, hats, clothes. Agnes was quite happy at her own table, Barkie at her feet in her special nest. She was earning her keep as a vigorous mouser; and once, with much tail-wagging, she had triumphantly delivered a huge, freshly dead rat to Agnes.

Jim didn't know whether to be horrified or pleased at her contribution. 'Not in front of the customers, Barkie, if ye don't mind.'

Agnes was enthusiastic about the tailoring work. There

was so much variety, and she was delighted to be given some of the finer stitching to do. Every day there seemed to be a new face coming in the door and calling from the counter: customers, of course, but also delivery men and travelling drapers, with their wares. She was learning who would bring the warm tweeds, and who brought the rolls of cotton. Big Jim was proud of his wares – not just the smart waistcoats, but also the varieties of plain and striped shirts he could offer; he would usually be seated at the treadle sewing machine, intent on a garment yet keeping a sharp eye on the workshop. Occasionally he would offer up a 'Wheesht!' to Margaret and Jane, when their nattering got too much for him; they would giggle, and be quiet for a moment, before starting up again.

'Hey, Agnes! He's got an eye for ye, young Davey!' said Margaret. The travelling draper's lad had just left the premises, his face a crimson red.

Agnes wriggled in her chair and looked down at her work. Then she looked up again, turning around to address the back of the room. 'Ah dinnae think so, Margaret. He's always asking for Jemima. He's interested in Barkie, not me. He's always stroking her.'

For some reason, the older girls found this hysterical.

Jim put his foot down. 'Girls. That's enough. This is a place of work, not a … a … place of ill repute. Settle down. The order book is full, there's work to do.'

Margaret and Jane bent over their workbenches once more, their shoulders heaving. Wiping tears from their eyes, they eventually managed to speak coherently.

'Aye. Aye, right enough.' Jane gulped, trying not to laugh again. 'He did always have a wee thing for Jemima.'

'A wee thing!' Her sister collapsed in giggles, searching for a handkerchief to wipe her nose.

'He's such a skinny big thing!' responded Jane.

The screams of laughter resounded as Jim got to his feet. 'Lassies. *That's enough*!'

Agnes bent over her work; she was smiling too. Under the workbench, Barkie was sitting up, ears cocked and listening to the fun.

It was at night, in her little bed at the front of the Market Place house, when she felt most alone. The cosy cottage in Wanlockhead, with her grandmother on the bench outside chatting with a neighbour, became an oft-visited reminiscence, where it always seemed to be summer, the sun shining in through the open door. Agnes would lay out all her treasured mementoes from that time – her grannie's little dish, the book of Burns poetry she had been given on leaving school, a ribbon that had belonged to little Lucy – and take her mind back to quieter times, easier times.

'My maw is happy, Barkie. That's the main thing. We cannae go back. And it used tae snow, something terrible. Mibbe Maw's right. It'll mibbe stop soon. Ah hope.' She would reach down for Barkie, who would respond with a lick to her hand.

It did get easier. Carluke had so many splendid streets, with solid stone buildings. There were grand houses sitting in their own grounds, with smart drapes at the windows, and many lamps extravagantly lit of a gloomy afternoon; terraced houses, like those in the Market Place, with gleaming front steps; big cottages, wee cottages, some well kept, others shambolic; and everywhere, so many folk. Agnes had taken to carrying the stone from the Priest's Pool again, rubbing the smooth pebble as she walked through the streets. As she gained confidence, she explored further. She recognised the miners' rows, similar to those in Wanlockhead but somehow grimier, poorer, less homely.

Barkie at her heels, she was walking towards a row now, listening to the women singing as they scrubbed at the communal laundry tub. Belting out the tune was a strong-looking woman, sleeves rolled tight above the elbows, her hands red raw, turning the handle of the mangle. Agnes recognised the tune to one of her favourite hymns: 'Praise, My Soul, the King of Heaven'. She stopped. Surely they were mistaken? Weren't these the wrong words?

> *'Once again we're doing the washin', hearin' not a word of praise.*
> *Praying for some decent weather, hopin' that it will nae rain.*
> *Steepin', soakin', scrubbin', washin', wringin' out the miners' claes.'*

The women were intent on their tasks, but the singer

lifted her head as Agnes scurried past. 'Did ye bring that wee dug with ye frae Wanlockhead?'

Agnes stopped, and nodded.

'That tail would make a fine bottle brush!' The woman laughed, pretending to brandish a knife as Agnes ran on, hoping it was just a joke.

Best of all, she liked to look at the shops. She could spend ages looking at the hardware store, with its kettles and pans, but the shopkeeper wasn't so keen on Barkie, so she moved on. It was difficult for Barkie to get past the butchers' shops, especially when the big meat pies were being made. She would be drooling and licking her lips. If she was lucky, a butcher's lad might throw her a treat. Barkie would always remember, and would want to return there every time she left the house.

And here was the singing man, shuffling along in his battered felt hat and his warped boots. Agnes would stop to listen to his strange tunes: half-familiar hymns, ancient folk ballads. Barkie was entranced, and would sometimes join in, in her own howling way. The singing man would bow, and smile. Agnes would bow back, then hurry away, unsure whether to speak or not. She knew her mother was giving him food, and she had once seen him in the kitchen, with his feet in a basin of water. Jim hadn't been too pleased about that.

It was late. Agnes was alone in the kitchen. She enjoyed the quiet; she liked clearing the last of the day from the busy room, and getting it ready for a fresh start in the morning.

Her eye fell on the cheese. Minnie Donaldson had brought it; a fine round Dunlop, sweet and fresh, it was in part payment on her new outfit. Big Jim's eyes had lit up when he saw it; although much had been made of the irregularity of the arrangement, everyone knew the tailor was partial to cheese. As was Agnes. She cut a thin slice, bit into it, and gave the rest to an attentive Barkie.

The dog turned abruptly to the door, hackles rising.

Agnes looked round. In the shadow she saw the outline of a figure. She let out a cry.

Then Barkie ran forward, tail wagging fast.

'Did ah startle ye? Sorry, Agnes!'

It was John, coming in through the back close.

'Lizzie heard there was a cheese. William is very partial. Is there any left?' He stepped closer, pausing to give Barkie a pat.

'Are you alright? Ye look as if ye've seen a ghostie!'

'Aye, aye. Ye gave me a fright, that's all. Let's cut ye a piece.'

John took the generous portion, now wrapped in muslin.

'I'd best be heading back across the road.'

'John, before ye go. Can ye tell me why Jemima doesnae like me? You and Lizzie are that nice tae me, but Jemima doesnae even come tae the house. She barely speaks. I've been thinking. Is it because of … my illegitimacy?'

John looked down at his hands. He noticed with a start how calloused and rough they were – real workman's hands. He tried to concentrate. He knew he had to get this right. 'It's no' you, Agnes. Jem still misses her mammy. This kitchen' – he paused, looked round – 'she'll remember it as her mammy's kitchen. It's been a big change for her, Martha coming, then yersel'.'

Agnes considered this. Maybe John was right; maybe it wasn't about her at all. Or maybe she just reminded Jemima of her loss. She thought of her grannie, and the sadness she still carried, and nodded.

'She'll mibbe outgrow it, Agnes. She'll find her own way. These things can take time.' He stood. 'I'd best get this cheese back for William, or there'll be trouble.'

As Agnes climbed the stairs to bed, Barkie at her heels, she remembered a recent encounter when Jemima had reminded her in no uncertain terms that she was quite aware of her status.

She had tried to respond, had tried to be brave like her maw. 'Ah've never tried tae hide it, Jemima. My name is Agnes Hewson Brownlee. Maw made a mistake when she was young, and here I am.'

'How dae ye think I feel, knowing a bastard is sleeping in ma brother's old bed? It's shocking!'

Agnes had bitten her lip to stop the curse as Jemima marched away, never once looking back.

MISS RANKIN PAYS A CALL

AGNES LOOKED UP. There was her maw, at the back door of the workshop.

'Agnes. Miss Rankin is here, and would like a word.'

Jim looked at her questioningly. 'What's this about?' He stood, and accompanied them to the front door of the house.

'Miss Rankin! How are ye? Won't ye step inside?' said Jim.

'Good day, Mr Lindsay. I just want a wee word with young Agnes here. We'll take a turn around the Market Place; I promise we won't be long.'

Jim nodded his approval. 'Off ye go, lassie.'

Puzzled, Agnes reached for her shawl and stepped outside. She recognised Sarah but didn't know her name. Miss Rankin undertook proper introductions, and they all started to stroll down the street. There was a woof, a rush and a commotion, and Barkie jumped over the step to join them.

'Yes. Your little dog.' Miss Rankin acknowledged the ginger terrier. 'Now, I am making you girls acquainted, because you have something in common. Something that is usually only whispered.'

Both girls started to look very uncomfortable. Sarah was blushing, looking down at her feet.

Miss Rankin proceeded, ignoring their discomfiture. 'Both you girls were born out of wedlock. I suspect both of you have been subjected to teasing and name-calling. It might be difficult to make friends.'

She paused. Agnes and Sarah continued to stare at the pavement. Sarah was scarlet to her ears.

'Sarah, your mother has never tried to hide your situation – and I understand that before moving here, Mrs Lindsay had taken a similarly straightforward approach in your case too, Agnes. After some careful thought, my brother Dr Rankin and I considered that an introduction might be helpful to you both. Even in a busy town, especially if you are an incomer' – she nodded towards Agnes – 'it can be difficult to get to know people.'

Realising a response was anticipated, Agnes said, 'Yes, Miss Rankin.'

'Now. Sarah, if you wish to call on Agnes of an evening, for a stroll and a chat, then we will gladly allow that. Agnes, might I ask your mother if this arrangement would suit?'

'Thank ye, Miss Rankin. I can speak to my mother. If Sarah is content with it, we might enjoy each other's company.' She glanced expectantly at Sarah.

'Why don't you girls walk on a bit, with the little dog. Sarah, I'll see you back at the house shortly. Goodbye,

Agnes. It was a pleasure to speak with you.'

Miss Rankin turned, and made her way back across the Market Place.

Sarah and Agnes looked at each other, and started to giggle.

'Well, I wasn't expecting this, when she asked me to step across the road with her. She is some woman!' said Sarah.

Agnes was full of questions. 'How does she know of my situation? Do ye mind her knowing your affairs? This is most … peculiar!'

Sarah spoke proudly. 'For myself, my situation is well known in the town. Particularly as my mother took my father before the Sheriff, to force acknowledgement of his part, and to require payment from him. He did oblige, and paid up as decreed, four pounds a year until I was seven years old.' The girls strolled on, and Sarah continued. 'My mother never hid matters from me. I took his name, and I learned to take a strange pride in her determination to seek justice from him.'

Agnes smiled. 'My mother made no such claim against my faither – although she is of a character that would make such a pursuit, if she had known it possible. And she too never tried tae hide my past from me. My faither was a blacksmith called Brownlee. She taught me tae hold my head up high. It is easier to say it than to do it, I am sure you agree.'

'I know that well.' Sarah nodded. 'Some are cruel, some less so – but quick with a judging look.'

'I know that look,' said Agnes.

'The Rankins have always been kind to me – to all our family. I was most grateful to be given a position there. Miss Rankin is strict, but she has a good heart.' Sarah looked over the Market Place. 'Look, your mother is waving from the door. Will I call for you tomorrow? We could walk down by Jock's Brae. Will you bring your wee dog again?'

'Aye, that will be grand. Till tomorrow.'

Agnes waved to her new friend, and walked back to a curious Martha, Barkie running ahead.

Martha listened to Agnes's account, then said, 'Well, if the Rankins think it a good arrangement, that you girls should be friends, why not give it a try?'

'Aye, Maw. Aye, I will.'

Agnes couldn't sleep. She couldn't stop thinking about Miss Rankin's visit with Sarah. She was excited about the possibility of a friend, someone who perhaps understood that feeling of being on the outside. Sarah seemed nice. And she liked Barkie, that was the main thing.

I can tell her the story of how I found her, thought Agnes. She opened her eyes in the gloom. How, though, did Miss Rankin know of her situation?

That was her first question to Sarah, the following evening, as they followed Barkie down the brae.

Sarah was clear. 'Agnes, everybody knows everyone's business here. Your circumstances are the talk of the town.'

'For the women at the water pump, aye. But even Miss Rankin?'

'Aye, even Miss Rankin. She would hear at the bakery, doubtless.' Sarah went on. 'Perhaps in a wee place like Wanlockhead, you just took it for granted that folk would know your history. But believe me, people still make it their business to know all about you here. Your mother's arrival caused quite a stir. Some folk are just eager to go on digging, looking for juicy morsels to gossip about.'

They passed a woman shaking a cloth out in her doorway, staring at the two girls.

'See her?' Sarah nodded over in her direction. 'She's a real clishmaclaver.'

'A what?'

The woman tutted and went inside, slamming the door.

'A gossip, of course. She'll talk to anyone that might know anything about you and your mother. And there are many others like her.'

'Aye,' said Agnes. 'Ah know all aboot gossips. Clishmaclavers. That's a great word. There are quite a few of them in Wanlockhead, too.' She thought, then said, 'Ah certainly feel eyes on us in the church.'

'That's the worst place. Full of clishmaclavers. Dr Rankin has no time for the Church. But he's different. It's all right for him to say he won't go. The doctor is well respected in the town, despite his strange beliefs … I attend with my family, of course, but I don't always feel very welcome.'

Agnes was quiet, remembering the minister's words to

her in Wanlockhead, that Jesus wasn't checking her birth certificate. She missed the services where the Reverend James Laidlaw would speak of everyone being part of God's family. She had felt she belonged.

'Me and my maw, we've started going to that big Church of Scotland on the main street,' she confided to Sarah. 'Ah cannae get used to it. It's strange being in a church where the minister doesnae know ye. The minister in Wanlockhead was different. He was awfy kind tae me.'

At least Tom Lee gave me a wave, she thought. She had been so relieved to see his ginger head in the congregation.

'Have you heard that Burns poem, *To a Louse*? I often think of that, when I'm sitting looking at all these fine bonnets and prim faces in the Kirk.' Sarah struck a pose, then started the verse. 'O wad some power the giftie gie us …'

Agnes finished the line. 'To see oursels as others see us!'

They laughed, mock-scratching their heads, finding imaginary lice.

'Your maw, Agnes – she's got the right idea, just like my maw. They keep their heads up, look them all in the eye. We've got to do the same.'

They linked arms and walked on – taller, brighter, bonnier.

'C'mon, Barkie. Time for a walk.'

For once, Agnes was pleased to be getting out of the house. It was lighter now in the early evening, and there was the possibility of spring in the air; she sensed it, somewhere beyond the overwhelming stench of cattle dung. The street was still filthy, and she had to be careful about mud on her dress. There had been a cattle fair that week – the first of the year – and although she still got a thrill from the bustle and noise filling the Market Place, she had learned that the slurry remained treacherous for many days afterwards.

It was doubtful she would see Sarah just yet. It was the wrong time: she would be busy preparing the tea at the Rankin house. Agnes enjoyed hearing the stories of the doctor and his fierce sister, and she sensed that Sarah appreciated the companionship of the quiet lass from the tailor's house. Blushing, Sarah had told her that she sometimes walked out with John, but that his shift work and her work made it difficult for them to find time to be together. Agnes wondered if John knew of Sarah's background. She found it difficult to imagine Sarah being anything other than straightforward.

She called Barkie to heel, and turned down the lane towards the abandoned hulk of Kirkton House, shivering as she remembered the stories Sarah had told her about previous inhabitants.

'The doctor is writing a history of Carluke, Agnes.' Sarah had spoken in a suitably serious tone. 'There are so many stories. One of the best is about the man who lived at Kirkton House, long ago. He was a wizard – imagine that!'

'That's so shocking! Nae wonder the house is a ruin. Who would want tae live there?'

'Sorcery, Agnes. Devilry, even!' Sarah had paused, then continued. 'Although the doctor thinks he was maybe ill, maybe demented, and that's what caused his ranting and debauchery. Imagine being burned at the stake. What a horror!'

Agnes shook her head, as if to cast the disturbing thoughts and images out into the early evening. She then adopted her usual tactic for passing the looming entrance gates of the abandoned property. She had learned a new hymn at the church, and she felt it appropriate for use when under threat from ancient malevolent spirits.

'*Onward, Christian soldiers …*'

'That's a fine tune, Agnes! Ah heard that ye could sing!'

It was John, with his mate Tom Lee. Agnes blushed red.

'Is Sarah no' with ye?' asked John, looking round. 'Hello, Barkie!' The dog had run up to greet him.

'Naw, it's a bit early for her. I'll mibbe see her later on. Is that you finished? Back tae Lizzie's, for yer tea?' said Agnes.

'Aye. Starvin'!' John grinned, his teeth white against the coal dust. Tom was also making a fuss of Barkie, crouching down to scratch her back.

'We'll mibbe see you two lassies later, then?'

'Aye, mibbe. Ah have tae help Maw, though. I'd best be goin' back.'

She turned and fled up the hill. As the lads started

whistling, she recognised the tune, and could hear the words of the hymn in her head. *Marching as to war …*

She'd never live that down.

'Is that you, Agnes?' Martha was waiting for her in the kitchen; she was holding a letter. 'Wait till ye hear the news frae Wanlockhead. It's aboot Catriona Ferguson.'

Agnes gripped a chair, her chest and heart starting to fill with a cold fear. Her hand sought Barkie's head.

'It says here that she was lifting a porridge pot from the hook, when the handle broke away. The poor lass has been badly burned. Yer auntie says they could hear her screaming right down the street. Dr Menzies attended right away, and she is now covered in bandages. She is in awfy pain with it.'

Agnes slumped in the chair and put her head in her hands.

Her mother looked up from the page. 'Agnes. I know it's a shock, but … Whit's wrong wi' ye?'

'It was me, Maw. It's ma fault this happened.' Agnes was crying. Barkie put her paw in her lap, looking up at her.

'But how could that be? She's miles away!'

Shaking, Agnes explained about the teasing, and about the curse. 'She was really mean tae me, Maw. For years – for as long as ah can remember.'

Martha was solemn. 'This is awfy serious. It's at a time like this it would help to speak with a minister.'

She paused, reaching a comforting hand to Agnes.

'No! No, Maw. It would be different if it was our old minister. But here, it's hard enough, being the incomers. Whit'll any Carluke minister think o' me? Have me burned at the stake, the bastard witch frae Wanlockhead?'

Martha ignored this. 'Whit would yer grannie have said?'

They paused, reflecting, both suddenly sad.

Martha pulled herself up and spoke again. 'Ah think she would say it's just a terrible accident. Mibbe she would suggest a wee quiet prayer at the Church, just to yersel', to say sorry. For cursing. And then mind no' more aboot it. She would certainly say that whit's done is done.' Martha emphasised these last words, repeating them. 'Whit's done is done. Ye cannae turn the clock back, Agnes.'

'Aye, mibbe that's whit she would've said. But I'm awfy upset, Maw. To say whit I did, that was a sin. Poor Cat – she was unkind, but naebody deserves that.'

'She was cruel, Agnes. But no, indeed, she didnae deserve a porridge burn. It's mibbe a lesson to ye, to bite yer tongue when someone says a vicious word. I always telt ye, it says more aboot them than it does aboot you.'

Agnes was crying again. 'Ah'll never forgive masel'.'

Barkie was whimpering, looking up at her, bewildered.

'We'll walk up to the Church later, say a wee prayer, just us. That might help ye. Now, I need a hand makin' the tea. Can ye see tae the tatties? And wipe yer eyes, before anyone sees ye.'

When Jim came through from the workshop later, all was industrious quiet, and the letter was in the fire.

Sarah called for her later, and found her friend even quieter than usual.

'I'll just fetch ma shawl.' Agnes picked up the grey blanket and wrapped it round her shoulders. Barkie was already at the door.

'Will we walk to the Cross?' said Sarah. 'We might see John and Tom.'

'Aye. I saw them earlier, in the brae. They were asking if we were out this evening.'

'At least it's stopped raining today. There is still so much mud, though.' She hesitated, and looked at Agnes. 'Are you ill? You seem worried. Is something troubling you?'

'No, ah'm fine. Well, not really. We heard some terrible news aboot a neighbour in Wanlockhead. A young lass. She was at school at the same time as me. She's suffered terrible burns.'

'That's shocking, Agnes. It is always difficult to hear news like that.' Sarah took her friend's arm, and they walked on to the Cross.

The friendly chat and teasing with John and Tom lightened her spirits. She did enjoy Tom's company, even if he spent most of his time petting Barkie. They even looked a bit alike: his ginger hair seemed to stick up, like a brush.

To take her mind off the letter, she was asking the lads

about the pit. 'Is it really dark down there? The lead mines at Wanlockhead weren't so deep. The men could walk in, or climb down a ladder. They were mostly near the surface.'

John started to explain.

'Aye, we go down deep into the pit in a metal contraption, like a box. We call it the cage. It's attached by ropes tae that big wheel; ye can see it frae the top of the Glasgow Road. That's whit pulls the cage up and down. And when we are working, it brings up the coal, in the hutches.'

'It is really dark in the pit, Agnes,' said Tom, 'but we've got lamps down there. You should see the gleam of the coal. It looks really different in the lamp light. Like jewels.'

'Dr Rankin was telling us that the coal seams are left over from a time when Scotland was a warm swamp. Imagine Scotland being warm all the time!'

'He's always talking about ancient times,' said Sarah. 'His sister says he is well known by many important men of letters. He certainly receives much correspondence.' She laughed, remembering. 'One famous gentleman from London tried to visit him. He wrote that he got as far as the railway junction at Carstairs, but found the inn there so unwelcoming and the food so unpalatable that he turned back to Edinburgh, without finishing the journey. The doctor read his account out loud, and was much amused by it, as was his sister.'

'They seem good employers, Sarah,' said Tom.

'Aye. They sought me out specially, Tom. In truth, they

do not really need my services. But they were determined to give me a start in work, and say they will furnish me with good references, should I need them.'

John nodded. 'They are fine folks, indeed. And your work there ensures we have nae shortage of excellent stories – even if the crocodile is no longer there!'

Agnes was, of course, intrigued, and had to be told all about the crocodile. More stories followed, about fossils and strange worms. By the time she was walking home, she felt lighter, easier. Perhaps this ghastly news from Wanlockhead was just a terrible coincidence after all.

THE MOLE-CATCHER

MARTHA HAD SLIPPED out early, wanting a few moments in the dawn to herself. She had a cloth bag under her arm and another in her pocket, ready for her hedgerow finds.

She was thinking about wishes, as she often did when she was alone. What would she wish for? A smile from Jemima? There was just one wish, really. It was that they might all come together and be a family.

She walked up the brae, towards Yieldshields, then further, towards Hare Hill. She was surprised to see a figure coming down the lane towards her through the gentle morning mist. He was a squat fellow, with big, working hands; he was wearing an unusual dark brown felt hat, which he wore pulled down over his ears.

'Mornin' tae ye, missus. A fine day. You'll be gathering plants, maybe?'

'Guid morning. Aye, there are some herbs best collected fresh.'

'Now. That's not a Carluke accent. Let me think.' The man pondered, then his face lit. 'The Lowther Hills. Thereabouts. Leadhills, maybe. South from here, anyway.'

'Aye, you're right! You must do some travellin' to know

voices that well.'

'Ah have ma circuit. I'm on my way to Braidwood just now. I'm a mole-catcher by trade.'

Martha had noticed the travelling bag and the tool pouch slung over the shoulder. 'That's an interesting profession. You will know the countryside well, I expect? The birds and animals?'

'Aye, indeed, missus. And I think there are some creatures looking out for you, over there.'

On the far side of the field, two hares were sitting up, gazing over intently towards Martha. She found herself grinning widely.

'They are bonny, are they not?' she said.

'Aye, and they are quite particular who they take to, hares. They are generally shy; it's unusual to see them watching someone this way. You wouldnae be wrong to think it a kind of blessing.'

'I have always thought that. There is a strange comfort in a connection with a creature.'

'Aye. Sadly, my task is to seek out their burrowing brothers. Just when they become too troublesome, mind.'

'Do ye leave the trophies, on the gateposts? That seems awfy cruel!'

'Ah have to advertise my services, Missus. And provide evidence of a job done. Now. Missus. Will ye be wantin' a mole hand?' He dug into his bag. 'Good against the toothache, or the rheumatism. Usually a florin a piece. To you, sixpence.'

Martha considered the offer carefully. She had heard tell of the benefits of the paws of this burrowing creature, and toothache was a constant concern for Jim. Perhaps if she hid it under the bed, it might assist.

'I have only fourpence at my disposal. Might that suffice?'

The mole-catcher sighed. 'Ye'll be gettin' a bargain. But you seem the right kind of person to make good use of it.' He handed over a large shrivelled claw, and Martha put it into her bag. Best keep it hidden till back in the house.

'Well, it was a pleasure meetin' ye, missus. Keep well. And all the best with the baby, when it comes.' He tipped his hat, and moved off.

Martha stood for a moment, holding the gate. *Of course.* The sickness, the tiredness, all explained in a second. She looked over at the hares. They looked back, curious, as she smiled, then laughed.

COURTING

AGNES HAD BEEN so excited that first time when Archie Campbell had called over to her.

'Are ye taking yer wee dug for a walk? Can I come along too?'

How long had she had a fancy for him? Since she had first seen him, jesting with the other lads at the Market Cross, perhaps? He had a careless mop of dark hair, and wore his cap back on his head. He had a way of walking – a saunter, one hand in his pocket; he made life look effortless, easy and seemed so much more mature than the likes of Tom Lee.

He came over and stood, grinning, while she gathered her shawl round her.

'C'mon, we'll take a turn down the brae.'

Agnes was aware of others looking, as she walked off with him. She frowned. Doubtless the clishmaclaver women would be hard at work, dreaming up some stories. Let them.

But she was tongue-tied, trying to answer his questions, trying to think of clever responses. He was asking her about Wanlockhead, and she just couldn't think of anything to say, even though just hearing the name of her old home filled her head with images and memories.

'It was a grand place tae live. Well, not grand like Glasgow. Well, I hear Glasgow is very grand – I've never been. Wanlockhead is just a wee village. Folk were friendly enough.'

'Is it true they found gold in a river up there?'

'Aye, there is gold in the river, if you know where tae look.'

Archie seemed very interested in the gold. Relieved, Agnes started to recount some stories, but she soon realised that he wasn't really listening; he was clearly in an imaginary world, where the gold would buy him anything.

'Think what ye could do wi' all that wealth. Do ye know what I would do?' He didn't wait for a response. 'I would buy a fine horse, like that black beauty the doctor used to have. Do you mind his horse? No, you weren't here then. Well, he had a huge black beast. He was such a sight, trotting down the street to visit some sickly soul. Must be dead now, that horse.' He continued at some length, describing different horses he had known and admired.

At last there was a moment when Agnes could speak. 'I'd best be heading for home, now, Archie. It was nice walking with ye. My maw is expecting me. Perhaps we'll speak again, sometime.'

Barkie was already halfway up the brae, looking back, as if encouraging her on.

Archie seemed taken aback that she was heading back so soon.

Agnes wasn't sure whether to mention the encounter to Sarah, then was surprised when her friend spoke in a serious voice. 'Agnes, Jemima called by. She wanted me to warn you. Is it true you were with Archie Campbell earlier?'

Agnes flushed. 'We were just talking, that's all. Is nothing private around here?'

'She was worried for you. He's not a nice lad, Agnes. He's got a reputation.'

'Why could she no' tell me herself?'

'She's right, Agnes. Watch yourself with him.'

Agnes thought ruefully that she should be pleased Jemima was looking out for her. Instead, she was feeling stupid, like a little kid.

CASTLEHILL

JOHN WAS CHATTING with Tom Lee on the way to work. They were reminiscing about their first days at the coalface: the strangeness, the smells, the heat – and, unspoken yet understood, the fear, the fatigue, the relentlessness of the shifts.

'Mind when wee Daisy bolted wi' that full load? Yer face was a picture!' Tom was laughing.

John recalled the gallop of the pit pony, the hutches rushing and rattling behind. 'It wasnae funny at the time. How was I tae know whit tae do?'

'Aye, lucky William was there. He's a sound man. He steadied her, nae problem.'

John was pleased that Tom admired his brother-in-law.

'Are ye near our seam today? Will I see ye at piece-time?'

'Aye, I'll see ye then.'

The lads went off to collect their tokens and lamps.

The lunchtime chat turned to the unions. Sanny and William – acutely aware of the need to keep the steady money coming in – were cautious about the renewed activism sweeping across the coalfields.

Sanny was uncomfortable about the increasing militancy.

'The bosses have a point. Ye cannae just walk out every time there's a dispute. We should try and settle it, man tae man.'

'Aye, and we dinnae get paid when we're out.' William's face was set.

'But how can we speak man tae man, when it's more like master and slave?' Tom had heard the speeches of the union men, and had been roused by their words, their passion. 'Our wages are a disgrace. They keep cuttin' them back, tae suit themselves. How are we supposed tae live? Ah was hearing aboot the strikes in Ayrshire, a few years ago. The colliery bands marchin' down the roads, gathering all the men behind them, all out on strike together.'

'Aye. Till they were starved back tae work. Either that, or they send in the strike-breakers. The Irish will put up wi' any conditions,' said William.

John was listening to the discussion, interested in the different points of view. He found himself torn – one moment in favour of keeping the status quo, the next indignant at a perceived injustice by the management and owners. The image of the marching miners was certainly exciting, but he too had heard the stories of terrible destitution during prolonged strikes.

'The union men sometimes just make the situation worse. It can damage working relationships. I've seen it over the years.' Sanny paused, sipped his tea. 'This union thing, it comes and goes. In a few months it'll all blow over. But right now, they're stirring it up right across the Lanarkshire collieries.'

'But wi' the unions we get tae hear what's happening in other pits. Aboot wage bargaining. Safety. Important things that the unions have won for us in the past.' Tom spoke with passion.

'The minister isnae keen on the unions, though,' said William.

'Is that MacKenzie, at the Free Kirk? He doesnae like new ideas, does he? I hear he says we should all know our place, not make trouble. I even heard that he says poverty comes frae idleness.' Tom grimaced. 'One of these union men used the word "patronising". And it made me realise that is how people like MacKenzie speak tae us. I'd like tae see him down the pit. He woudnae last five minutes.'

John nodded. 'See when he speaks like that? Ah just feel he's talking down tae us. Like we are no better than children. Patronising, right enough. And he doesnae like the unions. Mibbe I should come along tae one of these meetings.'

There was a cough, and an older voice spoke. 'Well, we'd all best be getting back tae work. And just mind this. Ah sometimes just wonder what's tae be gained by rocking the boat.' Sanny had the last word on the matter as the empty hutches rolled in.

'See ya!' The drawer gave his usual cheery shout as he ran back down the passage.

'See ya, Bert!' John turned back to the seam. 'William!

I'm just going tae take a leak.'

John moved back towards the main passage, then down the slip and around the corner, to the place they used for relief. He pulled up his scarf to cover his nose and mouth; it was a rank wee corner.

He said later that he had no idea how it happened; perhaps his scarf edge knocked the lamp. It was suddenly pitch-black, intense darkness. He put his hands out, groping. He had no idea where he was, where the passage entrance began. He became aware of the pressure of thousands of tonnes of earth above him. He felt buried alive. His chest was hurting.

John started to call for help, but his voice was useless. He heard it bouncing back at him, as if he were in a coffin. He shook his head. He had to get rid of the image of being in a coffin. A grave. His hand hit the wall. *Mustn't panic. That's what the old-timers say. Stay calm.*

His mouth was dry and he felt his heart pounding in his chest. He took a breath, then another.

'William. Sanny. Help me.' His voice was guttural, strange. 'I've nae light. Help me.'

Oh God. What was that scampering sound? Was there a rat?

Stay calm.

Another breath, deeper this time. And another. He found his shout.

'Hello! Can ye hear me? Ah've lost ma light!'

At last he heard the voices approach, saw the lamps

bobbing.

'Ye're all right, son. Here ye are. I'll light ye up again.'

'Aye. Thanks. Aye, I'm fine. Ocht. It's awfy dark down here, eh?' John tried and failed to keep the tremor from his voice.

'Why no' do what ye came to do, and we'll just wait round the bend for ye. Then ye might need tae rest for a minute. There's no shame in it, John. It's everyone's fear, losing the light.' William's voice was reassuring.

Later, back at the seam, Sanny and William recounted the story of a couple of pranksters who left their workmates in the dark, and how the culprits had been sought out by a gang of the older men and taken to a disused seam to be left there without lights.

'It was tae teach them a lesson. We only left them for a wee while, John. Honest. But by the time we went back for them, they were just wrecks. Crying like babies. They'll no' do that again. I'm not saying that ye cannae have a laugh. There are things that are a good joke. But there are things that are just never done in a pit, and taking someone's light is one o' them.'

'Aye. Right enough, Sanny. Ah can understand that.'

'John's had a bit o' an adventure!' William shouted over at Tom, as the work gangs converged at the wider rail passage.

His pal was curious. 'Whit happened?'

John managed a brief description of his ordeal, but was keen to change the subject, to try and forget. A thought from the lunchtime banter came into his head. A change of subject. 'Whit does your minister say aboot the unions, Tom?'

'Dinnae mind that just now. Ah need tae ask ye somethin'.'

Tom appeared agitated; it was John's turn to be curious.

Tom spoke again. 'Do ye think Agnes likes me?'

John was amazed. He had no inkling that Tom was interested in girls. He seemed to spend all his time avoiding any eye contact with females, and would crouch and chat with Barker rather than engage with her mistress.

'Ocht. Erm. Ocht. Whew. Ah don't know, Tom. That's the honest truth. Dae ye want me to ask her?'

'Naw! Naw, dinnae mention it. Just leave it, will ye?'

Tom pushed ahead and jumped into the one empty space in the cage, just as the whistle blew for it to rise to the surface. John was left in the dimness, wondering what had got into his pal.

William had caught up with his young brother-in-law. 'Whit's wi' him?'

'Ah don't know. Women trouble.'

William laughed. 'That can be some trouble, John! But I'm lucky there. Your sister Lizzie is the best.'

'Aye. She is. Ah don't know whit Faither would have done without her, when our maw was ill. She is like a mother to us all.'

'Your Faither has Martha, now.'

The cage descended noisily, drowning their talk.

Yes, it's all so different now, thought John. He was still staying with William and Lizzie and their young family. From time to time, he wondered about seeking new lodgings, but knew in his heart that he was most comfortable in the easy kitchen of his big sister.

THE RETURN OF THE FAIR

AGNES WAS WAKENED early with clamour and noise, as Carluke finalised the preparations for the spring market fair. She and Sarah had talked of little else for weeks. Agnes had been enthralled by the descriptions of the atmosphere and the attractions and at last fair day was here.

She lay there for a moment, grinning in anticipation and excitement.

Martha had warned Agnes to be careful.

'Ye dinnae want to be mistaken for a servant girl for hire. If anyone tries tae touch ye, tell them loud to keep their hands tae themselves. Stick with Sarah. An' here's some pennies for your purse, for sweeties. Or ye might want tae see the fortune teller. If you do see her, tell her Martha will see her later.'

Agnes and Sarah did want to see the fortune teller. They had speculated for hours about whether there might be news of husbands, or children. What colour might his eyes be? Would he be a miner? Think of the dirt and the washing. Might there be a daughter, to dress in bright ribbons?

'Naebody will fancy me,' Agnes said. 'At least, not if they know ma background. I'll be left behind, an old maid in the workhouse.'

'Wheesht!' said Sarah. 'The Right Man won't be caring.' The Right Man was a phrase they used often, a favourite from the story papers. She continued. 'The Right Man will see past all the gossip, and find your true heart.'

'True heart.' Agnes pictured her heart beating red and warm, filling her chest. She had so much love to give, if only she could find the Right Man. Perhaps the fortune teller could tell her if there was someone for her, right enough.

The booth was beside the Market Cross, and there was a long line of people waiting their turn. Agnes saw Jemima near the front, and waved. Jemima turned away. 'Will we come back later, Sarah? There might be fewer folk in an hour.'

'Aye, fine. Let's go and buy some sherbet. Ocht, Agnes, what do you think she'll say?' And they launched yet again into their hopes and fears, as they walked round the bright stalls.

There was a call; it was Sarah's turn for the spae-wife. Taking a deep breath, she pushed past the curtain, into the booth.

After a five-minute lifetime she re-emerged, hot-cheeked, from behind the mysterious crimson curtain. There was no time for Agnes to hear anything. It was her turn now.

'Here I go!'

Agnes could feel her warm, red heart beating fast as she entered the stuffy enclosure.

'Well, young lady. Let me see your hand.'

Agnes offered her palm.

'Left-handed! That's different, indeed. And I can see that you work with a needle. You have fine fingers for that work. Unusual in a corrie-fister. But what's this?' She traced a line on Agnes's hand. 'You have had some troubles in your life, for one so young.'

'Are these troubles finished, now?'

'I think you know they will always be with you, Agnes. But look, the line is strong. That means you will find the strength to be resolute – you will be more able to bear it.'

She looked at Agnes's wrist, turning it back and forth. 'There is a mark here, as if you have a tie around your hand. This means you have a strong attachment, perhaps to a place. A place of good fortune. Perhaps you have something from a lucky place that is precious to you?'

The stone from the Priest's Pool. It was in the saucer, beside her bed, in the tailor's house. Agnes's eyes widened. The spae-wife continued.

'Be careful with this talisman, Agnes. With it in your possession, you are stronger than you think. Even powerful. You would not want to wish anyone ill.'

Agnes stayed silent, the horrific nightmare image of Catriona Ferguson's burns playing in her mind.

'I will never wish anyone ill,' she said. *Again*, she thought.

'Now, are you not interested in love? All the girls want to know about a husband. Why don't you take a card?'

Agnes leaned forward, chose a card from the proffered pack and handed it over.

'What have we here? Dearie me, if it's not a seven of hearts. That's a lucky one for love, Agnes. There is someone out there for you, fear not.'

'And children?' Agnes followed the spae-wife's indication, and leaned forward to pick another card. She passed it over for inspection.

'Aye, there will be children. But be prepared for heartbreak in this regard. There is a possibility that not all will live to adulthood.'

Agnes felt a sudden chill.

She gathered herself together; perhaps that was enough fortune-telling for one day. She remembered to pass on the message from Martha, and the spae-wife nodded and smiled.

'Martha is your mother? I might have known, lass. You have the dark eyes of your kin. Tell her I look forward to renewing our acquaintance.'

Agnes left the tent feeling very thoughtful. Sarah was waiting for her outside, hopping from foot to foot.

'How did ye get on?'

Arm in arm, they wandered on round the bustling Market Place, sharing their news.

Agnes did not speak about the discussion of the lucky object, and she suspected that Sarah was not telling all of her experience, either. Both, however, had been promised luck in love, and so the day took on a particular glow all of its own. The run-down stalls and cheap spectacles seemed unique and glamorous; the girls laughed at Punch and Judy as if it were the funniest thing they had ever seen. Every group of lads that passed by seemed to look their way, and they would look back, with shy smiles.

'We should find you another shawl, Agnes. Something more flattering. That dark grey colour is too old for you.' Sarah was feeling buoyed up enough to give fashion advice to her friend. 'Maybe we can find you a bonny tartan.' Sarah tossed her own checked shawl over her shoulder. 'Or perhaps something with some red in it. That would look fine against your dark hair. Maybe Mr Lindsay has something in the back of the workshop. Will you ask him?'

'Aye. Aye, I might do that!' Agnes was smiling. Everything seemed possible today. 'Whit aboot sharing a bag of Soor Plooms?'

They stopped at the sweetie stall, and Sarah found a halfpenny for the treats. 'We can take the rest to the Cross, later. When we see John and Tom.' She pointed out some sticks of rock to Agnes. 'Look at these! A wee message written in every stick. That one says, "Kiss me!" Will we take a couple of these to the Cross?'

'Whit? For John and Tom? Ye dinnae think they are the Right Men, do ye, Sarah?'

Sarah laughed. 'They're just our pals, Agnes. The Right

Men will come galloping up in a fine carriage, and invite us to tea. Or they might even take us to Glasgow for the day. Imagine that!'

Agnes couldn't sleep. After the meeting with the fortune teller, there were many conflicting thoughts in her mind. Perhaps the Right Man was out there, parked in his fine carriage in the Market Place, looking up at her bedroom window. Maybe he was dreaming of a skinny wee bastard mousey-girl from the hills. She sighed. She knew she didn't stand a chance.

There was still a lot of noise and activity in the Market Place after the Fair, but it had progressed into the public houses. A peek out of the bedroom window confirmed that the inn was bursting at the seams, with much raucous laughter and high spirits in evidence. Fiddle music was scraping a jig, and some folks were cavorting in the street. Margaret and Jane were still out there, somewhere. Agnes suspected they were courting; she had overhead snippets of whispered, giggly conversations in the workshop and on the stairs. She and Barkie were cosy now in their little room at the front of the house. She still got a thrill from hearing the busy street, but it wasn't usually so loud.

Cutting across all the competing noise, a lusty voice started to sing, and was soon joined by other strong, male voices. Confused again by the familiar hymn tune, it took Agnes a moment to catch what they were saying. To the tune of her favourite, 'Onward Christian Soldiers,' she heard:

'Watch out you Carlukians
Here's the boys frae Law
Lock up all yer lassies
Especially if they're braw
We're looking for a battle
On this summer's night
Come and join us in the field
We're ready for a fight …'

Looking out, she could see a large group of lads, some holding tankards of ale, others with bottles of spirits – and all singing at the tops of their voices. They marched, stumbled and swaggered off down the street.

'They must be going tae the field, to fight, Barkie. Ah hope there won't be trouble.'

Ears flat and hackles raised, Barkie was clearly uncomfortable about the noise outside. She also wasn't keen on being lifted up to see out the window, and soon wriggled free, making her way under the bed and leaving her mistress to lean on the sill, taking in the street theatre below.

A BATTLE

IN THE STEWART Street house, Lizzie was trying unsuccessfully to keep John in by the fire.

'William. You tell him. It's no' safe out there. These Law boys are wantin' trouble. They'll make a rumpus.'

'I'm going wi' Tom. We're just going tae look, Lizzie. Ye know I'm no' a fighter.'

'Ye might get dragged into it, John.' She looked again at her husband.

'He's no' an age we can keep him in, Lizzie,' said William, pipe in hand. 'He's a working man. Just keep yer head, John. Don't be drinking any spirits. Half the stuff out there is home-made, and it will poison yer system as well as make ye half-mad. You and Tom, stick together.'

There was a brief knock at the door, and Tom burst into the kitchen. His eyes were shining, excited. 'Are ye comin,' John?'

'Just watch yersels, lads, eh?'

'Aye, William. Good night!'

And they were off out the door, away to the field.

An open area at the back of the Market Place, 'the field' was a misleading local name for a rough piece of scrubland. It had a variety of uses. The pit ponies spent two weeks here every summer, their one break from the relentless dark. Some of the Fair folk had parked their waggons there, and there were a number of unkempt, thin horses cropping at the meagre grass. With a start, John noticed Martha sitting on the steps of a waggon, chatting animatedly with a woman; he wondered how on earth she knew someone from the travelling folk. Tom nudged him back to the business of the evening, and they carried on. A little further away from the lights of the Market Place, there was an open area where traditionally young people would gather on Fair nights. The evening was still light, and it felt as if everyone under thirty was on the way there. In the distance, John could see his older sisters, Margaret and Jane, arm in arm with a couple of lads. He thought he recognised them from the pit.

'C'mon, let's see whit these Law boys are made of,' said Tom.

Law village, situated just a couple of miles to the north-west of Carluke, had its own distinct and proud mining community. The mostly friendly rivalry between the lads from Law and Carluke tended to erupt over Fair weekends.

'They're all well full o' drink,' said John. 'I think our boys will beat them easy.'

'Let's try and see whit we can; as long as we dodge the actual battles, eh?'

It started as usual, with name-calling and jeering. The

odd stone was thrown. John noticed Archie Campbell swaggering into the field; a bottle was dangling menacingly from his hand, and he was shouting obscenities. Tom and John backed away as the bigger, older lads started to move in on each other. In practice, the battle comprised four or five serious fights between lads known for brawling, and all the others shouting at the spectacle. It started to get ugly when a group of older men moved in on two younger individuals. John saw some vicious kicking and stamping. Some of the other men were shouting, 'Stop it now. That's enough.' Someone yelled, 'Get off me!'

Had someone sent for the minister? Or had the Reverend MacKenzie just been passing by?

Back in the comfort of the Stewart Street house, John later recounted the scene to Lizzie and William. 'So, the minister walks towards the stramash, hands up, tryin' tae calm things. He's just getting ignored. He's shouting for the boys tae desist, and they keep on, like he's no' even there. Then guess who came by?'

'C'mon. Who?' William wanted to hear the story.

'Dr Rankin. He strides in, wi' his big walking stick. Sticks it in the ground, stands holding it. He doesnae look like an old man. He looks like a chief, or somethin'. He had on that tall hat o' his.'

'Whit happened? Did they ignore him too?'

'He just roared at them. Told them tae stop actin' like children, immediately. He didnae spare them, Lizzie. Such a tongue-lashing. They all just stood back, hangin' their heads. Of course, he could point tae most of them, and call them out by name. Law boys, Carluke boys, they all started slinkin' away. He was yelling at them tae mind that it was the drink that does it, and that it would rot their brains.'

'He hates the drink, that's definite.'

'He's seen the damage it does in his profession, William,' said Lizzie. 'Families destitute, women and children beaten. No wonder he hates it.'

'So that was the end o' the fun, folks. The Law boys headed back tae their town. Till the next time!' Grinning, still buzzing, John headed off to bed.

THE CURSE

THE FAIR WAS gone now, but remnants of excitement still buzzed in Agnes's head like bright ribbons. She pulled her new tartan shawl around her, enjoying the softness and the colours.

She smiled to herself; there was Archie Campbell again. He always seemed to be hanging around these days.

'Good evenin', Agnes. Comin' a wee walk?'

'No, I was just getting a breath of air, Archie. I took Barkie out earlier.'

'Just a quick stroll. C'mon.'

What harm in a wee stroll?

They went down the brae towards the abandoned husk of Kirkton House, and he pushed at the gate. Agnes looked up at the house. The dark shapes of the old windows looked malevolent, sinister.

'That place is full of ghosties, Archie. I'm no' going in there at this time o' night.'

He grabbed her hand. 'C'mon. I'll gie ye a kiss. That'll keep the ghosties away.' He pulled her down the drive.

Agnes wasn't sure she wanted a kiss. She was feeling horribly uncomfortable. She realised she wasn't scared of the ghosts as much as of this big lad, bearing down on her.

Archie held her wrist and grabbed at her breast. She cried out.

'Whit are ye feart of, Agnes Brownlee? Yer mammy's a hoor, is she no'? Are you no' up for it as well? C'mon, ye fancy me, ah know ye do.'

His lips sought hers and pushed on to her mouth; then his tongue was thrusting at her teeth. He shoved her hard against the wall, pinning her with his body. Suddenly his hands were up her skirt, tugging at her, prising her legs apart. She tried to shout, to push him away, but was he was heavy, and his face was covering hers. Somewhere deep inside, she knew that this was what she deserved; that she was a whore's daughter, and a bastard, and that this is what she must expect.

There was a shout. 'Campbell. *Campbell*! Whit are ye doin', man?'

John was at the gate, then running down the path. She felt a surge of relief, of shame, of guilt.

'Are ye all right, Agnes? Get off her, Archie, for pity's sake. She's just a young lass.'

Archie Campbell grunted, and slackened his grip.

Agnes slipped from his grasp. Her knees were shaking, and she felt sick. But she was safe. She stumbled towards John, straightening her skirts. Archie leaned back against the wall, glaring at them both.

Agnes turned back. She found her breath and a scream came. 'A curse on you, Archie Campbell!' No sooner were the words out of her mouth than she regretted it. John put his arm round her shoulders, and steered her up the brae.

'Oh God, please forgive me. I didn't mean it. Please forgive me.' She was half crying, half praying.

John was puzzled. 'Whit are ye saying? It's him that needs the forgiveness, Agnes, not you. C'mon, we'll get ye home.'

'Give me a moment, John. I cannae go home like this. I need to calm myself. Don't tell anyone. Don't tell my maw. I shouldnae have cursed him, I shouldnae have.'

'C'mon, we'll sit on this step a minute. Ye've had a shock. He's got a really bad reputation, did ye not know? Thinks that he's God's gift tae the lassies, that one. He's not one tae walk out on your own with, Agnes.'

Agnes remembered the warning from Sarah and hung her head. 'I would die rather than let … you know … *that* happen. I cannae thank ye enough.'

'We're family, Agnes. Now, are ye feeling a bit better?'
She nodded.

'Let's get ye home.' He paused, looked around. 'Was Barkie not with ye?'

'Naw, she was asleep by the fire. Dreaming of chasing rabbits. I had her out earlier. Why?'

'I wonder if he would have dared try that, if Barkie had been with ye? I bet he'd have thought twice. Your wee dug would have lived up tae her name, if she'd been at your side. She would have made a real racket. Might have given him a nip in the ankle, an' all.'

Agnes stood, ready to walk up the hill. 'It would have

served him right. Barkie will be with me, from now on.'

And maybe I should remember the stone from the Priest's Pool, too, she thought, shivering. *Carry it with me. To protect me. And save me from cursing folk.*

Back at the Market Place house, Barkie was waiting for her, whining and jumping up and down.

'That dog has been barking and scratching at the door for the last wee while.' Martha turned from the stove, her new bangle clinking against the range. She looked concerned. 'Where have ye been? Are ye all right?'

'Aye. Aye, ah'm fine, Maw. C'mon, Barkie. Whit's the matter?'

Agnes bent down to her dog and stroked her. Barkie was lying on the floor, whimpering.

'Are ye sure you're all right? That dog knows something is amiss,' said Martha.

Agnes nodded, still bent down, her hair covering her face. 'Aye, I'm fine, I tell ye. I just thought I saw a ghostie near Kirkton House. Luckily John was there, and he walked me home.'

Martha watched her for a moment, then moved to the table, wiping her hands on her apron.

Of course she knows something is wrong. She's my maw. But I can't tell her. Not tonight. Agnes stroked Barkie for a moment, then the two of them headed up the stairs, for the safety of her room. She lay for a long time, listening to the blood rushing in her ears.

PLANS

THERE IS NEW life growing inside me. I hope for a boy. My mother taught me the natural rhythms and cycles of womanhood and, over time, I have come to understand these more thoroughly. I have applied certain precautions and preparations, so I am optimistic that I will give Jim a son. I have a longing for my kin, my dear cousins and aunts, to be near at this time, but that is not possible. I need to prepare. I will be very careful in choosing someone to assist with the birth, someone who understands and respects the old ways. Perhaps Lizzie will know of a good woman.

Jim is excited and proud about our news. I see him thriving in his work. I often hear him remark, 'Life is grand,' and this makes me very happy; although I know only too well such times must be appreciated, as none of us know what awaits us.

The unquiet spirit in the house has gone at last. The very day of my meeting with the mole-catcher, I returned to the kitchen and knew it as my own. The photograph in the parlour no longer alarms me. Instead, I feel a genuine sadness for the poor woman, who never saw her children grow up. She is at peace now.

I must take care to keep watch over Agnes. She has been unsettled, particularly since the dreadful news from Wanlockhead. She has grown into a fine young woman, and I think she is unaware of her striking looks. The stares she attracts are not just those of the gossips. I sometimes think of little Lucy, and wonder whether she too would have been a bonny lass.

It has taken a while, but I am becoming familiar with my neighbours. There are women who will not speak to me on the street; others who ask too many questions; and a few that I feel I can trust. Sometimes it is just a nod that tells me they are someone I might seek out if needed. Once more women are knocking at my door, seeking advice about how to make their skin glow, or how to be rid of a difficult problem. I know I must be careful and not become careless with pride or self-importance. I miss my old herb garden in Wanlockhead, but my patch at the back of the deserted house faces south, so is thriving and becoming most useful for my purposes. I am also learning where to find those plants that are unusual, and this takes me to some wilder places – places where I can breathe more deeply, places I might see a hare.

The creatures here are different to their kin in Wanlockhead – more cautious. They will not approach. Perhaps it is just that they know me less well. It brings me comfort to watch them watching me as I stand by the gate or on the path. Jim once told me of local men here in Carluke who will set dogs after hares; this made me feel ill, almost as if I had heard about my own child being attacked by the brutes.

I try not to think of the hare's skull I took from Jemima's room as a theft; more that I have borrowed something precious, to keep it safe. I will bring it back from the garden in time for the birth. I will be reassured, knowing that it is in my box of precious things, beneath my bed.

A DAY WE WILL REMEMBER

JOHN HEARD SOMETHING break. Something fragile. Then a wail.

'Aw, no! That's terrible bad luck! Ma guid mirror!'

Lizzie stomped into the kitchen. John and William looked at each other, then down again at their porridge.

'Is this ma punishment, for being vain?' She held up bright shards. John thought how tired she looked; how she was starting to resemble their mother.

'Watch yersel'. That's awfy sharp.' William pushed back his chair. 'C'mon, I'll help ye clear it. Before one o' the weans gets a nasty cut.'

'Sit down. I'll dae it. You need to get tae your work. Eat yer porridge.'

The worst possible start to the day: Lizzie in a bad mood. The men finished their plates quickly, then started to collect their piece-bags, jackets, caps.

'That's us. Are ye sure I cannae give ye a hand wi' that glass?'

'Naw. Away out my hair, both of ye. I'll see you the night. Mind and no' be late.' She grabbed the floor brush and left the room.

'Goodbye!' William shouted after her. A muffled sound came back.

'We'd best leave her. She'll be better by tea-time.'

The men tiptoed out, pulling the door quietly behind them.

John moved forward out of the cage to light his lamp. Tom was just ahead; William held back, waiting for Sanny, who was on his way down with the next descent. The cage lumbered upwards, and then stopped. They heard the faint shout of the winchman, and the next group of men were ushered in.

Then, a different sound: a loud, harsh grating sound. Instinctively, John looked up. The cage was creaking, tilting; the angles were all wrong. The men inside were shouting now.

'Get us out of here! For God's sake, stop the winch!'

John watched in horror as the cage started to move. Juddering at first, then faster, then careering out of control, it came hurtling down, down the shaft. The safety lines smacked uselessly. The men were screaming now, a terrible, unforgettable sound.

John and Tom turned as one, diving into the tunnel as the cage crashed into the bottom of the shaft. The noise behind them was huge, physical, overwhelming; then there were dreadful mechanical shudders and creaks, then silence. John had no idea how long they lay there, covered in dust and debris. He remembered to breathe, tried to clear his nose, coughed. He couldn't see; it was pitch-black, that terrible darkness. Perhaps he was blind. His ears were buzzing and ringing. He couldn't hear. He felt for Tom – his arm, his hand. He heard him cough, breathe.

Thank God.

'Tom.'

'Aye.'

'Ah cannae see.'

'Nae lights.'

'Are ye hurt?'

'Naw. Don't know. Whit happened, John?'

'The cage dropped.'

'Jesus Christ.'

They lay there, coughing, breathing, trying to listen.

'Where's William?'

'Back there.'

'We should mibbe try an' help.'

'Cannae see.'

'Let's try and turn around. There might be some light from the shaft.'

The lads shifted, moved, each taking comfort that the other was near. John rubbed his eyes, squinted into the darkness. Gradually he became aware of dim shapes through the dust, choking thick in the air.

'Hello?'

His voice sounded weak, feeble. He tried to clear the suffocating filth from his throat, coughing. He had no saliva, no spit. His mouth and nostrils were caked with dirt.

He hawked drily, tried again. 'Hello?'

He listened. He could hear something. Harsh breaths, beyond the frame of the cage. Moaning.

'Tom, I'm feart.'

'We'll move together. Best move slowly. We dinnae want tae dislodge anything.'

'Aye. We might be safer staying just here.' John stopped, thought of William. 'Naw. We've got tae help.'

A faint shouting came from above. At the same time, John became aware of calls from the tunnel, from men coming back from the coal seams. They had lights, thank God – lights – faint, yellow through the dust. He remembered the fear of losing the light before, and the relief of the return. Now he felt dread at what the light might show.

'Lads, lads. Are youse all right? Whit's happened? We heard a crash, shook the whole pit.'

'Christ, Marty, look. It's the cage. Ah thought it was the cage. Is there anyone alive, boys?'

'We've not looked. We lost our lights,' said John. Tom was still coughing.

'Youse boys were lucky, getting into the tunnel. Sit back there just now. Catch yer breath. Marty and I will go into the shaft. It might be dangerous. We'll shout if we need ye.'

'They're shouting from up top,' said John.

'It'll take a while, but they'll get us a rope down. First we need tae check out the cage, see about casualties.'

'Ma brother-in-law. William MacDonald. He's in there, somewhere. There was a group of men at the base, getting their lights.'

'Aye, son. We'll look for him.'

The kindness in the older man's voice was too much for John. He felt the tears well up, fought to control it. He took big, dusty, snotty breaths, and felt Tom's hand on his arm.

'C'mon. Best follow them. Best try and help. Dae something.'

Following the lights of the older miners, John and Tom crawled forward into the shaft. John was immediately confused, disorientated. Nothing looked as it should. The cage was flattened at a horrible angle, metal bursting from the top. Safety ropes hung uselessly on the sides.

John's stomach churned. The men in the cage had surely all been crushed. He became aware of sticky pools of blood beneath his feet, puddling around him. He smelled blood, piss, shit.

Gradually his mind started to make sense of what his eyes were seeing. A hand pushed through bars. Legs at horrible angles, bones protruding. A cap covered in blood, hair, brains. He turned away and retched.

Marty called over. 'There's some men round here. Alive. Must've been at the base of the shaft.'

Tom eased his way past the tangled mess of metal and

helped John through. There was Archie Campbell, semi-conscious; he was trapped, both legs beneath part of the cage. Two other figures were crouched in the corner, arms covering their heads. John could see them shaking.

'This fellow here didnae stand a chance. Look, he's taken the brunt. Poor chap.'

John knew. Before he heard Tom's cry, before he looked, he knew it was William.

The siren blares over the town. Everyone knows what it means. An accident at the pit; the day no longer a usual day, becoming instead *that day*. That day when lives are changed forever.

Jemima is at the Shieldses' house. She hears the siren wail, and fear is gripping her.

'Mrs Shields. Supposing it's John. I've got tae go tae the pit.'

'Jemima, it's maybe nothing at all. Even if something has happened, how can you help? We are all best staying away, unless needed. Our job surely is to try and carry on as normal, unless called upon to assist.'

'Mrs Shields. Ah need tae go.'

'Let's get a baking on, Jemima. If there is trouble at the mine, the men will need fed. We'll make scones.'

The siren is heard at Law, and the call goes up. Carts are loaded with men, ropes, tools; they move purposefully down the road to Castlehill. The word spreads to the bigger pits, at Wishaw; help will come from there, too;

help will be offered from far afield. As the news of an accident spreads across Lanarkshire, churches are opened and fervent prayers are said. Prayers for Carluke.

The townsfolk start to gather at the gates of the pit. Lizzie has run there, clutching her children; Jim and Martha find her in the crowd, Jim pulling her near. Margaret and Jane, both white-faced, arms around each other, stand beside Martha. All are asking, 'What happened? Is anyone hurt?'

A man speaks with authority. 'Look at the winch-wheel. It's broke. The rope's away.'

'Whit does that mean?'

'The cage is down. It's fallen down the shaft.'

'Oh, dear God. Dear God.'

There is crying and wailing. It quietens, gradually. Then waiting and waiting.

The doorbell chimes at the Shieldses' house, and Jemima rushes to answer. There is Agnes, Barkie at her heels.

'It's an accident. The cage has broken, fallen into the shaft. Are ye coming?' Jemima looks back to Mrs Shields, in the doorway of the kitchen; she nods. Jemima grabs her shawl, and starts to run up the path.

'Jemima. Ah cannae keep up with ye. You're that fast.'

Jemima slows, waits.

Agnes catches up, catches her breath. 'Jemima. They are all just standing, at the pithead gate. Lizzie, she's that worried, for John and William. And your Faither.' She pauses, then continues. 'We might no' be able tae do much.'

'Ah just need to get there. Ma family … John.' Jemima starts to run again.

The men from Law have set up a base. There is a foreman, organising the work; they are building a temporary lift. It looks like a big bucket. They are testing new ropes on the winch-wheel, preparing a rescue. Carluke miners, off-shift or retired, run to join them.

The Castlehill winchman and the managers are checking the hutch tokens and records. They are working to ascertain how many men are trapped. They are also starting to follow a drill: bringing out medical supplies, extra lights, water bottles. They all have tasks to do. Working and planning.

Those at the gate can only wait. It starts to rain.

Martha speaks gently, firmly. 'Lizzie. Why don't you let Margaret and Jane take ye home? This is going tae take an age. We'll come for ye right away if there's news. Ye'll be nae use to anybody if you become ill. They'll help ye with the weans.'

'If ah hadnae broken that mirror.' This is the umpteenth time that Lizzie has talked of that morning's incident. 'Ah never even said goodbye tae them. God forgive me.'

Martha puts her hand on her arm, looks into her eyes. 'Ye are punishing yersel' for a winch-wheel accident, Lizzie, and it isnae good for ye. Here's Jane and Margaret, tae get ye home.'

The three sisters huddle together, and start off down the street, carrying frightened toddlers.

'Jim.' Martha speaks with calm strength. 'Might ye wait here for news? Ye could take shelter with these other men, by the shed. Agnes and I will busy ourselves. We can make soup. Jemima – Jem. Would ye like to help us? There's a lot tae do.'

'Aye. I'll come, Martha. Let's make soup.'

Walking back through the town, they were stopped often, and news was exchanged. Women talked of trestle tables that might be taken from the church hall to the pithead; the men from Law would need tea and food. Hopefully soon the men trapped underground would be rescued, and they would need feeding, too. Someone knew of bandages and supplies in an aid post by the railway station. Another was knocking on doors, gathering blankets. The women were starting to work.

It is much better to work than to wait.

Martha paused.

'Jem. Before ye come to the house. Run and be sure Dr Rankin knows whit has happened. They'll need him.'

Jemima hammered at the door.

Sarah opened it. 'He knows. He's coming. He's getting his equipment. You could help to carry.'

Jemima was aware of activity within.

Daniel Rankin called to her. 'Just the person. We're going to need an extra pair of hands. Can you girls carry these bags up to the pit?' He was thinking aloud. 'Tell them I'm going to need a table. You girls will wash it down as best you can, then put this clean sheet over it.'

'The winch broke. The cage is down. There are men trapped.' Jemima spoke clearly.

'Right. That is useful to know.' He turned to his sister. 'We'll need the operating kit. And the amputation bag.' He saw the shock on Jemima's face. 'I just hope we don't need it, but best be prepared.'

In the Market Place, Martha and Agnes were just reaching the house when Martha paused again. 'We need tae go tae the garden.'

'Maw. Ah hate that Kirkton House. It's full o' ghosties.'

'Now's not the time, Agnes. Fetch the basket from the kitchen, bring a knife. I'll see ye there.'

Think of John, of Tom, of William.

Agnes gritted her teeth and walked down the path at the side of the derelict house; past the wall, where John had rescued her from Archie; around the corner, to the back of the property.

Even through the drizzle, she could see that this was a sheltered spot. Her mother was crouched over a bed of plants, her shawl up over her head. She was choosing carefully, selecting the finest, the strongest of the herbs.

'Pass me the knife. We need thyme. That's guid for yer chest, for coughs. Their lungs will be full of dust. We can make a tea, it'll help tae clear it.' She moved over to another plant and began filling the basket. 'Witch hazel. For bruising. Time to learn, Agnes.'

'Aye, Maw.' Agnes noticed a graceful rowan in the

corner, by the back wall. Looking closer, she couldn't help but see the little circle of stones by it, the ash piled inside. A wishing fire.

Martha's basket was full at last. She and Agnes started back up the brae.

'Agnes, I'll just fill that other basket with some jars from the cupboard, then head back tae the pit. You get the soup started. The big pot. Chop up all the vegetables we've got. Listen for the door. On my way back up the street, I'll be asking folks tae bring ye barley and the like, and tae give ye a helping hand. Guid lass.'

The waiting crowd felt a further shift into action as Dr Rankin strode into the yard. In front of him ran Jemima and Sarah, carrying bags and sheets. Bringing up the rear, walking briskly, was Miss Rankin.

'Thomson!' Daniel Rankin shouted over at the manager. 'We'll need this area here, under the overhang. Can we have some men to clear it? Get this equipment moved. We'll set up a clearing station.'

Men rushed to assist. Miss Rankin indicated where a trestle table was to be set up, and Sarah and Jemima set to getting it washed down. Women came over with bandages and supplies.

'Not yet, not yet. Let's get this area cleaned and set up first.'

From the shelter of the shed, Jim saw Martha approach the doctor with her baskets. As she moved across the rainswept yard, a tall man interrupted her progress. The

Reverend MacKenzie put a hand on her shoulder. He was gesticulating at the baskets, indicating that Martha should take the contents and leave. Jim watched as Martha removed the hand from her shoulder and pushed past the minister. He left the shelter of the shed, and started towards her. He heard her say, 'These will be needed, Minister.'

Dr Rankin hurried over. 'Excellent. Most useful. Take these over to the dressing station, Mrs Lindsay. I'll need you there. We need more hands, boiling kettles and preparing towels.'

Jim put his hand on his wife's back, both of them now facing the minister and doctor. He spoke, proud. 'Mrs Lindsay has quite a skill with the nursing, Dr Rankin. She learned it from her mother.'

'I am surprised that the doctor is taken in by such superstitious potions and brews. After all, he is supposedly a man of science,' said the Reverend MacKenzie.

'Well, Minister. I don't interfere in your work, so perhaps best you don't meddle in mine. There is something for us all to offer here, and I for one appreciate Mrs Lindsay's apothecary knowledge. Men of science understand that there are ancient remedies still useful today. As for you, sir, I am sure there will be many here who will need your prayers.' The doctor moved off.

'Apothecary indeed. One has to take care not to cross the fine line between that and witchcraft. From what I hear, you will be aware at least of the possibility of these blurred boundaries, Mrs Lindsay?'

'Minister. Ye cannae speak to my wife in that way. And at this terrible time. The doctor's right. Ye should be praying for us.' Jim stood firm before the lanky, black-suited figure.

Just then, a shout came from the pithead, calling for the doctor. Jemima ran to her father, clutched his arm.

'Whit if it's John, Faither? Ah couldnae bear it.'

'We all need tae be strong, Jem. This will be a testing day, whatever happens. It's good tae see ye, lass.' He gave his daughter a hug.

'Doctor.' Andrew Thomson was trying to stay calm. 'Doctor, we've sent down the bucket, with the Law foreman and a retired foreman from here – Hughie. He knows the men. It's on the way back up now. There will be news.'

The winch was turning as the rickety contraption jerked towards the surface.

The Law foreman got out, and everyone stared at his feet. His boots were covered in blood.

'Doctor!' he shouted. 'The cage is crushed, all men inside lost. Three men injured in the shaft space, also one fatality in the space.'

'Tell me about the worst injuries, of those still alive.'

'Right. The worst is a lad trapped under the cage.'

'Trapped how?'

'By the legs. The whole cage is lying across his thighs.

He's not really talking, but he's alive.'

'And the rest?'

'One we think has a broken ankle and bruising. The other is badly bruised. Both are struggling to get their breath. Maybe broken ribs.'

'Right … Thomson. We will need lights – as many as you can manage. I will need a small stool. A stretcher to be lowered in due course. Blankets and sheets. My sister and I will get the equipment, and we will descend. This information is very helpful. I will make a further, thorough assessment once I am beside the injured man.'

'Should we not try to free him, Doctor? Bring him up to the surface, for treatment?'

'If we move the cage without first stabilising his blood flow, he will surely die. I suspect that the only course open to us will be to operate on him where he lies.' Dr Rankin turned to his sister. 'Helen. Are you ready?'

The tiny figure at his side nodded. 'Of course, Daniel.'

He shouted over to Jemima and Sarah. 'Bring the bags, lassies. We'll be needing all that equipment.' Then he turned back to the manager and foreman. 'We need to move quickly. Miss Rankin and I will descend. The bucket should be sent straight back up, for the blankets and sheets and our bags and supplies.'

'Should we not start to move the men out, Doctor?'

'The less disruption and dust in the air, the better. Our priority is to save this life, if we can. Let's go.'

The makeshift hoist and bucket rattled down into the

cage space. The men were heartened to see Dr Rankin, surprised to see his sister with him.

Hughie stepped forward. 'Are we tae move the men out, Doctor?'

'Hughie. Good to see you here. No. Not yet. We must have calm and quiet. Come and show me the injured men.'

Hughie led the way over the tangled metal. The stench was suffocating. Miss Rankin put a handkerchief to her nose as Daniel Rankin worked quickly on his initial assessments. He saw the blank, unseeing stare of William's eyes, saw his crushed body.

'Can we spare something to cover this poor man's face?' He bent, and gently closed William's eyelids. 'Now, we need to move these injured men out of here. Hughie, perhaps you and another can help this chap out of the corner. I think the other may be able to walk, with assistance. We will need the room, so that we can operate on this poor fellow.' He indicated Archie, prostrate under the cage.

'Are ye operating here? Good God. Surely we'll take him tae the surface first?'

'No, Hughie. The best chance he has is if we operate here and now. If we try to move him, it is likely he'll bleed to death. The bucket is on the way back down with my equipment. I'll need your help to get organised.' He moved back and raised his voice so that the men in the tunnel could hear him.

'I know you will all be wanting to get out of here. But please be patient. By staying very still and quiet, you will help to save this man's life. I will need a volunteer to assist. Someone with a strong stomach. For the rest of you men, perhaps it is best if you sit on the ground, facing away from us. We need to minimise the movement of dust in the atmosphere, so quiet is essential.'

Marty stepped forward. 'I'll help ye, Doctor. My faither was a flesher. I worked in the butcher shop, so I'm used to it.'

'Good experience for this job. Now, help me unload these supplies.' The bucket had juddered down. 'My sister will need this little stool. She will be administering the anaesthetic.'

The injured men were helped, stumbling through the debris, to the tunnel space. Only the whites of their eyes showed in their faces; they were covered in filth and dust.

'Sit them up against the wall. Give them each a blanket. Small sips of water only.' The doctor barked his orders, but then spoke gently. 'You are safe, chaps. We will have you out of here soon.'

Daniel Rankin turned back to his sister, who was crouched by Archie, speaking to him quietly.

'We'll get this area set up, Helen. Marty here will be my assistant. Marty, we need the clean sheets down here, round the patient. All the lights you can manage. Put the stool there – Miss Rankin will need it. We will all require use of the carbolic.' He bent to speak to Archie.

'How are you doing?'

There was no reply, just an animal-like whimpering.

'We are going to put you to sleep, Archie. Then I will operate on your legs. You know they are trapped. I will try to save what I can, but you must prepare yourself to lose both limbs.'

The bags were opened, the laudanum identified and administered. Archie's eyelids fluttered as the powerful analgesic took effect. The anaesthetic mask was prepared.

'Helen, in such a confined space we can only use a very little chloroform. I will try to be as quick as I can. Remind me to tell you the joke about Mr Lister's speedy operation later. Marty, help me remove his clothing – here, use these scissors. Then we will use these carbolic swabs to clean the skin.'

All preparations made, Daniel Rankin turned to his amputation bag and lifted a large knife.

'Marty, I am going to cut the skin first. Then I will use the saw, to work through the bone. Your task will be to mop up the blood, and to keep my line of sight clear. We will then tidy up the wounds, and dress them. I shall undertake the suturing once we get back to the surface. At all times, I will require you to ensure I have good light, and that nothing impedes my movements. Helen, is the patient ready?'

His sister nodded; she was holding the mask over Archie's nose and mouth. A nauseating smell filled the space.

Daniel Rankin felt the familiar chloroform headache, and willed his confidence into place. 'Onwards and upwards. Let's go.'

The doctor worked quickly and methodically, speaking only briefly when giving his orders. Marty proved an able assistant, latterly anticipating the needs of the surgeon. The amputations were quite speedy, but it took much longer to close and dress the wounds. Marty's strength was invaluable, as he helped to apply the pressure dressings. All present knew they would never forget the sound of the saw, cutting through the bone, as Archie lost both legs.

John and Tom were huddled in the tunnel, with the rest of the men. John was finding it a huge effort, trying to be patient, when every sinew in his body wanted to be out of the pit, out in the fresh air. When Dr Rankin had arrived, his spirits had raised; surely now they could be moved to the surface? Eventually he had taken courage from the resignation and resilience of the men around him, as they all waited, cramped together in the poor light of the lamps, in the putrid, dusty air. When the operation took place, John had tried to cover his ears so as to block out the dreadful sounds of tearing flesh and bone. He heard Tom humming a tune quietly to himself, and joined in. 'Onward, Christian soldiers …'

'John.' Tom spoke at last. The atmosphere in the tunnel had changed; it seemed that the operation was almost over. Instructions for bandages were being given, and Dr

Rankin's voice sounded easier. The men around them were moving a little, changing position; quiet conversations were starting.

'John, I've been thinking about whit I'll do, when ah get out of here.'

'Me too,' whispered John. 'A scrub in the bathtub, for a start, and I want tae blow ma nose about eighty times.'

'I'm going tae ask Agnes to walk out wi' me.'

'Guid for you, Tom. Ah mean it. She's a nice lassie. Ah'm pleased for ye. For myself...' He stopped and sniffed, wiped his hand over his eyes. 'There's a lot tae take in.'

'Oh, aye. Aye, I know. William. Ocht. I'm that sorry, John. It's just ...'

'I understand, Tom. I do, really. Being stuck in here, it makes ye think, whit is important, what do ye want in your life? I'll need tae look after ma sister, though. And the weans.' He slapped his friend's leg. 'I'll come tae the wedding, though. I'll be yer witness.'

They lifted their heads at the sound of more activity at the bottom of the shaft, and a call for the stretcher. Surely not long to wait now.

Hughie was the expert in directing the next phase of the rescue. He and two others lifted and manoeuvred the stretcher through. Then, with some difficulty in the awkward space, Archie was eventually loaded on. The straps were secured in place and the signal to hoist given. Miss Rankin was to follow the patient up, in the bucket.

Daniel Rankin issued her with brief messages to take

back to the surface.

'Preparations need to be made for two more casualties in the clearing station. It will be useful also to make ready for more potential victims of breathing difficulties and shock. We need more fresh water down here. Send down my smaller bag – it has a splint that might be useful. Now go, quickly. That man will require constant attention.' He paused, considering, then spoke again. 'Once you are sure he is stable, you might ask Mrs Lindsay to sit with him. I have a notion she has nursing skills. That would free you to take charge of the clearing station.'

He turned to the remaining men, huddled in the tunnel. They all looked up at him, expectantly.

'Now, where is that chap with the bad ankle?'

Miss Rankin was surprised to find it was mid-afternoon when she reached the surface. She looked down; her skirts were filthy, sticky with blood and dirt. No matter. The women were waving her over to the clearing station, where lights had been set up; the place was busy with noise and bustle, as the first casualty was received. She would surely find a clean apron there.

The waiting crowd was restless. Rumour and speculation passed from one to the other. Why weren't they bringing the men out of the pit? Who might have been in the cage?

Jemima approached Miss Rankin, saw the blood on her clothes, on her boots. She felt her mind tip and reel. With an effort, she steadied herself. 'Excuse me, Miss Rankin.

I know ye are awfy busy. It's just that people are asking what's happening. They are getting very upset. You've been down there. Ye could answer their questions.'

'I'll speak to Thomson. He needs to make an announcement, try to calm things down. Jemima, there is a full shift of men coming up shortly, and all will need some tea and sustenance. As will my brother.'

'Agnes is making soup. We'll get it brought here.'

After a quick word with her father, Jemima sped off.

There was noise on the road, shouting; then a commotion at the gates. A gang of men from Wishaw were trying to get into the site. 'We brought the great tarpaulin. You'll need it for the cage.' Six men were carrying a huge canvas roll.

'Thanks, boys. Can ye just put it there? We'll try and cover the cage with it, right enough.'

The Law foreman stepped forward. Another Wishaw man came to meet him; he looked angry. 'Who is representing the rights of the workers here?'

The crowd murmured dissent.

The Law foreman shook his head. 'This is not the time, boys. Thank you for bringing the tarpaulin. Now, you need to back off.'

'This *is* the time. We hear that there has been a serious incident at this pit. Your men need proper representation. People asking the right questions.'

Andrew Thomson came up. 'The right questions will be addressed, but all in due course. There are still men trapped underground. That is where we are putting our energies. Now, we need you to leave.'

Another of the Wishaw men moved forward, pushed his face close in. 'And we can trust the manager tae tell us what tae do, eh?'

'Listen to the people here.' The Reverend MacKenzie came out of the crowd. 'Your views are not welcome just now.'

'The minister! Even better! Ye'll be on the side of the unions, then? I bet!' The Wishaw man was sneering.

A man was shouting from the rear of the Wishaw gang. 'Geordie. Alex. Back down, why don't ye? That's enough.'

Another voice spoke up. A female voice, this time. 'This is not about sides. This is about working together, rescue and care. Unless you are prepared to come and assist us, you had better go.' The crowd parted as Miss Rankin stepped through. The blood was still sticky on her boots.

'With all due respect, madam. Ye wouldnae understand.' The angry Wishaw man was still insistent.

'I understand perfectly well. It is you who is showing ignorance. Look at these people. They cannot hear your arguments now, whilst they are waiting, afraid, grieving. You are alienating them, turning them against you. You may be men of principle, but you are woefully inadequate at the basics of human nature.'

'Aye!'

'Aye, she's right! Away an' leave us alone!'

'Or ye can join the minister in a prayer – that might be some use!'

The Law foreman raised his hands towards the Wishaw group, conciliatory. 'I'm sure you boys mean well. And it was good of ye tae bring the tarp. But Miss Rankin is correct. Time tae go.'

The Wishaw men exchanged looks.

The voice from the back of the gang spoke again. 'Might ye need a hand wi' the winch, gaffer? Big Drew here knows all there is tae know.'

The Law foreman brightened. 'Aye. That would be grand. Any winch expertise would be very welcome.'

A few of the Wishaw men stepped forward, including the man from the back; an older chap, he took off his cap to speak. 'We'll be happy tae help, gaffer. We cannae go back an' prevent this, but let's try tae do whit we can.'

A few of the Wishaw gang withdrew off up the road, muttering; the majority walked towards the pithead, rolling up their sleeves.

Andrew Thomson strode purposefully back into the site, and found a crate. He carried it to the middle of the yard and stepped on to it.

'Listen, everyone. An update. As you know, one individual has been retrieved from the shaft. This individual sustained such serious injuries that Dr Rankin had to operate on him in situ. The doctor has explained that it was essential to perform this procedure as quickly as possible, and with little disruption to the surrounding environment. Therefore, the decision was made to leave the men in the tunnel until he had finished and the patient was brought to the surface. We will now be bringing up the remaining men. Please leave us space at the top of the shaft, in which to work.'

Miss Rankin spoke up. 'We will bring the men to the clearing station, where we will check them over for injury. Medicines and nourishment will be provided.'

A voice called out from the crowd. 'Whit aboot the men in the cage?'

The Law foreman stepped forward. 'I regret to inform you that it is most likely all those in the cage have perished.'

There was a terrible collective groan; sounds of howling, crying and weeping.

Andrew Thomson spoke again. 'We will try to identify them as soon as we can. In the meantime, I entreat you again to allow us to work without impediment.' He looked over at the clearing station; at the tables in the yard, where women were setting out food; at Jemima and Agnes, arriving with a huge, steaming pot of soup on a handcart. He continued. 'Thanks to you all for your efforts today. The people of Carluke are showing their very best.'

Daniel Rankin was still in the pit. He had made it clear to Hughie that the waiting men should be taken out first. Each one was checked before getting into the bucket, and gentle words of advice given – about looking out for breathing problems, about bruising, about shock.

On the surface, the word spread that the miners were coming up. At last. Thank God, thank God. Jim moved forward, tears in his eyes. Here was John and his mate Tom, grey with filth, being hoisted up in the bucket. Names were checked against a list, hutch tokens retrieved as an extra identification. Blankets were put round their shoulders as they were helped out. They could hardly stand and had to be assisted over to the clearing station. Jim ran to join them there.

'John, ma boy.' He pulled him close. 'We've been that worried. Thank God ye are all right.'

'Faither.' John leaned into Jim's shoulder. 'I'm no' all right. William. It's William. He's dead.'

Agnes was at the food table when she saw John and Tom being helped into the clearing station. Her heart leapt; she found herself crying.

The baker's wife nudged her. 'Away and see the lads, hen. I'll watch the soup.'

Agnes sped off towards them, and Tom held out his hands to her. He was completely covered in grime, even his ginger hair; just his eyes were showing white.

'Agnes. I'm that glad tae see ye. Whit a terrible day.' He was crying too.

'Tom. Ye're all right. You're all right.' She found herself laughing with relief and hysteria through the tears. 'Ah cannae touch ye, ye're so dirty. Hurry up and get checked over, come and get some soup.'

She looked over at Jim and Jemima, huddling together round John. She looked back at Tom, afraid, questioning.

'It's William, Agnes.' Tom could hardly speak. 'He …

he's away.'

Someone would have to tell Lizzie.

It took a long time to bring all the shift workers out of the mine, and it was dark when Dr Rankin came up in the bucket, clutching onto the ropes for dear life, his medical bag at his feet. Hughie had volunteered to stay down until the cage was moved, until they could retrieve William's body. Some of the men from Law had gone down to see to the ponies; they would then stay to help stabilise the cage, ready for its grim upward journey. Andrew Thomson helped Daniel Rankin out, and turned him gently towards the yard. There was a spontaneous loud applause from all around. From the clearing station to the food tables, from the Law rescue station to the manager's tables, from the gates to all corners of the site, there were the helpers, the families and the men, all nodding their heads at him, all clapping. He bowed his head for a moment, then put up his hand.

His strong voice carried over the site.

'You do not need to thank me. I am merely a citizen, doing his duty. This has been a hard day for us all, and it is not yet over. The hardest is yet to come, I fear. However, we need to keep our strength up, do we not? Did I hear there might be soup?'

His sister hurried towards him and took his arm, guiding him to the waiting steaming pots.

'I kept you some leek and potato,' said Sarah briskly. 'I

ken you like it.'

'And there are cheese scones, Doctor.' Agnes was still a little shy of the tall figure.

'Cheese scones. Ideal. I wonder if we can send some of this down to Hughie and those other men? I am sure they will be hungry too. Helen, how fares our patient?'

'He is doing well, Daniel. Respirations are steady. The pulse is somewhat weakened, but the rhythm is normal. Mrs Lindsay is sitting with him now. I must say, she is very attentive; and she has a calming presence.'

'Good. I will attend to the suturing after some nourishment. I will need the best lighting – I expect Thomson will see to it.'

'Everyone has been more than helpful – but we must make sure that you do not overtire yourself, brother. Will the suturing not wait until tomorrow?'

'I think I should attend to it sooner. And whilst my old body has the benefit of all this ghastly excitement coursing through it.'

'I will get everything prepared. Supplies of carbolic have been sent from the hospital, and more dressings than we know what to do with.' She touched her brother's arm. 'Daniel. A thought. The lad will require further anaesthetic for this procedure, will he not? Mrs Lindsay might be interested to assist you with the suturing, whilst I administer it. I also wondered if she might be called on to attend to the wounds as they heal?'

'An excellent idea as ever, Helen. Tell her I'll be over

shortly. Now – where are these cheese scones?'

Lizzie had insisted on returning to the yard; she said that she wanted to wait until William's body was retrieved. It was early morning, a soft light. The crowd was different. Remaining now were those whose loved ones had not come up, those who feared the worst. Sanny's wife was there, with her children, faces drawn and wretched. But they had been joined by others: by neighbours, friends. The people of Carluke had come to support as best they could. The Reverend MacKenzie was still there, too, moving from group to group. He approached John and Lizzie, held out his hands. Jim asked him to say a prayer.

They all bowed their heads. Then Martha called him over to the clearing station; the families there wanted to hear some words of comfort too. The minister knelt by the crude stretcher and prayed with Archie Campbell's parents. The lad was still unconscious, breathing in a heavy, drugged sleep. He then turned to the next: a man with a leg in a splint, a badly broken ankle. He too was woozy with laudanum, but he was awake. His wife was gripping his hand, as if she would never let it go.

'Minister. Ah've something important tae tell ye.'

The Reverend MacKenzie moved closer. He could hear the rattle of phlegm, dirt and dust in the man's throat and chest. His wife offered him a sip of thyme tea. It smelled surprisingly fresh and cleansing.

'Minister.' He coughed, breathed. His voice was clearer

now. 'Minister. Ah've got tae tell ye. It was William MacDonald that saved us. He pushed all of us tae the back of the shaft. He saw that cage coming down, and he acted. Never thought of himself. Ye need tae tell Lizzie MacDonald that her husband is a hero.'

'Aye. That I will. I will tell her.'

'Minister.' The man's wife spoke up now. 'Can we say a prayer? We need tae give thanks. But we also need tae think of those who have not survived. Their loved ones.'

They all closed their eyes, and prayed.

The off-duty Carluke miners, alongside the Law and Wishaw men, had been busy all night with ropes, hooks and slings, and the winch was once more operational. With some deft teamwork, the tarpaulin had been draped over the cage; but all anticipated the dripping of blood that would be inevitable as it was hoisted to the surface. The foreman conferred with the manager, and another announcement was made.

Andrew Thomson stood on his crate.

'Thank you for your patience. Thanks to the skill of these men, we will now be bringing up the cage. Even with the tarpaulin, there is no way to shield you from this shocking sight. Prepare yourselves for the worst.'

The minister stepped forward from the clearing station, ready to say a prayer, as the winch started.

Then a familiar voice rang out. A clear, loud, singing voice.

The singing man limped into the yard, his hat in

his hands.

'The Lord's my Shepherd, I'll not want.
He makes me down to lie.
In pastures green, he leadeth me,
The quiet waters by.'

The crowd started quietly, then gathered strength. The strength and power of terrible shared heartache, of deepest sorrow. As the cage came up slowly, into the dawn, the old psalm rang out. They all stood around to greet it, heads high, singing.

PART FIVE

We will never be the same

RAW

Six weeks later. The wind was raw across the Market Place, and there was an iron hint of sleet in the air. Martha and Agnes wrapped their shawls tighter round their heads. Martha stooped to place a wrap of oatcakes and cheese on the step for the singing man; then arm in arm they crossed the rutted roadway, skirts hoisted, weaving to avoid puddles and horse manure. After much painful discussion, they had decided to speak to Dr Rankin.

'Good day, Mrs Lindsay. Oh, hello, Agnes.' Sarah was smart in her cap. 'May I help you? Are you wanting to speak to the doctor?'

'Aye. Is it convenient, Sarah?'

'Mrs Lindsay.' The booming voice of Dr Daniel Rankin rattled down the corridor. 'Come in. How are you today? Miserable weather we are having. And Agnes, too. Come in, both.'

Sarah opened the door wide and stepped to the side as Martha and Agnes entered the house, before disappearing into the kitchen.

'Thank you, Doctor. Just some words of advice, that's all.'

'Of course. First of all, I have to ask what you make of young Archie Campbell's recovery?'

'Aye, he's doing fine. I'm only going in every third day, now. The surgery is healing up well. Ye did a grand job.' Martha was shaking off her shawl.

'He's a young, fit man, Mrs Lindsay, and that is his biggest asset, believe me. Your frequent attendance to his wound care has also assisted his recovery. His mother speaks very highly of you, although it took her a little while to accept some of the methods which you use for wound dressing.'

Martha laughed. 'Aye. Spider webs. It's an old trick, for areas that are difficult to heal. My mother taught me that. It seems tae have worked well. Although when I asked for as many as possible, Mrs Campbell thought I was passing some sort of judgement on the cleanliness of her home. However, soon enough she had all her neighbours gathering them.'

'Interesting. There must be some sort of antiseptic and protective quality in the natural gossamer,' said Dr Rankin. 'What we hope for is that young Archie has the mental robustness to adapt to his new circumstances. What is your judgement in this regard?'

'It's still early days, Doctor, but I would say that his mood is low. I wonder if it might help him tae meet someone in a similar circumstance? Do ye know of anybody who has adapted well to such an injury? A person that might speak tae him, let him know all the practical ways he could help himself?'

'That is an excellent idea. I will ask the doctor in Wishaw and see if we might identify someone. Now, come in to the fire. What am I doing, chatting in the corridor?'

Martha and Agnes followed him down the passageway to the back parlour.

'Guid day, Miss Rankin.'

'Good day to you both. Won't you take a seat?'

Daniel Rankin sat in his winged armchair by the fire as his sister indicated two smaller chairs for Martha and Agnes.

'What can I help you with? Will it do in front of my sister?'

Martha looked at Agnes, who nodded. Then she cleared her throat and spoke. 'As you know, sometimes we have to explore some ideas that are unusual, Dr Rankin. I am sure we could be confident that Miss Rankin wouldnae judge us if we were tae ask some rather strange questions – and that the discussion will stay private, in this room?'

'Of course, Mrs Lindsay. My sister often has a useful female perspective on matters. We both completely understand the need for confidentiality, fear not.'

'We have come tae see you because ye are a wise man, Doctor,' said Martha.

Daniel Rankin laughed. 'Not wise, Mrs Lindsay. Perhaps old and experienced in the ways of the world, but I would not claim wisdom.'

'There. That is what makes ye wise; that you do not

believe yourself tae be so. If only other men had such wisdom!'

They all laughed.

'As you know, Agnes and I are from a small village,' Martha continued. 'There are many superstitions and beliefs that date from days gone by that are still strongly held. There are also stories in my own family of a long-ago relative who came frae travelling people, and remedies that have been passed down since. Some of the old ways are useful – as we found with the witch hazel, for bruising. Other traditions are less so. I was embarrassed for ye to find out about the mole's hand, Doctor.'

Miss Rankin looked surprised, so Martha explained.

'I had been given tae understand it was useful against the toothache, Miss Rankin. Your brother corrected my views.'

'Yes. I did not mean to be cruel, Mrs Lindsay, but I did have to laugh. Such things are myth, only – and perhaps a means of generating extra income for the mole-catcher. It is as ridiculous an idea as spells being responsible for an infectious illness.' He shook his head.

Martha leaned forward. 'That is why we are here today, Doctor. We need tae know if Agnes has an evil gift, or if it is just a myth.'

'Go on. I'm curious.'

Martha and Agnes together told the story of the Priest's Pool, of the stone, and of the cursing of Catriona Ferguson and its dreadful consequences.

'Worse was tae come, Dr Rankin,' said Agnes. 'A few weeks before the accident at the mine, I cursed Archie Campbell. Does that mean I have tae take some responsibility for the accident? It didnae just injure Archie. All those poor men were killed.' Agnes looked anxious, fearful.

Miss Rankin pursed her lips. She could guess why Archie Campbell might have provoked a curse.

'We don't feel able to speak to the minister here in Carluke about this,' said Martha. 'He doesnae know us as well as James Laidlaw, our minister in Wanlockhead. But we don't know what tae do about this matter of the cursing of Archie Campbell. Should Agnes confess? It might be the right thing tae do. Yet as ye know, her life is already quite difficult here, given the circumstances of her birth – this might make things worse.'

Daniel Rankin addressed the young woman. 'I can understand that this could prey on your mind, Agnes. However, I wish to reassure you emphatically that the only cause of that accident was the worn ropes on the winch. Other than in folklore, there is absolutely no evidence that cursing someone results in actual injury. Please be completely assured that your angry words did not cause any adverse events – be it a nasty porridge burn, or a dreadful mining accident. It was entirely coincidental that these individuals went on to suffer an unfortunate incident. If you so desire, you might seek forgiveness for uttering cross words – but that is the limit of your responsibility, Agnes.'

Agnes visibly relaxed.

'Thank you, Doctor,' said Martha. 'That is most helpful. We respect your knowledge of the world. I hope ye don't mind that we brought you this concern.'

'Not at all, Mrs Lindsay. Indeed, you would be surprised how many unusual queries come across this door. It is important to try to heal the mind as well as the body, don't you agree?'

Martha looked troubled. 'Aye. And the mind takes longer tae heal, does it no'?'

'Are you thinking of all the poor folks, grieving?' Miss Rankin spoke gently. 'Right enough. These are the invisible pains that will take a long time to ease.'

'Poor Lizzie MacDonald.' Martha shook her head. 'I just dinnae know how tae reach her.'

'You are right to be concerned, Mrs Lindsay. I will endeavour to see all those who were bereaved again soon. That is indeed a long-term commitment that we all need to make.' Dr Rankin was silent for a moment, then said, 'I believe that the physical injuries – perhaps even those as grim as poor Archie Campbell's – are almost easier to bear than the terrible pain of grief. If you are in good health, like young Archie, you certainly recover much more quickly.' He stood. 'Thank you, Mrs Lindsay. You have given me something to think about.'

'And thank you, for listening to us. We are much reassured. And Dr Rankin, perhaps one day ye might have time tae tell me more aboot this idea that we come from apes.'

'Mrs Lindsay, it has been arranged that I give a lecture about this very subject, in the Reading Room. Perhaps you might like to attend?'

'I will see whit Mr Lindsay thinks, Doctor. I understand it is principally the menfolk that would attend there. Good day to ye. And to you, Miss Rankin.'

THE QUIET CHAIR

THE SUNDAY SERVICE was over at last, and John had managed to catch Jemima.

'How are ye, hen? Fancy a wee walk? It's not raining, for once. It'd be grand tae get some fresh air.'

'Aye. Will we walk down the brae? We might get as far as the Clyde. Hope these boots'll make it.' Jemima looked down at her Sunday shoes, then back to her brother. She smiled, and took his arm. They joined a procession of others, strolling out in the Sunday sunshine.

'How are ye, John? Ye've been back at work a few weeks now. They weren't slow at getting the pit working again.'

'Ocht, I'm just getting used to it. It's different. Everything is different. I keep thinking that I had life without care before it happened, and now it's all changed, here in the afterwards times. Everything feels empty, somehow. I cannae explain it right.'

'I think I understand.' Jemima nodded slowly. 'I feel like that when I go into the house at Stewart Street. There's an absence, isn't there?'

'Aye. It's the wee things that get tae me, Jem. Like his pipe is still there, on the mantelpiece. It chokes me up, every time.'

She squeezed his arm.

'It must be hard in that house just now, John. I've got to admit, I've been avoiding the place. Lizzie just looks so grim and annoyed all the time. And she'll bite yer head off, soon as look at ye.'

'We're all tiptoeing round her, Jem. Even the weans. She could really do with a hand, she's so behind with all her work. I dinnae like to say, but I've nae socks to wear. They're all in this big pile of stinkin' washing. I've been fishing the dirty ones out, tae wear again. I'll be getting complaints frae the boys.'

'I've offered tae help, John. More than a dozen times. But it's like she's pushing us away.'

'Martha says she's mentioned it to Dr Rankin, that she's not herself. Mibbe he'll help her snap out of it,' said John. Then he corrected himself. 'Ye cannae snap out of somethin' as big as this, though.'

'No. It'll take a long time. After Maw died, I suppose I wasnae myself for months afterwards. It felt like I was just getting through every day, like wading through treacle. And we were expecting her death. This terrible thing that happened tae William – it was such a shock.' She squeezed her brother's arm again. 'And I know it must hurt you sore, too.'

'Aye. I think aboot him all the time. I hear his voice talking tae me in my head, especially at my work. He'll be giving me wee tips, like "put that pick at more of an angle, John-boy, ye'll get a better result."' He coughed, trying to cover his emotion.

They walked on quietly.

Jemima broke the silence. 'Do ye remember when we climbed the Hare Hill? That was such a fine day out. That was before. I know what ye mean, John. Life is now divided into before the accident, and after. And after seems very dark.'

'Aye. It's like a big cloud over us. Hopefully it will shift.'

'When I felt like this, when our maw died, I didnae realise, but it was slowly shifting all the time. I just didnae notice. Then when we went that walk, it dawned on me that I felt better.'

'Aye. We'd best let time do its work.'

'Whit were you thinking aboot, during the sermon? Did I see ye looking pretty annoyed?'

'It's that MacKenzie. He can't seem tae talk aboot anything that I can agree with. I've been thinking of stopping going tae the Kirk. Or changing tae Tom's church, like Martha and Agnes.'

Jemima was shocked. 'John, ye cannae do that. Faither would be so upset. Particularly just now, with Lizzie not going.'

'I know, I know. Now isnae the time. But it is really getting to me, listening to him going on aboot his ideas of what is right and what is wrong. The worst was at William's funeral. All that talk about God's mysterious ways, and Jesus waiting at the gates. Perhaps Lizzie was comforted, but my heart was just cold, listening to it. Nothing aboot William, how he was a staunch man. Then today, when he was laying into the trade unions. Saying that good Christian men should be above the troublemakers and rabble-rousers. The unions are the ones that got us more pay, a couple of years back. They are the ones trying tae make the mines safer for us all. I just don't know whit the Kirk stands for.'

'Mibbe it doesnae have to stand for anything. It's just the Church. It's there tae help us understand the Bible, and to be good folk. Tae marry us and bury us.'

'MacKenzie has different ideas aboot who are good folk and who are not. They dinnae always match mine. He doesnae much like Dr Rankin's ideas, either. I sometimes wonder, is it the Kirk that doesnae like these ideas, or is it just our minister?'

'Are ye going tae the lecture? I heard Dr Rankin is giving a talk, at the Reading Room.'

'Aye. Me an' Tom are thinking of going along. Do ye fancy it?'

'I might. I might go. I'll see. Is it no' usually just men?'

'Not sure. Mibbe see if any other lassie might want to attend?'

'I'll see.'

'Jem, can I tell ye something?'

'Aye. Whit is it?'

'It's that hard, goin' into the cage at work. I hate it. I know I'm not the only one. But I dread it, every day.'

'Oh, John. I'm not surprised,' she said. 'But did I not hear that they've made it safer?'

'Aye. There are two ropes now, and all these checks being made every time. And they've put barrels at the bottom of the shaft, to ease any sudden fall. But I hate it, Jem.'

Jemima looked at her brother; his face was set. She squeezed his arm.

'It cannae be fair, sending ye all down again so soon after.'

'Their priority is getting the coal out, making a profit. There's going tae be a big enquiry, but in the meantime, it's business as usual.' He sighed. 'The managers, they're no' bad men. They have their jobs tae do. And they have all made big contributions to the relief funds for the families.'

'Aye, and there have been these community events as well, raising a lot of money. I hear funds are coming in frae all over Scotland, especially when the *Daily Herald* put out that appeal. The folk from Law and Wishaw have been most generous, too.' She added, 'Mr Shields gave five pounds. And Faither says the Masons have raised huge amounts.'

'Aye. Folks have big hearts.'

'How are the funds tae be managed, John? Do ye know? Will Lizzie be able tae claim against it?'

'Aye. Aye, I'm sure she'll be fine. Dr Rankin is helping to organise it. All the funds raised are to go into the

Savings Bank. There is tae be a Board of Trustees, who will administer it. The main thing will be looking after the children's futures, of course.'

'Good. That's good tae hear. That might ease things for Lizzie.'

'She cannae take anything in, Jem. She's … she's kind of stuck.'

'Aye. I know. We have tae keep trying with her. It's all we can do.'

'It's good to talk to ye, Jem. It's always been good.'

They linked arms and strolled on, John pausing from time to time to breathe in the fresh, clean air.

STEWART STREET

'Oh. Martha. And it's yourself, Doctor. Can I help ye?' Lizzie peered reluctantly round the door. Martha could sense her discomfort and knew that the last person she wished to see was Dr Rankin.

'Aye – I wonder if we could have a word, Mrs MacDonald.'

Lizzie hesitated, then relented. 'Ye'd better both come in.'

She motioned them down the dank passageway and into the kitchen. The smell of unwashed clothes and stale food pervaded the room. There were piles of dirty laundry on the floor, and unwashed pots in the sink; Lizzie's hair was unkempt and her skirt was stained.

'Excuse the mess, Doctor.' She scooped up a toddler. 'It's these weans. I never get a minute to myself.'

'How are things with you?' His voice was concerned.

'Ocht, don't ask.' Lizzie's eyes filled with tears. 'It's best if ye don't ask.'

Dr Rankin continued, gently. 'I've been hearing the stories from the mine, Lizzie. Your husband was quite the hero.'

'Aye.' She jutted out her chin. 'Well, he shouldnae have been. Whit aboot us? He should have thought of his own family before diving in tae save others.' She stroked the child's hair and sat. 'Take a seat if ye want, Doctor. Martha, sit yersel' down. Whit can I help ye with?'

Daniel Rankin pulled up a chair, and Martha found a seat in the corner by the fire. She placed a heavy basket by her side.

'Mrs MacDonald, I have been lax in my duties. I should have been here to see you before now. Part of my job is to attend to the bereaved, as well as the injured.'

'I dinnae need your help, Doctor. I'm fine. There's nothing wrong with me.' Lizzie pushed back her lank hair and challenged the doctor with a stare.

'Grief brings a terrible pain of its own, Mrs MacDonald, and it can be as hard to bear as any broken bone.'

'You dinnae know the hurt of this pain till ye've suffered it.' Lizzie's voice was sharp. 'And we both know there is no cure, Doctor.'

Her tone sent a chill into Martha's heart. She spoke up. 'There are things we can do tae help ye bear it. And there are people all around you who want tae help.'

'I dinnae need anyone's help.' She stared hard at Martha.

The doctor spoke again. 'Mrs MacDonald, I think that you would gladly assist others in a similar situation. It is a sad fact of life that one never knows when one might be called upon. But for now, this is a time for you to ask for help.'

'Help with what? It's all inside me. I'm so angry, Doctor. I'm angry with myself, for being like this.' She gestured round the room. 'I'm angry with the weans. Angry with my family. Angry at the world. I'm more than angry. I'm furious.'

'I suspect that the person you are most angry with is William.'

'Aye. Aye, ye're right. I cannae help it. I think I'm going mad, I'm that angry. Everyone telling me how brave he was, I cannae stand it. How is he brave if he left us here alone, tae manage without him? How could he do that? Leave us? He's no' coming back.' She was shouting, red-faced, eyes brimming. 'And another thing. I'm really, really angry with myself. I broke a mirror the day it happened. Terrible bad luck. Then he left the house, and I never even said goodbye. That's the worst.'

They sat in silence for a moment. Lizzie's breathing slowed.

'These feelings are normal, Mrs MacDonald. This anger is part of grief. It will ease.'

'Normal? How can this be normal?'

'Others who have experienced sudden loss in difficult circumstances also describe feelings of rage. You are not alone. You are not going mad. You will get through this difficult time.'

'It doesnae feel like I ever will, Doctor.' Lizzie started to weep. 'I just want my William tae walk back in, through that door. That's the only thing that could make me better.'

'We all know that is not going to happen.'

'Did ye come here just tae tell me that?'

'I came here to see how you are, and I can see how hard it is for you just now. I have a prescription that will assist.'

'I cannae afford medicines. I cannae even afford tae have you sitting in that chair.'

'As you have no physical illness, there is no charge for this visit, Mrs MacDonald. In truth, it can better be described as one concerned neighbour calling on another. And my prescription is free. I suspect the medicine will be quite difficult to take, however. It will require much effort. But your family, including Mrs Lindsay here – they will all assist.'

'Well? Whit is it?'

Daniel Rankin stood up tall from his chair. His rich voice resonated in the kitchen as he walked up and down, gesticulating his message, counting on his fingers. Martha was mesmerised.

'One: a daily walk in the fresh air. A short walk at first, then a bit further every day. Mrs Lindsay here will call for you. Two: the consumption of regular meals of good, wholesome food. Broths. Custards. Mrs Lindsay has brought you some soup today, to get you started, along with some oatcakes. Three: ask Mrs Lindsay and your siblings for their support with the children, and with your housework. Three small things, but they will help.'

He sat down again, and spoke more softly.

'I have two observations. Firstly, the broken mirror

bringing misfortune. I am aware that this is a very ancient and deeply held superstition. But that is all it is – a superstition. It is a place for you to put your anger and grief. Blame the broken mirror, if it helps. But we both know that it was not the mirror that caused the accident. Secondly, you did not have the chance to say goodbye. I presume that relations between you and your husband were normally amicable?' Lizzie nodded, her eyes filling again. 'Well, then. He will never have doubted you, Mrs MacDonald, not for a second. Neither of you were to know that he was not to return. For all the men that perished that day, there was no opportunity to say goodbye. That is the real tragedy.'

They sat quietly for a moment, then Daniel Rankin spoke again.

'This is going to take time, Mrs MacDonald. It is not for nothing that they say time is a great healer.'

He stood again and stepped back, grasping the back of his chair.

'Now. Here is some practical advice. When the feelings of anger are upon you, find a chair. Hold the back of it, like so. Close your eyes, and take three very deep breaths.' He lifted his head, tossed back his long white hair, closed his eyes, and took a dramatic inhalation. At the same time, he swept his arm towards the ceiling; then, with a flourish of the hand and a loud sigh, he lowered it. He opened his eyes again. 'Three times, Mrs MacDonald. It will help to calm you.'

'It will certainly surprise the children!' Despite herself, Lizzie was smiling.

'It is a proven method of managing these feelings of anger, Mrs MacDonald. Do give it a try. Now. I must leave you both. I hope you won't mind if I call again in a week or so?'

'Aye. Thank you, Doctor. Ye're a tonic in yourself. My mother always used tae say the same. She loved your visits.' She paused, tears welling once more. 'I'm sorry if I was rude to ye, Doctor. Do you know one of the hardest things? I dinnae have my mother here tae comfort me. I miss her too, Dr Rankin.'

'That must be hard, indeed. But your siblings are all most fond of you and are ready to assist, in their own way. You Lindsays are quite a remarkable family. Strong. Robust. Resilient. That is why I know you will come through this.' He patted her shoulder and nodded towards Martha. 'I leave you in good hands.'

Lizzie stood. 'Thank ye, Doctor. And I'll mibbe try that deep breathing thing, too.'

A LECTURE

'THAT WAS GOOD of ye, to speak to Dr Rankin. Aboot Lizzie. John told me.' Jemima spoke shyly. She was drinking tea with Agnes and Martha, sitting in the kitchen in the Market Place house. She had taken to calling in since the accident, and at last a truce was being established. More than a truce: a real warmth. Barkie had crept over to her chair and she was scratching the ginger head.

'We've all been so worried aboot her. If she's going tae listen to anyone, it'll be the doctor,' said Martha.

'Aye,' said Jemima. 'She's known him all her life. And he was very good to us when my mother was ill.'

'He's a guid man,' Martha observed. 'Carluke is lucky tae have such a doctor.'

'There was a guid doctor in Wanlockhead, too,' said Agnes. 'Dr Menzies. He was always looking in, when Grannie was ill. And wee Lucy, of course. He was awfy kind tae her.'

'Aye, it's true,' said Martha. 'He was a guid soul, as well.'

'Wee Lucy. Was that …?' Jemima hesitated.

'She was ma half-sister. She was only three years old

when she died. I loved her that much. She's gone tae be an angel.' Agnes looked down at her hands. Barkie crossed the room to her, and she rubbed her head.

'That must have been awful hard.'

'Aye. And we're a long way frae where she lies, with my mither,' said Martha.

'Oh. Yes.' Jemima hadn't really thought about that. 'At least I can visit my mother's grave.'

'Now,' said Martha more briskly, 'let's speak of something more cheery.' She laughed. 'Or mibbe not. I wondered if ye've heard that Dr Rankin is to speak of these ideas of Darwin, in the Reading Room?'

'Aye. John mentioned it. I think he is planning to attend, with Tom.'

'I wondered if ye might be interested in accompanying me, Jemima? Agnes isnae too keen, and your father is concerned that the minister wouldnae approve, so he will not attend. Myself, I think we should be open to new ideas.'

'Hearing that we come from apes?' Agnes grimaced, and shook her head.

Jemima said, 'Thank you, Martha. That's kind. Yes, I agree. It is important tae hear new ideas. I think I might be interested. We could report back about our monkey ancestors, Agnes.'

'I'll cover my ears! I'd rather hear that I'd come from a dog, like Barkie. Sometimes I think she understands every word we say.'

Agnes looked down at Barkie, who was enjoying her head scratch. The dog rolled over, and smiled.

There was quite a crowd at the Reading Room, and much noise and talk as the audience filed in.

'I'm prepared to hear whit he has to say, even though I think it is all a bit far-fetched. We know that the doctor is a man of learning.' Martha recognised the voice of Archie Campbell's father, and waved. He looked quite surprised to see her, but nodded his head in greeting.

'Will we find a place here at the back? There are not many womenfolk.' Martha indicated two seats in the back row, and she and Jemima settled in.

The imposing figure of Dr Rankin strode into the room, with his sister at his side. All present clapped.

'Enough, friends, enough.' He held up his hand. 'I have not yet spoken! Save your applause for the end, if you survive that long!' He took his place at the front of the room and lifted a book in his right hand.

'This tome is called *On the Origin of Species by Means of Natural Selection, or the Preservation of Favoured Races in the Struggle for Life*. It was written by Charles Darwin, in 1851. And this' – he lifted another book, in his left hand – 'this is called *Descent of Man and Selection in Relation to Sex*.'

Martha was jolted at the mention of the word 'sex' in a public place.

Daniel Rankin continued. 'This second book was published

more recently, in 1871. We will begin by discussing the theories put forward in the first book, in order to better understand the arguments being made in the second.'

With his habitual dramatic style, pacing up and down on the floor, Daniel Rankin proceeded to outline the theory of evolution to his attentive audience.

'It's much more complicated than ah thought,' whispered Jemima, at a break for questions. 'But that phrase, survival of the fittest – that makes sense.'

'Aye. It is complicated. I still cannae understand why some say it's blasphemy,' responded Martha.

As if in response, several seats forward, Tom put that very point to Dr Rankin. 'Why is the Church not keen on these theories?'

'There are certain voices in the Church who are adamant that the creation of Man occurred separately to other species. They completely embrace the narrative that is outlined in Genesis, in the story of the Garden of Eden. However, the Bible is a relatively modern book. There has been life developing on earth for many millions of years. Since the publication of Darwin's first study, more and more scientific evidence has accrued that leads us to conclude that humans are mammals, and are therefore also subject to the laws of natural selection.'

Another voice called out from the floor. 'Selection from apes?'

'It was my friend and scientific associate Thomas Huxley who first explicitly made this link. Yes, from apes.

And before that – many millions of years before that – from fishes, and marine creatures.'

'How come there are no fossils of humans, Doctor?'

'Fossils are, in fact, very rare. They are created in particular physical conditions such as a swamp, or a lake bed. They also date from extremely ancient times, from before the evolution of mankind.'

There were many more questions. Finally, the discussion concluded with applause, and the audience began to leave the room. Martha and Jemima found themselves jammed in, waiting for an opportunity to move outside. Jemima was waving at John and Tom, indicating that they should wait for her, when a booming voice rang in Martha's ear.

'Mrs Lindsay. Jemima. So pleased that you came along.' Daniel Rankin had walked down the side of the room and was there beside them.

'Oh, guid evening, Dr Rankin. That was most interesting. We enjoyed the discussion and questions, too,' said Martha. Jemima nodded in agreement.

Martha spoke again. 'I have a question, though. Perhaps just nonsense, I don't know, but it is something that I've wondered about for some time. I didnae feel able to speak up during the debate, but perhaps I might ask ye now?'

'Of course. Wait, I'll just locate my sister.' He waved to the front, where Miss Rankin was deep in conversation. She saw him, and waved back. 'Go ahead, Mrs Lindsay.'

Martha took a breath and started. 'This evening, you described very clearly the ideas about natural selection and evolution, Doctor. My question is about our relation tae other animals – animals with which we might feel an affinity. Might evolution continue after death? I have been wondering – might we become another creature, when we die? Or is it blasphemous tae think so?'

'Ah. Interesting. That is a separate debate, Mrs Lindsay. Darwinism does not address this matter. However, this is a fundamental belief of one of the great religions of this world, and many millions of people do, in fact, think that this is the case. Buddhists believe that animals are sentient beings. That is why they will not eat meat. I do have a book about the religions of the world with a chapter on Buddhism, if you might find that of interest.'

Martha nodded. 'Sentient beings. Thank ye, Dr Rankin. There is so much to learn, is there no'?'

'Even at my age, I am finding that it is a never-ending process, indeed. Ah, here is my sister. Good evening, ladies.' He moved off with Miss Rankin.

Martha turned to Jemima anxiously. 'I think your faither might not like tae hear me speak of such matters. I wonder whether …'

Jemima smiled. 'I won't say anything, Martha, don't worry. Best not tae rock the boat.'

Daniel Rankin and his sister were strolling home, arm in arm.

'Aye, that seemed to go well enough,' he said.

'It was a packed house. They asked good, thoughtful

questions, Daniel. The community is fortunate to have an opportunity to debate such matters, and with such a knowledgeable citizen to lead them in their discussions. Many that I spoke to said that it was a most informative and enjoyable evening.'

'Wheesht, Helen. Enough flattery.' He smiled, then was thoughtful. 'I used to relish such meetings. We had some fine topics in the past, did we not? Electricity. I especially enjoyed that one.'

'Aye, you have quite a history of encouraging expansion of the mind in Carluke, Daniel. Now. I have a question.'

'Aye, what is it?'

'That dreadful day, in the pit. You said you would tell me the joke about Lister and the amputations. I've been waiting to hear it.'

'Oh, Helen. It really isn't suitable. It is coarse and irreverent. My mind must have been seeking distractions for me even to mention it.'

'You have certainly piqued my curiosity now, Daniel. Come on. Out with it.'

Daniel Rankin sighed, then nodded. He stopped and took up a pose. 'Here follows a highly inappropriate tale from Glasgow Medical School. It goes like this. Did you know that Mr Lister is the only gentleman who has performed three amputations in twenty seconds?'

'Goodness! How can that be?' responded his sister.

'Why, the patient's leg, the patient's penis and his assistant's thumb, of course!' Daniel Rankin burst into laughter, then stopped abruptly. Had he overstepped the mark? He looked down at his diminutive sister, only to see her shoulders shaking with mirth.

BUNTING

JIM WAS RUMMAGING in the stock cupboard.

'Ah cannae believe that we're out of black ribbon, Jane.'

'Aye, Faither. The order should be in today, wi' Davey. Ah think everyone in the town is still wearin' a piece, either in their bonnets or tied on their arm.' Jane was cutting out a large pair of trousers; she paused to push her hair from her eyes, and looked up the workroom. 'Your black lace trims are doing well, Agnes. Keepin' ye busy.'

Agnes turned and smiled, then stitched on.

Jim closed the cupboard, and shook his head. 'Ah don't know how ah feel, making money frae sorrow.'

'It's as well ye're no' the undertaker, then!' said Jane.

Margaret laughed, then covered her mouth.

'Aye, true enough,' said Jim. No offence had been taken.

The shop door opened, the bell tinkling, and Davey stepped in.

'Guid day, folks. How are ye all the day? Ah've got those reams on the waggon, Mr Lindsay. And more black ribbon.'

The supplies duly dealt with, Davey drew up a stool at the front of the counter and perched his long body on it. He looked somewhat precarious. Agnes imagined him like a giraffe; she had seen a picture of the animal in one of the papers, and had thought the likeness striking.

Davey cleared his throat. As he prepared to address the room, the redness crept from his neck to his face.

'Ah was hearin' aboot the parade, for the opening of the school. There are marching bands comin' from all over. It's going tae be some spectacle. How will they fit everyone into the Market Place, that's what I want to know?'

'Aye, Davey. It's going tae be some occasion.' Jim's position in the Masons meant that he was party to much of the planning; the Masonic lodges were sponsoring the laying of the foundation stone.

'What it is,' Davey continued, 'ah was thinking aboot the bunting.'

'Bunting!' Jane and Margaret left their work and moved forward. 'That's a great idea, Davey!'

'Aye. Of course, I had been thinking of that too,' said Jim, hastily. 'Just never mentioned it.'

'What dae ye think? Make Carluke look special. We've got some rolls of tape on the waggon, ends that have been left. Have ye any scrap pieces of fabric we could use?' Davey was enthused.

Margaret and Jane were already deep in the scrap boxes. A tumbled rainbow array of different cloths was starting to gather on the floor.

'Davey, this is a great idea. Well done, lad.' Jim was gracious. 'We'll get started. As ye go about your deliveries,

329

mibbe you could gather up some more material for us? Get the other tailors onto it. I'd be pleased to co-ordinate the effort frae here. Look.' Jim walked to a side table, piled with boxes. 'We'll just move these tae the back. C'mon lad, give me a hand – and this will be a handy workbench. Whenever we've got a spare moment, we'll be cutting triangles. Pile those scraps there, lassies, off the floor.'

'Some touches of lace might add to it, dae ye think?' Agnes was keen to join in.

'Aye, that would be bonny! No black, mind,' said Margaret.

'No black,' said Jim. 'This is a chance tae bring some colour back to the town. We'll make the bunting up, Davey. For free, of course.'

Sunday, so no work. Agnes was itching to get back to the bunting, but knew this was the day of rest. She called up the stairs.

'Maw! Have you the wee scissors? Ma nail is catching.'

'Agnes, no! Ye cannae cut yer nails on a Sunday. It's bad luck. It'll have tae wait till tomorrow.'

'Sorry Maw. I forgot.'

'Are ye ready for the church?'

Martha came slowly down the stairs. She had adapted a robe that sat high, but her pregnant belly still protruded boldly, a statement. A new brother or sister. Agnes felt a rush of joy.

'Aye. Just aboot. It's awfy long, the service, Maw. Poor

Barkie will be on her own, all that time.'

'Barkie knows it's Sunday, Agnes. The Lindsays have already left for their Kirk.'

Barkie was curled in her corner, fast asleep.

AND THE BANDS PLAYED

THE REVEREND MACKENZIE was enjoying his habitual scan of the congregation as they sang out the first hymn. As it finished, he gathered himself ready for the sermon. He looked sombre.

'It is some weeks now since that terrible event at Castlehill sent waves of shock through our town. Weeks to grieve, yes. But also, time for reflection. We are perhaps asking ourselves, "Why did God let this happen? Why did He not step in, and prevent it?"'

He looked around the congregation as if seeking an answer, and then went on.

'Rather than questioning God, it might serve us better to reflect on the words of the scriptures. From Romans one, verse eighteen: "For the wrath of God is revealed from heaven against all ungodliness and unrighteousness of men".'

The Minister repeated the phrase, raising his voice dramatically.

'*For the wrath of God is revealed from heaven against all ungodliness and unrighteousness of men.*'

He paused, and looked around.

'It is for all of us to look into our hearts. *All of us.* It saddens God that we are so full of sin. Such as, the sin of lust.' He looked down at Jim, shaking his head. Jim looked down at his hands. The minister continued, looking around, as more and more of the congregation dropped their heads. Some put their heads in their hands; others covered their eyes, as if to look into their hearts.

'The sin of pride. The sin of vanity. The sin of profanity and ungodly thoughts. Then there is the sin of sedition.'

He looked over at John, who glared back.

The minister continued. 'And what of those who indulge in heathen practices? To all of you sinners, I say this: *Beware of the wrath of God.*'

The church was tense, the congregation holding its collective breath, chastised.

'In this house of God, we can reflect on our sins. We can ask for forgiveness. We can ask for mercy. And we can reflect on the words of the apostle James: "Therefore to him that knoweth to do good, and doeth it not, to him it is sin." And where there is sin, *beware the wrath of God.*'

There was a noise at the back. All turned to see John pushing past Jemima, into the aisle.

'Ah'm no' listening to this!'

Like his grandfather before him, he strode out of the Kirk.

All of Carluke was out in the Market Place, for the great occasion. There was speculation that over a mile of bunting had been strung up between buildings and lamp posts; certainly there was a most festive air. The Provincial Grand Master of Lanarkshire was to lay the foundation stone for the new school. Even the singing man had been spotted on a bench, at the far end of the square, humming quietly. John and Jemima had Lizzie's weans with them; when Tom and Agnes joined them, they were quite a little crowd.

'Room for one more?'

John's heart lifted and filled; here was Sarah Kennedy. Smiling shyly, she put her arms out, and he passed her a wriggling toddler.

'See what ah've got?' Tom had a bag of sherbet.

'Sweeties!' The children whooped with delight.

'When are the bands coming?' Agnes was straining to see down the street, past the crowds.

'The procession is supposed tae start at two o'clock,' said Tom, running his hand through his brush of ginger hair. He was grinning. 'It should be braw. They've been practising for weeks. The bandmaster says ah'll be joining them next time.' He mimicked playing a cornet.

'Aye, it should be a fine noise indeed.' John clapped his hands together. He was looking forward to it. 'Do ye think Barkie will be all right?'

Agnes looked worried. The dog was standing on a low wall, looking at the unusually busy square.

'We can always take her back tae the house, if she doesnae like the noise,' said Jemima. She grabbed her brother's arm; she was excited too, full of anticipation. 'There are bands coming from all over the parish. I've heard the Volunteer Band is playing, and the Flute Band, as well as the Carluke Brass Band. And there are so many lodges taking part in the parade, from all over.'

There was a smell of roasting sweet chestnuts in the air. Many of the stalls that had last been seen at the Fair had appeared in alleys and corners. At last, the distant sound of a march could be heard; the stirring sound of 'Highland Laddie'.

The Carluke Masonic brothers marched proud at the head of the procession, dressed in their robes and finery, and carrying their banner. Jim was there, in the second row, looking suitably serious in his elegant gown – as ever, the dapper man. He gave a little wave to Martha, who was standing in the doorway of the house with other neighbours. She raised one hand high above her head in response, the other resting on her pregnant belly.

'Here they come! Listen to that drum!' John was grinning in delight.

Smart in their uniforms and caps, the lads of the Flute Band marched into the square. The big drum beat a deep rhythm, almost hypnotic; the snare drum cracked through the air. The children begged to be released. Once on the ground, they jumped up and down, squealing, clapping their hands in time. The others looked at each other, smiling broadly; then John took up the beat, clapping his hands high. Everyone was joining in.

'Ye cannae help it!' John shouted in Agnes's ear.

'Aye! It's grand!' Agnes was grinning, and clapping. 'But ye were right. Barkie's not keen. I'll run her back to the house.' The dog had jumped down from her perch and was lying against the wall, as if hiding.

Tom was there, by her side. 'Ah'll come wi' ye. Tae help.'

What a show. The Carluke Masons gathered by the confluence of bright, fluttering bunting where the new school was to be, watching and clapping as the band marched in. Then came more Masonic parades as the neighbouring lodges put up a show, all in their bright colours and regalia. Behind them were groups of miners from Law, Wishaw and further afield, returning once more to the town in this happier time, to support Carluke in recovery. The air rang with cheers and shouts. More bands were coming down the street. The Flute Band finished and stood to one side, as the Volunteer Band started up with 'Bonnie Dundee'. More groups of marching men arrived into the square; and yet another band. No sooner had the Volunteer Band finished than the joyous sound of the finale from Burns's 'Jolly Beggars' struck up. All the bands joined in, faster and faster.

Tom and Agnes re-joined them, breathless from running across the Market Place.

'Do ye think it's allowed tae dance? We could dae a reel to this!' Tom extended a hand to Agnes, and they joined the toddlers in a wild cavorting.

'Um ... f-fancy a wee turn around the square?'

Jemima was surprised to see Davey, the draper's lad, there at her side. She could hardly hear him over the music. He was looking down at her most anxiously, his face its customary beetroot red.

'John, can ye watch the weans for a minute? I'm away for a dance!'

'Aye! Of course!'

Davey grasped Jemima's waist, and they set off in a mad semblance of a polka. Not to be outdone, Sarah and John took a toddler each and swept them up in their arms in a mock dance hold. They paraded around the Market Place until they were all exhausted and slumped against the wall. John heard another tune and jumped up once more.

'This is ma favourite. Look at the union men!'

The Scottish Miners' Association banner was being held high by the men from Wishaw. They were shouting and singing the well-known words of Robert Burns, 'A Man's A Man for a' That'. John's fist clenched to his chest – then, along with many of the men present, he raised it high for the last verse.

Then let us pray that come it may,
(As come it will for a' that,)
That Sense and Worth, o'er a' the earth,
Shall bear the gree,[1] an' a' that.
For a' that, an' a' that,
It's coming yet for a' that,
That Man to Man, the world o'er,
Shall brothers be for a' that.

_____
[1] victory

The bands signalled the last tune – then they were off, back down the road out of the square, with a rousing rendition of 'Onward Christian Soldiers'.

'Oh, that was grand, was it no'? That piece by Burns was the best. I'm going tae the union meeting next week, Sarah. That's for definite.' John was out of breath. 'Whew. Home time for these two, don't ye think?' He looked at Sarah. Her eyes were shining and her chest was still heaving from the exertion of dancing while carrying a toddler.

'That was fun, aye – although very tiring! You're right, we'd best get these weans home to Lizzie. They are starting the speeches soon – we can miss that.'

The children were protesting. 'Don't want tae go home, Uncle John!'

'C'mon, you two,' said John.

'I'll help,' said Sarah. 'Though I'd best get back to the Rankins, before too long.'

'Aye. Ah hope it's no' fossils for tea!'

Sarah laughed. 'No, it will be their usual fare. Buttermilk and oatcakes.'

'Jemima made a tasty pot of stovies earlier, at Lizzie's,' said John. 'We could mibbe have a plate, before ye head back.'

Sarah looked over the crowds in the Market Place. There was no sign of Tom or Agnes. Jemima and Davey had disappeared, too.

'Our pals have deserted us! Aye, that sounds a good

338

scheme, John. Come on, let's see how Lizzie is faring.'

The reluctant toddlers were gathered up, one each, under John's strong, brawny arms.

The kitchen at Stewart Street was full of chat and the smell of food. Lizzie wanted to hear more about the processions and the bands, and John was enthusing about the snare drum. He was beating the table with a spoon.

'It makes a "drrrr" sound, Lizzie. Like this.' He leaned forward and rolled out a beat with a rat-a-tat-tat.

'Not with my cutlery, John Lindsay,' said his sister. 'You'll mibbe have to find out where they practise, if ye are serious? Ye've got a good sense of rhythm.'

'Aye, I'm serious. I don't know how ye get the instruments, though. I'll need tae ask Tom.'

'Could ye no' learn something quieter than the snare drum, John?' said Lizzie.

Sarah laughed. 'Aye, it's quite a racket! You'll have to practise away down Jock's Brae, so we're not all deafened.'

'Imagine all the rabbits, with their paws over their ears!'

The weans joined in the laughter, imitating cowering rabbits. Jumping up and down, they began to show their mother their best marching skills, swinging their arms in time to Uncle John's beat.

Everyone was busy, caught up in the excitement of the day. Martha crept upstairs to her bedroom and opened the drawer in the bedside cabinet. She pulled out an old biscuit box and placed it on the eiderdown, lifting the lid. Inside there were two locks of fine hair, tied with blue ribbon. She lifted these, one by one, and imagined that she smelled the faint baby smell before carefully placing them back. Two tiny wraps of paper contained baby teeth – she rubbed these between her fingers, feeling their unexpected sharp hardness. Another lock of hair, white this time, was tied in a tartan ribbon. She laid it in her hand, caressing it, feeling a rush of emotion as she thought of her mother. And here was the fragile skeleton of the lucky heather, from her wedding chest. The bangle, from Carrie. And a lucky silver coin. Finally, she started to collect up the many tiny pieces of paper that had been pushed into the box in haste, over the past few weeks. She didn't need to re-read them; the words were already inscribed on her heart. She pushed the fragments into her pocket, and replaced the box in the cabinet. Downstairs, she found the matches by the fireplace; grabbing her shawl and her herb bag, she slipped out of the door and down the hill, towards Kirkton House. It was time to make some wishes; and it was time to bring the hare skull back into the house.

Agnes was walking home on cloud nine, when a charred wisp of paper settled on the track in front of her. She picked it up and read it, smiling to herself. In beautiful copperplate handwriting were the words '*Tom and Agnes*'.

A NEW ARRIVAL IN THE MARKET PLACE

IT WAS GETTING dark. Agnes was lighting the lamps; Jane and Margaret were out courting, expected back soon. Barkie was restless, whimpering.

'Whit's the matter? Ye cannae lie still.' Agnes bent to pat her dog, then straightened. 'Whit's that noise, Barkie?' She was still apprehensive about ghosties.

She decided it was coming from upstairs.

'Is that you, Maw?' She went into the corridor, and shouted up.

'Agnes. Is Jim back from the lodge meeting?' Martha's voice sounded strained, breathless.

'Are ye all right, Maw?'

Agnes ran upstairs to the bedroom. Her mother was leaning over the bed, clutching a pillow. Agnes could see the film of sweat on her face, and felt afraid.

'Ah think it's the baby coming, Agnes. Ah thought I'd eaten too much cheese, and it was disagreeing with me …' She groaned. 'Ah cannae get comfortable. Oh, whit's this? Oh my. It's ma waters breaking. Can ye run and fetch Lizzie? Tell her tae bring any spare cloths. And ye'd best put on a big kettle of water before ye go. Quickly now.'

'Should I no' stay with ye, Maw?'

'I'll be fine for a few minutes. Fetch Lizzie.'

Agnes ran downstairs, and put on the kettle. She grabbed her shawl and set off across the street, heart pounding, Barkie at her heels. She hammered at the door of the Stewart Street house.

Jemima opened it, candle in hand. 'Whit's wrong? It's awfy late, Agnes.'

'It's Maw. The baby's started. She's asking for Lizzie. Can you stay and look after the weans, Jem?'

'Aye, of course. I've been sleeping over anyway. It's fine, as long as I can get to my work first thing. *Lizzie!*' She hollered into the house, then turned to Agnes again. 'She's upstairs, putting them tae bed.'

'Whit's the matter?' Lizzie was coming down the hall, wiping her hands on a cloth. 'Is the baby coming, Agnes?'

'Aye. She's asking for ye, Lizzie. She asked if ye could bring cloths.'

Jemima rummaged in the cupboard, and came out with a pile of assorted linen.

'Not the good stuff. It's going tae get ruined. Get those old towels and sheets from the chest.' Lizzie had a sense of purpose about her. 'Jem, can ye wait here, with the weans?'

'Aye, I've already said it's fine. You go on. Let me know what's happening.'

'We will.' Lizzie was wrapping her shawl round her. 'Let's go, Agnes.'

Back at the tailor's house, the groans from upstairs were more audible. Lizzie lifted her skirts and galloped up the stairs.

'I'm here, Martha. Take big breaths. Ye're going to be fine.'

'Lizzie. I'm that pleased to see ye.' Martha let out a long howl, then some gasping breaths. 'It's coming that quick. Do we need the howdie wifie frae up the street?'

'Aye. She delivered all of mine. Like I told ye before, she's got good hands. And she's clean. Agnes, it's Mrs Shaw, beside the bakery. Run.'

Agnes watched on, impressed, as Mrs Shaw and Lizzie worked together. She was called on to run errands; even in labour, Martha knew what needed to be done. All the mirrors in the house had to be turned over so that the soul of the baby could not be captured. Doors and windows were to be unlocked, to ease the passage of the birth. There was a mixture made of rowan berries, already prepared in the cupboard in the hall; Martha asked for it specially. She had to drink some, to ward off evil spirits and fairies. Butter was brought, ready to be put in the mouth of the newborn, for protection. Agnes also prepared the oatmeal and water, for all the womenfolk to take after the birth; this would bring luck and good fortune. Martha seemed much calmer now, knowing they were there and that the rituals that meant so much to her were being fulfilled solemnly and thoroughly. All was progressing in its inevitable way.

'Whit aboot a wee song? Help the wean find its way out?' Lizzie was preparing the cradle. 'Have ye heard this one?' She started to sing, and Mrs Shaw joined in. Agnes knew the hymn tune – it was 'All Things Bright and Beautiful' – but these were different words.

'Pushing out the baby, it's surely on its way.
Warming up the swaddling claes, it's coming, come what
may.
All the weans around us, they come from heaven above,
We thank the Lord, we thank the Lord, for all His love.'

'Lizzie. Whit aboot that one like "Yield Not to Temptation"? That'll dae the job, Mrs Lindsay.' Mrs Shaw was tucking towels in under Martha.

'You're having a baby, push with all your might,
Push hard now, lassie, don't give up the fight.
Aye, it won't be long now, we'll see this wean here,
Whether a lad or a lassie, let's greet it with a cheer.'

Lizzie gave a whoop, as she finished her verse. Agnes dashed downstairs, to fetch more water.

Margaret and Jane were chattering in the kitchen, trying to keep Jim calm. 'Listen to Lizzie singing. She's got a braw, strong voice, has she not, Faither? And Agnes, you sing well too. They'll get that wean born quickly, wait and see.'

Jane spoke. 'Ye're upsetting Barkie, Faither, pacing aboot like that. Come and have a seat.'

'Has she got all she needs? Mibbe we should fetch the

doctor. She's not a young woman,' said Jim. 'Lord, listen to her! Dearie me. Mibbe it's the minister we should be fetching.'

Jane and Margaret chortled. 'She's fit and healthy, Faither. It's not her first. She'll be fine. Sit down, why don't ye,' said Margaret.

Jim collapsed dramatically into a chair. 'What a strain. I wonder if I shouldnae have a wee drink?'

'Mibbe afterwards, Faither, if all is well. Just now, we all need tae keep our wits about us, in case assistance is required. The last thing Martha will need is an inebriated husband to worry about.'

'Aye, true, true.'

'It's as well that it's women that have the weans, and not men,' said Jane.

'How do ye mean?' Jim was indignant.

'She means ye need to stay calm, Faither. Let nature take its course.' Margaret's voice softened. 'After all, our mother had so many weans. How many times have ye sat in this kitchen, listening to a woman labouring upstairs?'

'Ah'm no' getting any younger,' said Jim. 'It cannae be good for my constitution.' He reached down, and scratched Barkie's head. The dog pricked up her ears, then stood, her tail wagging.

'Is that a baby's cry? Aye, it's here!' Agnes followed Jim as he rushed upstairs, to be met at the door of the bedroom by a grinning Lizzie.

'Just give us a minute, Faither. We won't be long.'

'How's Martha? And the wean?'

'Martha's fine. Very tired, but fine. My word, she's a strong woman. And it's a wee boy, Faither. A healthy wee boy.'

Jim turned away, but not before Agnes saw his eyes fill. Lizzie put a hand on his arm.

'A new baby, such a joy. And the howdie will do a wee christening, just till Martha gets him tae the Church on Sunday. Keep him safe.'

'What's to be the name?' He turned back, wiping his eyes. He looked at his daughter, and she nodded her head. They both knew what the child would be called.

'Martha says he must be called William, Faither. And I agree.'

It was dawn, the early light coming up. Agnes was still bursting with excitement.

'I'm that proud of ye, Maw. Ye did so well. He is such a bonny wee boy. My wee brother.'

Martha was sitting up in the bed, cradling a tightly wrapped little bundle. She managed to lift her eyes from his face. 'Ye were a great help, Agnes. And you, Lizzie. I was so glad to have ye here, by my side. Both of ye.' She looked down again at the baby in her arms, and then back again to her daughter.

'If you are not too tired, Agnes, might ye run and tell John and Jemima that they have a new brother? Be sure to tell them that they are welcome to step in any time to see him.'

'Aye. It's about the time that John gets up for his work,' said Lizzie. 'Oh. And Jemima will need tae get back to the Shieldses' house for her work.'

'I'll wait with the weans, Lizzie,' said Agnes. I'll get some laundry started, whilst I'm there.'

'Thank you, Agnes. Though I think Jem has done most of it. Mind you, John just keeps on adding tae the pile, doesn't he? Now, Martha.' Lizzie turned to her stepmother. 'Whit aboot some tea?'

John was bleary-eyed walking up to Castlehill, after a restless night. It had felt strange to have Jemima giving him his breakfast and making sure he had his piece-box. He was so relieved that all had gone well for Martha. He wasn't sure he could have coped with anything more.

Sarah saw him across the street – tall, broad-shouldered, a man now. She waved, and ran over to greet him.

'It's good news, Sarah. Martha's had a wee boy. They are both in good health.'

'John, I'm so pleased for you. Have they given him a name yet?'

'Aye. Martha insisted. He's tae be called William.' His voice caught. 'Lizzie's delighted. Ah just wish ...'

Sarah put her hand on his arm. 'We all wish, John. Every day. We wish that William was still here.'

'Will ye walk with me a bit, Sarah? Have ye time?'

'Aye. I'm always early for my work. The Rankins won't

mind this once. They'll be pleased to hear this news, too. Delighted.' She looked at him. 'What's bothering you?'

'It's just …' John looked down, kicking the cobbles. 'Well, I know that Tom and Agnes are walking out together now. I just wanted tae say …' He struggled to find the words.

'It's alright, John. I know you need to be with Lizzie. It's fine. She needs you. She's your family. Just so you know, I will wait as long as it takes. I'm not going anywhere in a hurry.' She looked up the street, then looked back, into his bright blue eyes. 'Here's Tom, looking for you. I'll see you soon, John Lindsay. Just remember. You're the Right Man for me.'

A RETURN TO WANLOCKHEAD

THEY HEARD THE skylark lifting, singing its heart out strong. Agnes and Tom lay on a bank by the track, looking up at the clean blue sky. A bunch of sweet wild flowers lay beside them.

'Ah wish we could take this day back tae the beginning. This wonderful day. I don't want it ever to end. Stop the sunset from coming, stop the night coming.' Agnes curled into the crook of Tom's shoulder. Barkie lay stretched out a few feet away, glorying in the warmth of the sun.

'Aye. I know what ye mean. But we'll always have today, Agnes. All our lives.'

Tom sat up and looked around.

'I can understand ye better now, aboot this place. It's not exactly bonny, but there is something special aboot the wildness. There's a sense that it's just us in the whole world.' He turned and looked at Agnes, stroked her hair. 'There is a great smell, too. After the mine, it smells glorious. Gorse, heather, moorland. Ah could lie here and breathe it in all day.'

'I'm glad we came, Tom. I wanted tae show you my home, right from when I first knew you. It's important, that ye know where I'm from.'

'And ye took me to that bonny pool, Agnes. What a lovely, secret spot. What did ye say it's called again?'

'It's the Priest's Pool. There is a story frae long ago. Well, a few stories, actually.' She laughed. 'A polite version, and a rude version.' She paused. 'But my maw and my grannie, they always gave it a different name. It's a healing well. It's called the well of St Agnes. I was named after it, like many of the firstborn women of the family.'

'Whit was that ye were throwing in the pool? Were ye making a wish?'

'Sort of. But I was also returning something that I had borrowed, long ago. When I was a wee girl. I dinnae need it any more.'

Tom looked into her dark eyes, full of hope, full of love. 'Did I hear that ye have an interesting birthmark, Agnes Hewson Brownlee? On your leg?'

She laughed. Barkie looked up.

'That old story! Who told ye that? Well, ye'll have to marry me, Tom Lee, if ye want tae find out.'

'They say it's the shape of a wee dog.' He leaned over, and made as if to lift her skirts.

'Do they, now!' She laughed again, swatting his hand away. 'All things come tae he who waits, Tom. And my cousin is waiting to give us our tea. So, come on. We'd best get back. We can take these flowers tae my maw.'

Tea. Barkie was already on her feet and trotting down the hill, towards Wanlockhead.

Martha was waiting for them on the bench in front of her cousin's cottage, cradling baby William.

She's sitting just like Grannie used to, thought Agnes. And here was Jeannie stopping by, just like the old days, clearly delighted to see Martha.

'Och, we miss ye something terrible, Martha. I'll never forget your wise words. They were a great help. And all that time ye took, dressing ma arm.' She rolled back her sleeve. 'Look, it's healed up a treat.'

She turned to Agnes. 'Ah don't suppose ye've heard the latest news aboot young Catriona Ferguson. Is she no' the same age as yourself? Anyway, she's in the family way. Nae sign of the father. Such a shame for the lassie. It seems just one thing after another, what with her own faither in trouble wi' money going missing at the Kirk, and then that nasty scar she's got frae the burn.' She looked at Martha again. 'It's a shame ye weren't here to help her wi' it.' She went on, shaking her head. 'That poor girl. Ye'd think she'd been cursed, would ye not?'

Martha put her arm round her daughter. 'We dinnae believe all that, do we, Agnes? Now, please excuse us, Jeannie. We have an important visit tae make.' She stood, wrapping baby William into her shoulder, and addressed Tom and Agnes.

'Yer grannie would have wanted tae meet Tom, would she no'? And we must introduce her tae her new grandson.' Martha started down the path. 'C'mon. Let's take those bonny flowers tae Meadowfoot.'

ACKNOWLEDGEMENTS

This book was inspired by a foray into family and local history. However, although it features some characters who did live in Wanlockhead and Carluke at the time, it is a work of fiction.

The 1870s was a fascinating period in Scotland's history, spawning many books. There are books about the growth of the railways, the industrialisation of the central belt, the people who came to work in the mines. Alongside the Statistical Accounts and detailed histories, I found myself drawn to books with pictures and illustrations of life at that time; for example, 'The Scottish Home', edited by Annette Carruthers (1996, The National Museums of Scotland). The faces look out at us across the years. They are familiar, Scottish faces, often chapped and red after exposure to weather and work. 'Historic Clydesdale, Parish by Parish' (2016, Lanark and District Archaeological Society) was another invaluable source of background and detail and I spent many happy hours on their website (www.clydesdaleheritage.org.uk). 'Bygone Carluke' (1991, Iain Somerville and Christine Warren) provided pictures and stories galore, as does the Carluke

Parish Historical Society's website. (www.carlukehistory.com).

The Scottish Mining website (www.scottishmining.co.uk) is a rich source of information; it was there I found the gruelling details of pit accidents and their aftermath. There are also excellent descriptions of conditions in the colliery cottages and the concerns of the housing inspectors.

I had a wonderful day at the Scottish Museum of Mining and can recommend the visit. In the research centre, David Bell and volunteer Bill were most helpful and gave me access to copies of memoirs by miners. 'Down the Mine at Twelve' and 'Memoirs of John Milligan' are first-hand accounts of the experience of going into the pit to work at a young age.

The Leadmining Museum at Wanlockhead was another great visit, particularly the reconstructions of miners' cottages through the years. Margaret answered my e-mails with patience and I apologise for inventing the miners' canteen, for the purposes of the story.

The libraries at Dumfries and Stranraer hold wonderful historical collections; and librarians at Carluke and Lanark also pointed me to some useful local material, especially Paul Archibald.

Eventually I had to stop reading and start writing. In November 2019, I spent a week at Lumb Bank with the Arvon Foundation. It was there that I was given permission to let go of the ties of history and just tell a story. It was an inspiring week, not least because of the company of all the fellow aspiring writers.

Friends and family were encouraging early readers and gave great feedback. A big thank you to Andrew Bannister, proof-reader extraordinaire, Eke Bont (now McGowan), Jen Cooper, Catherine Corr, Alison Hannah, Rowena Herbert, Peter Laurence, Alan Lindsay, Andrew Lindsay, Lucile McLeod, Jane North, Helen Philpott and Judith Scott. The Rhins Writers also provided boost and challenge at just the right time. Your support means a great deal, Elaine Barton, Lyn Lowenstein, Sarah Austin and especially Jane Fuller.

Thanks to Mary Holmes, who gave helpful publishing guidance. Sam Boyce provided excellent editing and re-drafting advice – thank you. Catherine Cousins and all the team at 2QT were first rate, supportive and professional.

And to all those not mentioned by name here but who supported me along the way, many thanks.

Last but not least, Alastair McGowan has been consistently enthusiastic and interested, accompanying me in all weathers on visits to some very obscure places. Thank you, best husband.

AUTHOR'S BIOGRAPHY

Marion McGowan grew up in the West of Scotland, to a family descended from miners and weavers. She splits her time between Yorkshire and the Rhins of Galloway.

The Priest's Pool is her first book.